Peyton grimaced at the black pistol he'd placed into her hand.

"It's small enough for your grip, but will suffice if someone threatens you."

Her heart raced as she handled the weapon. A dim memory tugged at the edges of her mind. She'd handled guns before, but this was different.

This was home defense, not sporting events.

"I don't know if I'm ready to shoot someone." She set the gun down on the bed.

Gray's dark brows scrunched. "If it comes down to shooting someone to save your life, you'll be ready."

"I can't do it. Kill someone?"

Gray sat on the bed, picked up the pistol. "Sweetheart, you never know what you're ready for until you face the situation. Knowing you're armed and this is with you while I'm gone gives me a little peace of mind."

Warming at his use of the endearment, Peyton looked doubtfully at the gun. Gray handed it back to her.

"You point the barrel at whomever you want to shoot."

Glancing up, she saw his faint, teasing smile. Peyton sighed. "All right. Give me the basics."

Dear Reader,

Sea turtles are a passion of mine. There are strict regulations to protect these beautiful animals from extinction. Several hospitals and sanctuaries in Florida are dedicated to saving sea turtles. These include the Turtle Hospital in Marathon and Loggerhead Marinelife Center in Juno Beach, where I conducted some of my research.

When I set out to write *Her Secret Protector*, I knew I wanted to incorporate sea turtles. This is how Peyton came to life. Peyton is a sea turtle biologist threatened by a dangerous stalker. The only way her worried parents will let her remain in Florida to do the job she loves so much is to hire a bodyguard to keep her safe. Peyton dislikes being watched over every minute. Gray is determined to do his job, even if it inconveniences Peyton.

Gray has a secret and troubled past. A former navy SEAL, he will do anything to keep Peyton safe, including risking his own life. He respects Peyton's work and her dedication, even if she is stubborn about his services as her bodyguard.

As they gradually learn to trust each other and eventually fall in love, Peyton finds out she needs more than Gray's protection to stay alive. Just like the injured sea turtles she loves and protects, she needs him to help her navigate her way home.

I hope you enjoy Peyton and Gray's journey in *Her Secret Protector*. Happy reading!

Bonnie Vanak

HER SECRET PROTECTOR

Bonnie Vanak

HARLEQUIN

ROMANTIC
SUSPENSE

HARLEQUIN®
ROMANTIC SUSPENSE™

Recycling programs
for this product may
not exist in your area.

ISBN-13: 978-1-335-59380-1

Her Secret Protector

Harlequin Enterprises ULC
22 Adelaide St. West, 41st Floor
Toronto, Ontario M5H 4E3, Canada
www.Harlequin.com

Printed in U.S.A.

New York Times and *USA TODAY* bestselling author **Bonnie Vanak** is passionate about romance novels and telling stories. A former newspaper reporter, she worked as a journalist for a large international charity for several years, traveling to countries such as Haiti to report on poor living conditions. Bonnie lives in Florida with her husband, Frank, and is a member of Romance Writers of America. She loves to hear from readers. She can be reached through her website, bonnievanak.com.

Books by Bonnie Vanak

Harlequin Romantic Suspense

Rescue from Darkness
Reunion at Greystone Manor

Colton 911: Chicago

Colton 911: Under Suspicion

The Coltons of Red Ridge

His Forgotten Colton Fiancée

SOS Agency

Navy SEAL Seduction
Shielded by the Cowboy SEAL
Navy SEAL Protector
Her Secret Protector

Visit the Author Profile page at Harlequin.com.

In memory of Susan Renn Mongiat. You loved fiercely and were taken from us too soon, but your loving spirit lives on in the causes you supported and the family who misses you so much.

Chapter 1

Society luncheons were as exciting as a slow internet connection, except here she was safe from her stalker. If Crazy Man was here, maybe he'd die from boredom and she'd finally be free.

Stifling a yawn, Peyton Bradley smiled at the gaggle of women clustered around her mother offering congratulations. Dr. Amelia Bradley was being inducted into Sea Grape Beach's Women's Hall of Fame. Yet another plaque the esteemed physician and philanthropist would place on her office shelf.

Her jaw hurt from all this smiling. Smiling came with the territory of being a Bradley. She'd learned to smile and never show feelings in public as soon as she mastered tying her shoes.

Peyton wished she'd found a reasonable excuse to skip the luncheon and walk the beach. She itched to see the possible sea turtle nest her coworker at the Sea Turtle and Marine Life Institute had found early this morning. Sand beneath her toes, waves splashing at her bare ankles, that was her joy.

Not this smiling at strangers who cooed at her mother as if she were a reality show celebrity. But family obligations, as her parents frequently reminded her, came first.

She sipped her water, glancing around the darkened room, illuminated with blue spotlights and accent lamps on each table. Sparkling zirconia diamonds and fake pearls tastefully arranged on mirrored centerpieces glinted under the soft blue lighting. Red roses had been placed on each table napkin next to the silverware. Around her, real diamonds and pearls dripped from the necks and ears of more than two hundred women.

Nearby, in a corner, trying to look inconspicuous, was the shadow. Tall, dark and brooding. He refused to let her walk the beach alone, go anywhere alone. Peyton couldn't even wander into the bathroom to wash her hands without him lingering outside the door.

Gray Wallace, the bodyguard Dad hired to protect her from Crazy Man. He blended in like shorts and a T-shirt at a formal wedding. Gray's gaze swept over the room, landed on her.

She waved, gave him a mocking smile. He did not return the gesture or the facial expression. Did the man ever crack a grin? So serious all the time. She supposed he was handsome with that stock of short raven hair, intense brown eyes under black brows and a wiry, athletic body hidden beneath a tasteful black suit, white shirt and navy tie. The slight scar marking his left cheek made him appear dashing and a bit dangerous himself. A few women passing near eyeballed him as if he were part of the buffet. Peyton could almost see them drool over what they must have thought a fine-looking morsel.

Paid to be here, to tail her, but it was unnecessary. Guy

could use a break. For two weeks starting in late May, he'd been shadowing her. The threatening love notes on cream-colored paper left on her car at work and wherever she went had stopped. She hadn't seen one in three days. Sometimes Crazy Man left a dead rose instead of a note, but she hadn't seen that, either.

Either Gray scared the stalker off or Crazy Man had found someone else to terrorize.

"Peyton? Mrs. Hutchinson asked you a question."

Her mother's clipped voice cut through Peyton's thoughts. She smiled harder.

"Sorry. I was studying the decorations. So lovely this year," she murmured.

"Are you still working at that marine place, Peyton? I thought you'd be headed to California for your PhD by now." Bright, inquisitive eyes made beady by the reduced light studied Peyton with the same intensity she used when analyzing specimens under the microscope.

She opened her mouth to answer when her mother cut in. "Peyton's taking time off to stay close."

"Oh? Are you headed to your summer home in Nantucket in May?" Mrs. Hutchinson asked.

"We've decided to remain in Florida for the summer," her mother responded. "Family and work obligations."

Leaning back in her chair, she stifled a sigh. Why bother talking at all when Dr. Amelia, the area's foremost cardiologist, did it all for her?

"Oh. Well, I suppose that's nice. There are so many more qualified men here for you than the hippies in California." Mrs. Hutchinson shook her head.

Peyton's smile slipped a notch. "I'm not interested in my MRS degree, but my PhD. UC San Diego has one of the best programs in marine biology, including marine microbiology and biodiversity and conservation."

Mrs. Hutchinson flapped a hand, making the diamond tennis bracelet on her wrist bounce. The women wore enough diamonds and pearls to buy a country.

"Very nice, Peyton, but I don't know why you didn't choose to become a doctor like your mother or work with your father in his business. He is a CEO." The woman sniffed. "Instead, you work with those…animals."

Peyton opened her mouth to let the woman know she preferred the animals over opinionated socialites who failed to understand how important environmental research was when miles and miles of coastline surrendered to development every day. Her mother shot her a warning glance. Instead, she shot Mrs. Hutchinson a wide smile.

"That sounds great," she murmured. "Excuse me. I need some water."

She sauntered over to the refreshment table, filled her glass. At least this luncheon had glassware instead of plastics that took years to degrade in a landfill.

"You're quite thirsty today. This is your fourth trip to fill your glass," a deep male voice murmured.

Startling, she turned, spilling her water. Damn, did he always have to creep up on her?

"You scared me. You're too damn quiet," she retorted, staring down at the water spot on her designer dress.

The shadow handed her a paper napkin with his usual efficiency. "I'm paid to be quiet."

Muttering a thanks, she mopped at the wet spot. Fantastic. Right on her left breast, as if she needed any more attention drawn to herself. The shadow didn't notice. Instead, he kept scanning the room.

"Listen, you don't have to follow me around."

"I do when you leave my line of sight, Ms. Bradley. I'm here to keep you safe."

"That sounds great," she muttered.

Peyton felt as if she had the man tethered to her by invisible strings. It was getting beyond tedious. Never any privacy or a moment alone.

"Well, as long as you're here..." She found an empty glass, shook it. "Juice or water?"

A brief frown touched his expression, then he nodded. "Water."

She filled the glass, handed it to him as he murmured thanks.

"I drink a lot of water because the people at these society luncheons are so dry it's like being on an excursion through the Sahara, except with lots more bling."

To her shock, he suddenly smiled, as if finding her little joke amusing. Wow. When he smiled, he lost the robot-like persona and almost appeared human.

"*Bling* is an interesting adjective to describe four-carat diamond necklaces. Do you suppose the food will be equally colorful?" he asked with a wry look.

Seeing his rigid shoulders relax, she decided to engage him further. "We may hit the jackpot for that. I saw the caterer earlier and the salmon and beef medallions look delicious. As long as there's no chicken, we're good. Rubber chicken was never my favorite."

His smile was like candlelight cutting through the darkness. "Mine, either."

They drank more water. The shadow, no, Gray, refilled his glass. "Florida can be quite warm in June, Ms. Bradley."

"Please, no formal last names. I'm Peyton. As for the weather, well, August is the worst, and September, the height of hurricane season. Walking outside is like having a wet, warm blanket wrapped around your skin. My parents usually like to spend time at the summer home in Nantucket. They wanted to send me there when the notes started showing up on my car windshield."

His dark eyebrows arched. "Why didn't you go, Peyton?"

How could she explain that everything that meant anything to her remained in Florida, despite the sticky heat? Most never understood her job as a sea turtle biologist, or her passion for the environment and saving sea turtles. Not even her own family. Last week her attorney brother tried to coax her into fleeing north. She'd told him she needed to stick around for nesting season to count hatchlings. Marc stared at her as if she'd confessed to dancing naked under a full moon on the beach.

Peyton shrugged. "It's not too bad at the beach. The ocean breeze is nice."

He seemed to consider this. "Why did you tell that woman 'that sounds great' when your face said otherwise?"

She finished her water. "'That sounds great' is my personal code phrase to someone to shut up and butt out. Much more polite than the truth."

No smile now. He clenched his jaw, the scar on his left cheek flaring. Always looking out for danger, never relaxing his guard.

Suddenly she realized what she'd just said. "Oh. That sounds great… I didn't mean when I said it to you earlier… I meant…"

"Thank you for the water." He set down his glass on the table.

Then he stepped back several feet, assuming a military-straight stance, hands folded in front of him, staring straight ahead. The camaraderie vanished as if it never happened. Guilt raced through her. She hadn't meant to hurt his feelings. She was simply exhausted from keeping up appearances and strained from the demands of both parents and profession.

On the stage, the MC called for quiet.

Peyton returned to her seat, noting the shadow had resumed his stance close by. On the room's opposite side was FBI agent Jason "Jace" Beckett, close friend of Jarrett Adler, who owned the security firm employing Gray. Jace was visiting on vacation. He was tall, dark-haired and as charming as Gray was grim.

Guess my shadow figured he needed extra help for this.

She slid out her phone from the beaded cobalt-blue clutch purse that matched her dress. With furtive glances, she studied the photos taken on the beach. This was familiar territory, where she didn't have to worry about what to do or how to act.

Peyton texted her good friend and co-worker Adam at the institute. He'd found another sea turtle nest this morning on the beach by her home and sent her the latest reports on nests. She scrolled through them with growing dismay. They had a record season last year, except for the private beach on Bradley land.

An elbow in her stomach and she looked up to see her mother scowl, shake her head. Peyton slid her phone into her purse.

Rigorous applause filled the room as the MC talked about her mother and her generous donation of time and talents to the community. Peyton felt her eyes glaze over. Much as she loved her mother, hearing those accolades over and over was like listening to someone read a medical journal.

Worse, several women at these luncheons had already told her what a blazing path her mother had forged for her to follow. It was ludicrous. How could she even expect to walk in her mother's footsteps when her own were etched on the sand while her mother's remained in a sterile surgical theater?

She supposed saving a sick sea turtle paled in comparison with transplanting a new heart into the city's mayor.

Finally, the MC announced it was time to eat. Each table was called to stand in line for the sumptuous buffet in the adjacent room. Though their table was first to be called, her mother remained seated, chatting with the well-wishers who wandered over to offer congratulations and ask for selfies.

Surprisingly, they didn't ask for an autograph. Peyton almost snickered at the thought of asking one for herself.

Finally her mother signaled she was ready. Taking her own china plate, Peyton rose and followed her mother dutifully to the buffet table. She selected the fish, some green vegetables and sped back to her table. Briefly she thought about filling a plate for the shadow, who had tailed her as she wandered through the buffet line.

Then she reached her seat and all thoughts of appetizing food vanished.

The red rose at her table napkin was gone.

In its place was a black, dead rose, lying atop a small cream-colored note. Her name was emblazoned in bold black letters like an accusation. The same handwriting she'd seen for the past three weeks. The same foreboding letters.

PEYTON, MY LOVE.

Her heart raced, her muscles tightened as if she'd run a marathon. The plate of food tumbled to the floor with a loud clatter. She tried to form words, but nothing came from her mouth except short, panting breaths. Her mother, caught in a throng of people as she tried to return to the table, looked at her with real emotion for the first time that day.

Gray was at her side immediately. Peyton's chest constricted as she pointed to the ugly object on the table.

All she could manage was a whisper.

"He's here."

Chapter 2

The bastard had snuck in and out with vicious efficiency. Grayson cursed his failure to catch her stalker yet again. His hand shot out, gently wrapped around Peyton's wrist as she reached down toward the note. People crowded around her, expressing alarm, and he needed to get her away from them.

"Don't touch anything," he said quietly.

Her welfare was his first concern. Blood had drained from her face and she looked ready to either pass out or vomit. Gray spoke into a small microphone just inside his shirtsleeve as he held Peyton's elbow to support her. Beneath the warmth of his fingers, her skin was soft but cold.

Two men cordoned off the room, allowing no one to leave as he'd instructed. Another suit, quiet and efficient, jogged over to the table, took control of the sitch. Gray breathed relief and hustled Peyton over to a quiet area near the refreshment table. He snapped an order to a nervous waiter, who rushed to pour a cold cola into a glass.

Gray made her drink it, his gaze centered on her face. Finally color returned to her cheeks and, though her skin was blotchy, she no longer looked in shock.

"Put your head between your knees if you feel ready to pass out," he ordered.

She shook her head. "I'm okay."

Peyton set the glass on the table, her hand no longer trembling. "Now I know why you always wear those suits. It's to speak into the mic in your sleeve like the Secret Service does."

"No, it's because I like to talk to myself and this way people don't think I'm a nutcase."

She stared at his deadpan look and then finally managed a smile. "Good one."

The smile faded. "The real nutcase is the one who left that note. How did he get in here?"

"Unknown." Reassured she was herself again, even if she acted snobbish and aloof, he squeezed her hand. "Remain here. I'll send your mother over to sit with you while I find out."

"My mother won't want to…" Her voice faded as Dr. Bradley reached them, already intent on joining her terrified daughter.

The woman hugged Peyton, her expression fierce. "Oh, honey, are you all right?"

He left them, glad the composed and detached Dr. Bradley had morphed into a worried and caring mother. More than Gray's protection right now, Peyton needed her.

Jace had brought a kit to dust for prints. The FBI agent was efficient and brisk. The local police would be notified and a crime scene cordoned off later, but their presence now would create chaos and he wanted a minimum of disruption. Too much fuss now, everyone milling about, wanting to know what happened, why the distinguished

Dr. Bradley in her pearls and short black cocktail dress sat in a corner, hugging her only daughter.

A short, precise command Gray uttered to those in charge and the MC restored order to the room. Servers cleaned up the spilled food and the table was moved to the side. Another table was set up with quiet efficiency a short distance away. A quartet of singers nervously took to the stage and began the luncheon's entertainment.

Dr. Bradley's guests were escorted over to the new table, with the MC telling people to please continue their meal, a guest had felt slightly ill but the esteemed Dr. Bradley was attending to her.

Much better than the truth—telling everyone the man who wanted to kill Peyton Bradley walked among them.

Finally he ushered Peyton and her mother over to the table, pulled out a seat and helped Peyton to sit. Color returned to those high, patrician cheekbones, and her lips, so lush and soft, were no longer reddened from her biting them.

As if biting back a sharp cry for help. His admiration kicked up the smallest bit. He knew from experience how tough it was to mask your emotions when all you wanted to do was scream and run away.

Her mother glanced around.

"All these men who are here now... I had no idea they were present at this event. Did you expect trouble?" Dr. Bradley asked.

"I'm always prepared," he informed her, his gaze sweeping over Peyton. "Jace, will you stay with Peyton while I find out how this happened?"

Jace nodded. He had already bagged the rose and note. Taking both, Gray walked off. Maybe now Peyton would understand, and her parents as well, that he took his job damn seriously. He wasn't window dressing to hover like a statue. When Charles Bradley hired Jarrett Adler's SOS agency and Gray to guard his daughter, he hired the best. SOS, Security Operations Specialties, offered protection to corporate executives and civilians, and taught self-defense techniques and gun training.

In another room down the hall from the luncheon, he dusted the note and rose for prints, not surprised to find both were clean. Perp wore gloves again. Still, maybe Jace's connections with the FBI could find something. He snapped on latex gloves and opened the note.

Same as before. Large, black letters in block style, almost childlike. Nothing childlike about the message, however.

PEYTON. YOU STOLE MY HEART AND YOU WILL BE MINE. I WILL FIND YOU ALONE, AND CUT YOUR HEART INTO TINY PIECES SO NO ONE ELSE CAN HAVE YOU. I'M WATCHING YOU.

In minutes he organized interviews in a separate room from the luncheon as to not interrupt the agenda. His men had found each person around Dr. Bradley's table and arranged to bring them into the room for questioning.

While he grilled each person, Jace stood by Peyton's side. The man was rock solid. If Peyton moved an inch, he'd move as well.

Unfortunately, in the hustle of the crowd, no one saw anyone drop a rose or a note at Peyton's place setting. Even the servers denied seeing anyone. Trouble was, there were too many people clustered around Dr. Bradley. It was like trying to identify one bee in a swarm.

An hour later, he got answers.

Mystery solved. A woman named Marcy Caldwell smoking outside admitted she'd been approached by a man who asked her to put the rose and the note at Peyton's place setting. He claimed he was an old boyfriend and it was a joke. Marcy tittered nervously.

Gray failed to laugh.

He scribbled down the description. Medium height, dark hair maybe, because he wore a dark hoodie and sunglasses, blue jeans and a white T-shirt, no distinguishing marks or scars or jewelry. Could have been any one of thousands of Floridians or tourists, except the man wore gloves. Marcy hadn't thought anything of it as she claimed they looked like bike gloves.

Yeah, right. Something was off about this.

He trained his gaze on the woman. "Why did you do it? You saw it was a dead rose."

"Seemed fine to me." She shrugged, flicking her gaze sideways.

Liar. He leaned back, stretched out his legs, gestured around the room. "This luncheon honoring Peyton's mother is quite an event. Nice they chose to recognize her this way."

"She's not the only inductee into the society, but the way everyone acts, you'd think so."

The scathing response told him everything he needed to know. Jealousy. "I'd like you to sit down with our sketch artist to get a description of the man."

She shook her head. "I'd rather not get involved. If you have any more questions, you can call my attorney."

She rattled off the name of a high-profile criminal defense lawyer. Biting off a juicy reply, tempted to use Peyton's own code phrase of That Sounds Great, he handed her his card.

"If you remember anything else, call me. That's my cell."

She stared at the white square and the discreet bold print. SOS Executive Protection. Grayson Wallace, Senior Security Consultant. "You're a secret agent? Is that like the CIA or something?"

Unsmiling, he regarded her. "Or something. Good day, Miss Caldwell."

Thirty minutes later, he'd interviewed everyone who might have been outside and seen the suspect. Nothing concrete. Same as always—white guy of medium height wearing a dark hoodie and jeans. Some said the hoodie was black. Others navy blue.

Returning to the luncheon, he was relieved to see Jace sitting next to Peyton. The man looked normal, comfortable at the table. He fit in. Jace had the personality for these types of social events. He could relax and make interesting small talk. He even smiled and laughed.

Gray seldom did either.

Jace had everyone at the table laughing. Even Peyton lost her terrified expression and looked amused. For a moment, Gray suffered his own flash of jealousy.

Shrugged it off. This was a job, and Peyton his charge. Nothing more. She'd created distance between them with her smart-ass remark. He welcomed it. For a few minutes, he'd actually enjoyed her company.

Never get involved with a client, Jarrett had warned him. Jarrett, the owner of SOS. Former navy SEAL like himself, who understood Gray's past and asked him to do this last job, because he was damn good at protecting people. Jarrett knew he needed to work out his ghosts. Even though Gray had no intentions of staying, he deeply appreciated his buddy giving him a chance to do something good. Not many people trusted Gray.

Especially not with his history.

Finally it looked as if the event was coming to a close. Breathing a sigh of relief, he headed to Peyton's table. Jace had already stood, calling in Gray's detective contact at the police department to alert him about the latest threat.

He stood military straight, ready to escort Peyton outside. Nodding at Dr. Bradley, he held Peyton's elbow, guiding her past the throng into the fresh air and sunshine.

Outside she drew in a deep breath. "This feels wonderful to be outside."

"You held up quite well." Casual remark, not a compliment, more an observation.

"Today's theme was diamonds and pearls. I kept with the luncheon theme. They're gems created under pressure." Peyton smiled again. "I understand pressure."

He gave her a second, more appreciative look. It wasn't Jace's conversation or jokes that had her smiling. Peyton made that facial gesture to hide her true self from the world.

Gray escorted her over to his vehicle, a black Mercedes with darkened windows. She glanced over at her sleek red Jaguar.

"I suppose you want to take me back home in your car because of what happened."

He unlocked the car and helped her into the passenger seat.

"Your vehicle is conspicuous and easier to track than mine," he murmured, sliding into the driver's seat. "I'll send someone to retrieve your car and bring it to your home."

Gray punched in a security code and then switched on the engine, and the dashboard lit up. Peyton whistled. "Talk about the latest gadgets. Nice electronics."

At least she hadn't gushed like Marcy had and asked if he was in secret agent mode.

"Do you have a tailpipe that spits out nails if enemies are following you?"

Her teasing tone coaxed a smile from him. "No, but the passenger seat is an ejection seat if someone unruly is with me, so behave."

"Fan of the old Bond movies."

"Am I living up to the stereotype?" He drove out of the parking lot and headed for the road linking the beach to the mainland.

"Not unless you wear a dinner jacket and start cultivating women named Bambi wearing tiny bikinis."

He kept glancing in his rearview mirror to see if anyone followed him. Out of his peripheral vision he saw Peyton grip her hands tightly.

"Do you think he will try anything else today? My day is wrecked, but I'd like to salvage what I can of it."

"Salvage how?" He turned onto the bridge leading to the exclusive, tight-knit community of Sea Grape Beach.

"Back to the institute. I need to get to work."

He shook his head. "No."

She sighed. "All right. I knew you'd be against it."

She pulled out her phone as it buzzed a message. Peyton studied it intently. "Adam says there was a sighting of a female loggerhead. If I time this right, I can be there when she comes ashore to lay her eggs. The season is off to a great start and I'd like to be there to record any nesting."

He glanced at the clock on the dash. "I will go with you this afternoon to the beach. But no more beach visits at night. It's too risky. Too many access points, from the sand to the water."

An exhale of breath. Glancing over, he saw her expression of pure disbelief. "Are you saying you can't protect me? Isn't that what you're paid for?"

He gritted his teeth. "I'm paid to keep you safe and that means keeping you from areas where you're vulnerable to this predator."

Peyton shook her head. "You can't put me in a box, lock it and guard the key. I have a life and I intend to return to it. I made a deal with my parents. If they let me stay here for the summer instead of going to our home in Nantucket,

I'd agree to a bodyguard." She made a small sound of disgust. "A bodyguard. Not a babysitter. Might as well have the housekeeper accompany me everywhere."

Keeping his temper under control, for he sensed fear masked by frustration, he turned onto the oceanfront road leading to the Bradley mansion. "That can be arranged as well, with a housekeeper cleared by my firm who has an open-carry permit and is skilled in mixed martial arts."

"Licensed to kill? Like everyone who works with you for this SOS company?"

No masking the sarcasm in her voice now. Gray kept his voice mild, though he grew irritated. The Bond jokes were fine regarding him and his car, but mocking the agency took things too far. "Licensed to protect with both weapons and body. Trained to spot assailants and potential trouble, like all agents at the SOS agency. Some of us have extensive military experience. Jarrett, the owner, is a former navy SEAL. Jace, who sat with you at the luncheon, was with the army rangers."

"Which kind are you?"

Gray didn't answer. They were at the ornate iron gates guarding the oceanfront mansion. He rolled down his bulletproof window and punched in a security code. Since starting this assignment, he insisted on changing the code each day. Didn't care that it was a pain for the family and the service workers.

"Answer my question. Which kind are you?" she demanded.

The kind that makes them look like Boy Scouts. "My past is none of your business. If you desire to question my creds, talk to the owner of SOS."

For a moment she didn't say anything. Then sighed. "I'm sorry. I didn't mean to insult you. I'm…a little jumpy."

Nodding, he guided the sedan past a sweep of trees

overhanging the road, green sentries that created a soothing path of foliage.

"What did I do to deserve this?"

He almost didn't hear her whisper over the crackle of static on his radio. Gray glanced at her as the gates shut behind them. "Not a thing. It isn't your fault. It's his."

He pulled into the curved drive in front of the two-story elegant mansion and parked, then turned to her. "Miss Bradley, the police explained you met your stalker someplace, somewhere and it could have been a totally innocent and casual exchange. This man is mentally deficient and fixated on you. There's nothing you could have done to prevent this."

She looked away. "I know you're trying to cut me some slack, but there had to be something I could have done. Because…the alternative is pretty scary to consider. That a simple, friendly greeting could get me killed."

Without waiting for an answer, she slid out of the car and strode to the front door.

A flicker of pity raced through him. With ruthless intent, he squashed it. Pity wasn't an emotion he could afford when protecting her life.

Peyton reached the door. She punched numbers into the keypad to open the door.

The pad flashed red. She groaned. "You changed the code again. What is it? Dammit, I live here. Must I have you unlock the door to my own home?"

Telling her the new code, Gray keyed it in and opened the door for Peyton. She stormed inside. He followed her upstairs to her spacious bedroom suite.

She tossed her clutch bag onto the four-poster bed and glared at him as he entered the bedroom.

"I'm showering off the stink of what happened. Now, you want to watch or can I have a little privacy?"

He walked over to the French doors leading out to the

balcony, wishing her parents had acquiesced with his request to move her to a bedroom with less visibility and entrances. Gray tested the doors and the new double locks he'd installed. Satisfied, he inclined his head.

"I'll be down the hall if you need me. Don't leave the house unless I'm with you."

She snapped him a military salute. "Yes, sir. You could bring me fresh towels while you're at it," she shot back, kicking off her heels and then heading into the bathroom.

Gray left her room and headed down the hallway to the linen closet. He selected two fresh white towels and marched back to her bedroom. The bathroom door was open, steam fogging the room as the shower ran. His heart sank as he heard the unmistakable sounds of crying. Gray leaned his forehead against the wall, experiencing his own vulnerability. He could kill a man with a single twist of his neck, scored headshots all the time at the gun range, but as much as he could protect someone physically, he couldn't do anything for their emotional well-being.

The strain clearly got to Peyton. She'd hate knowing he witnessed her breaking down.

Straightening, he pounded loudly on the opened bathroom door. The shower curtain featuring an array of swimming sea turtles jerked aside, and Peyton's scrubbed, dripping-wet face appeared.

She shrieked. "What are you doing?"

"You did ask me to bring you fresh towels."

The outrage on her face was worth it as he left the towels on the vanity. Gray chuckled. At least he'd stopped her from crying.

When he reached the guest room assigned to him, all amusement fled. He worried about Peyton. Not only because she was his assignment. Every day he felt a stab of pure fear of what would happen if someone extinguished her bright, shining light, hidden under a crabby layer of sarcasm and sharpness.

He'd already failed one woman in his life who trusted him to keep her safe. She'd died a horrible death.

He couldn't let anything happen to Peyton as well.

Chapter 3

Fresh towels. The shadow's smart-aleck side showed, but she had stopped her bawl fest. Briefly she wondered if he did that on purpose.

Beneath the gentle spray of her custom-designed rain shower head, she scrubbed her body with zealous energy. Peyton felt violated, as if the stalker had touched her. She supposed he had in a way, touching her mind and disrupting her composure.

She recited the scientific names of sea turtles to calm herself. *Dermochelys coriacea*, the mighty and endangered leatherback. *Lepidochelys kempii*, the most endangered of all sea turtles, known as the Kemp's ridley, whose breeding grounds were mainly one strip of beach in Mexico. *Caretta caretta*, the loggerhead turtle, more commonly seen in the United States. Most of the nests on the stretch of sand in Florida and Sea Grape Beach were loggerheads.

Usually it worked and she could focus. Not today. Today had been too close. Her stalker had actually been on the grounds outside a social event. He could have circulated among them, touched her as she'd made her way into the building.

Peyton leaned over, her gorge rising. Bracing her hands on the wall, she drew in a deep breath to keep the excellent salmon and rice in her stomach.

Why was this happening to her? She had no enemies, no admirers, dated some men, but nothing serious. Both the police and Gray had been over and over with her on her history. Nothing proved to be a red flag.

It was her fault she'd brought this upon her family, and yet she couldn't find a single reason for it.

Gray insisted the stalker's singling her out wasn't her fault. The stalker was mentally troubled and fixated on her. It could have been something as simple as saying hello in a coffee shop or the gym.

Remind me never to say hello again to strangers.

She twisted off the shower knob, stepped out and used one of the towels Gray left. After drying off herself and her long blond hair, she dressed in khaki shorts, a blue Marine Institute polo she always wore to work and water shoes that would protect her feet from the sand and let her walk into the ocean without scraping her soles.

After consulting her phone and seeing the latest text from Adam, resolve filled her. At least here she could work.

Time to check on her guard dog and see if he would let her go to the beach. Alone.

The door to the guest room was open. Peyton walked around the bedroom. Military neat, nothing of any personal nature left on the dresser. It was as if he truly was a shadow and did not exist.

She returned to her room and shook her head. "You think he'd be nice to me," she muttered aloud.

"I'm not paid to be nice to you. I'm paid to keep you safe," a deep male voice droned.

Peyton startled and looked around the room. To her shock, Gray stepped out of her walk-in closet.

"How long have you been there?"

"Long enough."

"Were you spying on me as I dressed?"

"No." His mouth compressed. "I would never violate your privacy that way."

"Did you find anyone other than yourself lurking in my closet and how did you get in there?"

"I was checking the outer perimeter and came in through your balcony door. You need to keep it locked at all times, Peyton. Your room is two doors on the same oceanfront side, the side that is most vulnerable to intruders because there's no traffic. I'm removing the trellis. I never should have allowed your mother to keep it."

Peyton groaned, thinking of her mother's shrieks when she saw her prized pink *Mandevilla* vines cut down. "You may need to hide yourself for a while when Mom finds out."

"Your mother should have planted bougainvillea. They're pink flowers with sharp thorns that deter intruders, not invite them to climb the walls to break into the house."

"Now you're a landscaper as well? Last time I checked, the security system does a good job."

"Security systems can be hacked. One can never be too safe. Not when a well-attended event with hundreds of eyes upon your table can turn deadly."

A shudder raced through her as she realized he referenced the luncheon and her stalker's note. Peyton drew in a breath. "Then you'd best change. Suits and polished shoes get ruined at the beach, and I have work to do. I'll meet you downstairs in ten minutes."

She raced to her room to retrieve her backpack with the 35mm camera and her notebooks.

When Gray came down the stairs, she couldn't help but stare. He wore a starched white shirt, tie and charcoal trousers. Same as previously, except he'd removed the jacket. His polished shoes remained on his feet.

"You're going to ruin your pretty shoes," she muttered.

His gaze was level. "I can remove my shoes."

The shadow was such a stick-in-the-mud.

They started for the living room and the sliding doors leading out to the pool deck.

"Where are you going?"

Peyton wanted to groan as her brother descended the stairs. He looked dressed for a tennis match in white shorts and polo shirt, with a red sweater around his neck.

"Beach."

"Good. Mom and Dad need a walk, so we'll join you."

Her parents came out of the kitchen. Both wore casual clothing, her father in white shorts and a white polo. Probably playing tennis with her brother. Despite the relaxed air, lines of strain were evident on her parents' faces. Guilt stabbed her. *This is because of me. They're worried sick.*

For that reason only, she resigned herself to the shadow's protective services. Peyton forced a smile for their sake. "It's lovely out."

Though June was usually warm in Florida, the weather had been cooler this week. After leaving the house, Peyton headed for the white flagstone path leading from the pool deck, marching past the verdant lawn toward the private beach.

Dad had kept the lighting low on the beach out of her request, but Gray wanted to light up the beach like a Christmas party to keep anyone from using the ocean to access the mansion. She was firmly against this.

He'd also wanted to install night vision security cameras on the vacant beachfront property. Peyton vetoed that as well to protect the turtles. Turtles were visually oriented and infrared lighting could spook nesting females, or worse, disorient them as they returned to the ocean after laying their eggs.

They'd compromised with extra security cameras on the landscaping. The mansion had a view of the beach, but most of their beachfront property had a thicket of sable palmetto, gumbo-limbo and sea grape trees, and mangroves. The vegetation and trees buffeted the vacant land they owned adjacent to the mansion and made beach access difficult by land.

Excellent for nesting turtles, however.

Gray punched in a code to the gate and opened it. She walked down the short flight of stairs to the sand. The scent of brine, fresh air and ocean relaxed her rigid muscles. This was her true home, here amid the natural elements.

Not a crowded ballroom filled with society mavens, eager to get their photos in the local newspaper.

To the south of the beach was a fence and locked gate, which Peyton unlocked with her personal key. This was the private beach on Bradley land, known for nesting sea turtles. A turquoise ocean stretched for miles, the lacy whitecaps rushing onshore as wind blew off the water. Overhead the bright yellow sun and blue sky, punctuated by a few fluffy clouds, showed no signs of rain. Clay-colored sand squished beneath her footsteps. By summer, the sand would be far too hot to walk upon in bare feet this time of day.

A few hundred feet from the fence line, Adam Russell squatted down by a U-shaped set of fresh tracks as Clive Powell made notes on an electronic pad. Both had security clearances issued by Gray and the SOS agency to have beach access from the mansion's property. Peyton's family had their own rules. Only Adam and Martin Gauthier, the institute's acting director, had keys to the gated beach. Interns were allowed on the beach if accompanied.

Brimming with excitement, Peyton dashed over to them. The huge tracks were unmistakable. Leatherbacks were massive sea turtles, weighing up to 1,500 pounds.

Adam beamed and shoved a suntanned hand through his shoulder-length dark curls. He'd worked at the institute for two years and she'd come to rely on his excellent instincts and hard-work ethic.

"Leatherback. Big girl. Look at those tracks!" Adam chortled.

"Wish we could have seen her." Clive's grin matched Adam's. "I've always wanted to see one up close."

Peyton smiled. "I thought you wanted to study agronomy, too."

Clive was their summer intern from Jamaica.

"This is more exciting than irrigation systems," Clive said.

Her bodyguard squatted down by the tracks, but not too close. "Sea turtle nest?"

"No." Peyton examined the sand. "If she laid her eggs there would be signs of the nest."

"I thought sea turtles nested in the middle of Florida's summer," Gray remarked.

"About ninety percent of the nesting takes place starting in May, ending in October, but the season itself runs March through Halloween." Adam told him. "Getting a leatherback here this early is a good omen for the season."

"Leatherbacks usually start the nesting season March first. They're the first to nest. She wasn't laying, though." Peyton studied the sand. "Scouting out the area to see if it was a good spot. Or she was ready to lay her eggs and got spooked by something."

False crawls weren't unusual. But considering how the nests on this stretch of beach had produced few hatchlings late last season, she worried.

Did the turtles know something?

"This has always been a productive area for nesting," she muttered. "Clive, let me see your tablet."

She consulted her notes from last year, which she'd meticulously logged in to the institute's system. As she figured, this was the area producing dud eggs last year. Peyton dug into her backpack for her notebooks. Every season she logged her observations by hand as well as electronically for easy reference.

A notation in last September's log caught her attention. *Ask Fletcher about activity at high tide.*

Frowning, she shut the notebook. "Dad, remember Fletcher Richardson?"

Gray glanced at her. "Who's that?"

"A retired fisherman who fell on hard times. I gave him a job as a handyman on the grounds," Mr. Bradley answered.

"He was my friend." Peyton zipped up her pack and squelched her annoyance at her father's casual dismissal.

"Fletcher was retired military. Spec ops. He was stationed in Malaysia and used to go to the beach during nesting season to watch the leatherbacks. Made it a hobby of his. Fletcher was great to hang with. He'd patrol our beach early morning during turtle season. He had great instincts, could tell when a storm was coming and when the females would come ashore to lay their eggs, and kept track of when the eggs hatched."

"Why did he leave?" Gray asked.

"Got bored, moved to Florida's west coast about a month

ago. Those types, they're nomadic." Mr. Bradley shrugged. "Just another man finding it difficult to stay in one place."

Fletcher had moved away suddenly and his sudden decision to leave had hurt. She missed their chats. "I should look him up, ask him about last year's nests. He may have observed something we missed," Peyton mused.

"Where did he go?" Gray asked.

"Who knows?" Her father shrugged. "Maybe Clearwater."

Something about Fletcher bothered her deeply. They'd been friends, but earlier this year he told Peyton she should have more staff patrolling the beach because her family's land was prime territory for young people to trespass and go skinny-dipping.

She'd written off his remarks as a man who was overly protective of her family's property. Then suddenly one day he'd quit and left, with only a hurried goodbye.

"Adam, Clive, I want to do a geographic cyber profile of the sand, overlaying a grid of nests that produced more hatchlings and those that did not."

A gentle cough interrupted her.

"There's time later for that, Peyton." Her mother pointed to the slim gold watch on her wrist. "We have the ball to prepare for. Marcia is coming over at four to go over the seating arrangement."

Peyton sighed. "Mom…I'm working. Let me do my job. Do you know how endangered leatherback turtles are? This is more important."

"What ball? I wasn't notified about any other social events this week."

Gray's quiet voice cut through her consternation. Peyton offered a sheepish smile. "Oops."

His grim expression warned he didn't like this oversight. "What time is this ball and where?" he asked.

"We're hosting it, rather, our foundation is, so Peyton and the family are expected there at seven Saturday night at the Beach Club," her brother answered. "All the family will be there."

Gray looked thoughtful. "Isn't it late in the social season for a fundraising gala?"

How did he know about the social season in exclusive Sea Grape Beach?

"Yes, but this is a special gathering of my clients and my parents' friends who support the Marine Institute. They look forward to it each year before everyone leaves the island for the summer."

"Black-tie?" he asked.

Peyton's dread increased. "You're not going. Invited guests only. It's an exclusive gala. Security will be extra tight, so I'll be safe."

He gave her a level look. "It will be once I gain access. Where you go, I go. You were supposed to alert me to any schedule changes and it seems you've known of this event for a while."

"But I'm supposed to mingle with the guests and do a public relations spin! How am I going to raise money with you following me around like a puppy?"

"Peyton, don't be rude," her mother exclaimed.

"You can't come. It's black-tie."

She doubted her security guard had a tuxedo among his severe suits.

"I will be dressed for the occasion and at your side."

Then Gray nodded at her parents. "I've arrangements to make for added security."

"Gray…" Her father glanced at her. "We'll have plenty of security."

Gray's grim expression never changed, as if he prepared for a war instead of an elegant ball. "You cannot have enough if you want your daughter to remain safe. Dr. Bradley, if you'll accompany me to the house. I need to know everything about where this gala is being held and a layout of the property."

As her mother left with Gray, Peyton sank onto the sand and hugged her knees. "Dammit! One night off. That's all I wanted."

Her father joined her. "Honey, after what happened today, we can't take chances. It's for your protection. He needs to do his job."

"I thought his job was finding Crazy Man," she snapped.

"What happened today?" Adam asked.

She'd almost forgotten about them. "It's nothing. Just that lunatic who keeps stalking me. I don't even know how serious he is. Guys, why don't you continue working here and report the results to me later. Continue with the grid and measurements."

Adam nodded. "No problem. You okay, Peyton? We need you, so please, don't let anything happen to you."

He squeezed her hand, his blue eyes filled with concern.

Though they'd never be more than friends, she liked Adam and didn't want him to worry. Or Clive, who should be immersed in learning instead of her personal troubles. "I'm fine. Family stuff. Finish up here and remember, you're expected at the ball as well."

To lighten the mood, she grinned at Adam, who took pride in his curly hair. "I expect both of you to be polished and shining, and Adam, make sure not to spend an hour on primping."

He laughed and returned to taking measurements.

She walked back with her father and brother toward the house. The job she loved, and the animals she wanted to save, should come first. The man who threatened her life and well-being must be found soon. Peyton felt a keen sense of failure as she trudged through the sand.

How could she save sea turtles if she couldn't even save herself?

Chapter 4

Peyton was one stubborn woman, and she worried the hell out of him.

Hard to perform his job if she kept him in the dark. He understood. No one wanted someone tagging along after them, especially a free spirit like Peyton.

A day after the ominous incident at the luncheon, all the red flags sprang up. Someone slipped past him. Her stalker was out there, and hell, the damn stalker knew more about Peyton's schedule than Gray did.

He never planned to be a personal protector after what had happened two years ago, let alone guard a wealthy family's daughter. But he vowed to do his job to the best of his ability.

Today he felt personally responsible for that incident.

If he had to sleep in her damn bedroom, he would. Gray smiled grimly as he followed her up the stairs. Not that the prospect would be unpleasant.

Right. Back off, buddy. Never get involved with an assignment.

After he showered and dressed in a gray business suit and powder blue shirt and blue tie, he headed for Peyton's room. When he knocked on the door, she answered, her manner sleepy. Wearing a tank top and pink sleep shorts, she looked languid and sexy. Gray drew in a breath.

"I hope you slept well. I'll be here, outside your door."

Peyton paused and narrowed her eyes at him. "Do you mind?"

Hands folded, he positioned himself against the wall. "Not at all."

"Look, I know you must do your job…"

"Then allow me to do it."

"Go get a cup of tea. I'll be fine."

"I don't drink tea."

His response failed to make her smile. Gray inwardly sighed. She was so stubborn.

She sighed. "Today's an important day. I have a noon meeting with a former coworker on Manatee Island at the town's aquarium."

Gray pulled out his cell phone, plugged Manatee Island into maps. "About an hour's drive north. Less if we take the turnpike."

Peyton eyed him with that look of hers as if she wanted to slug him. "Alone. It's an important meeting."

"I won't get in your way."

"I don't suppose you'll let me go alone."

Gray considered. "No."

She bit her lush lower lip, nodded. "Figured as much."

He palmed his cell phone. "I need to know where is this meeting, who is the meeting with, everything about this place."

Peyton sighed.

"I can't do my job if you don't communicate with me."

She rattled off information, which he plugged into his

cell phone. "We'll leave around ten thirty. That will give me enough time to sweep the place before your meeting."

Her gaze swept over him. "If you don't mind changing into something less…severe. You look like you're going to a funeral. Or a board meeting. Or both."

"Sometimes they're interchangeable," he deadpanned.

For a moment she stared, then broke into a loud laugh. Finally. It was carefree and he liked the sound of her laughter.

"All right. Go change into something casual and meet me downstairs at ten thirty."

Gray resisted the urge to salute her as if he were still in the navy.

If only Peyton obeyed orders like the men in his unit had, his job would be much easier.

The shadow was stuck to her side, and she realized he had no intentions of leaving her alone. Honestly, after the fright at the luncheon, she felt relieved he insisted on going with her.

Not that today would be easy, and having him there during a personal and private time would be challenging. But the man did take his role seriously.

In a powder blue polo shirt and khaki shorts and her running shoes, she paced downstairs.

When Gray arrived, she felt tempted to whistle. The man was sophisticated and businesslike in a suit, but this attire…

He looked striking and like someone she'd want to date, if not for the severe expression.

Black cargo shorts showed the curve of muscle and sinew on his trim, athletic legs. The black polo shirt was softened by white trim on the sleeves and neckline. He'd donned running shoes that looked worn.

The outfit made him look relaxed and human. Almost. For the first time, she wondered about this man paid to stick to her side.

She gave a pointed look to the black polo shirt. "This is Florida. We're going to be out in the sun, so I advise changing into a lighter-colored shirt, unless you want to sweat. A lot."

"I never sweat."

As she stared, his lips twitched slightly upward. "That's a joke, Peyton."

The shadow turned and went upstairs. When he returned, he wore a powder blue polo shirt with the SOS logo on it. She resisted a smart-ass remark that they looked like twins with their colored matching shirts.

At least he'd paid attention to her. Maybe he'd pay attention to her when she asked for private time on the jetty.

"I don't think I've ever seen you out of a suit. Were you born in one?"

His lips twitched. "My sister-in-law would have agreed with that statement."

"Oh?" She tilted her head. "I bet I'd get along with her."

His mouth tilted up in a faint smile. "You probably would."

"Is everyone in your family so serious like you? Are they all in the security business? Are they here in Florida? Do you get to visit often with all your high-profile assignments?"

No signs of a smile now. "No. I seldom see them. My family is my business, not yours. Are you ready?"

Back to the stiff formality. Fine. She didn't need to be friends. Still, she was curious. "What happened to your gun? I thought it was attached to you, like your nose."

His mouth quirked in a smile, as if he liked her sarcasm. "My sidearm is more attached to me than my nose, which was realigned when I got a nose job to enhance my good looks."

As she stared, he added, "The plastic surgeon was the best."

Peyton blinked. He grinned. "Joking."

As she rolled her eyes, Gray lifted his untucked shirt. Tucked close to his body, in an inside hip holster, his pistol sat close to his body.

She had to admire his tact, along with his dry humor. "If you keep joking, you'll start to grow on me, Gray."

"Like a fungus?"

She rolled her eyes again. "Bad science joke. That's my forte, not yours."

Keys in hand, he gestured to the front door. "Shall we? I'm driving."

Peyton sighed again. "My car gets terrific gas mileage."

He gave her a pointed look. "My car is fast and I'm expert in losing people…when I need to lose those tracking me."

Terrific. Once more the situation was out of her control.

She'd been too upset to pay attention to his car after the luncheon, but when he escorted her into the garage and unlocked it, she now stared with awed fascination. Wealthy as her parents were, they didn't have a car like this.

Nor did they need one.

"What is this, a tank?" Peyton rapped on the thick passenger side window.

Gray opened the door for her and didn't answer until pulling out into the circular driveway.

"Not quite. Mercedes. Interior windows have a coat of polycarbonate to prevent passengers from glass splinters in case the windows receive gunfire. It can take explosions on the bottom or the sides—it is specially protected to guard against those. Bulletproof, even against an AK-47."

Gray patted the leather steering wheel. "Onboard fire extinguisher in case of gas attacks. Even the tires can run for another sixteen to eighteen miles if punctured."

Peyton didn't know what to say. A car like this had to cost at least half a million dollars with all the enhancements. "Gas attacks?"

"Yes, and not the kind suffered by those who indulge in too many Taco Tuesdays at a popular fast-food restaurant."

He said this without cracking a smile, but she sensed the humor beneath the words. "Bulletproof car. So tell me, bodyguard, where have you been hanging out lately that you need a bulletproof car?"

Gray's expression remained level. "In my work, it is needed. I am an executive protection agent, Peyton. This is a car equipped to protect heads of state…"

"Or mafia bosses, bodyguard."

Now he did glance at her. "My name is Gray."

"Sorry," she muttered.

Manatee Island was an hour's drive from her home. At first she didn't talk, and then he pried her with questions. Soon she was chattering. Sure beat the radio silence.

"I'm debating going for my PhD," she told him in a low voice as if confessing state secrets.

He glanced over at her. "Why?"

She looked out the window. "I love my work. I want to continue with marine biology. The extra education…my parents think I need it. My mother wants me to be more than I am."

He changed lanes. "What do you want?"

The question startled her. Few ever asked her preferences. Her parents usually dictated what direction her life should take. "I'm not sure yet. Guess I was going to take this summer to figure it out, until this jerk started interfering in my life."

"You can still plan your life. This jerk is my business and I will take care of him."

For the first time, she really paid attention to him. The grim tautness of his jaw, the determination in his steely eyes. Her gaze slid over to the pistol strapped to his side. Her father had assured her Gray had an open-carry permit and though she disliked guns, the sight of it proved a little reassuring.

Peyton toyed with her cell phone, finally asking the question she dreaded. "How dangerous is he? Is it a secret admirer or someone who might seriously hurt me?"

Here, in the confines of his Mercedes, without her worried family overlooking her every move, she expected more frank answers.

Gray consulted the GPS before answering, and kept glancing in the rearview mirror. "It depends. The police seem to think he's a harmless admirer."

"But you don't," she blurted out.

"No."

Gray flexed his fingers before settling them on the steering wheel again. "About one in twelve women nationwide experience some form of stalking during their life. It could be a harmless admirer, but then again, could not. Most of the female victims are stalked by someone they knew, perhaps intimately."

"You mean had sex with?"

That dark gaze glanced at her again. Impassive, cool. "Perhaps. But the women knew their stalker when he finally was caught. It's a domestic case where the stalking can occur during the actual relationship. Not after the relationship ceases."

"What about my stalker? Any idea who he is?"

Gray frowned. "Your stalker exhibits signs of the classic symptoms—wishing to evoke fear, because he covets power and control. He wishes to control you, and make you fear him. It may be someone you know. Therefore domestic."

"Not a prank." She was hoping it was a friend with a terrible sense of humor.

"No." Now he glanced at her again. "More than half the women who are stalked are also physically assaulted by that person. About twenty-five percent or more of cases result in lethal violence."

"The victim is killed by her stalker."

Gray nodded, his jaw tight again.

A chill ran down her spine. Now she began to understand the worry her parents felt. Maybe they knew these statistics as well.

I'm not going to be a statistic.

"What did I do to deserve this?" she blurted out, fisting her hands in her lap. "I'm not a bad person."

"No one said you were. You're the victim, Peyton. You did nothing to encourage or elicit attention from this person. Do you understand?"

His voice carried a deep note, threaded with anger, and she sensed grief as well.

"Yes. Thank you."

Finally he relaxed a little. "I loathe victim blaming."

"Even when the victim places the blame on herself?"

"Yes. Most women in these situations don't report the crime. They fear the police will not take them seriously, or worse, they blame themselves for their stalker's behavior. It's like men pointing at a woman being…assaulted and blaming her because perhaps she wore a short skirt."

His knuckles whitened as he tightened his grip on the steering wheel. Gray was human, and she was glad he didn't view her as a socialite who encouraged her stalker. In fact, he seemed the opposite.

"What was her name?" she asked quietly.

He threw her a quick, startled glance. "Who?"

"The woman you knew who was stalked, and no one paid attention to her complaints until it was too late."

Was that a swear word he muttered under his breath? Peyton waited. Her family and friends sometimes noted she was intuitive, perhaps too much. But she'd felt those waves of anger mingling with grief here in the car.

Gray blew out a breath. "It doesn't matter."

As if to switch off their conversation, he punched a button on his phone and music began to flow through the speakers. Light classical music, the strains of horn and flute. Peyton got the message. No personal talk.

For the next thirty minutes, she consulted her notes on her phone as he drove. Finally he pulled off on the turnpike exit.

Gray dutifully followed the GPS instructions off the mainland to the causeway. Peyton put her phone down, her excitement growing at seeing her friend again. Today was a day of remembrance, yet she hadn't seen anyone here in months.

The parking lot of the Manatee Island Aquarium was full, so Gray parked in the dirt lot adjacent to the building and near the marina.

"Stay here while I do a perimeter check."

For once, she waited for him, slinging her laptop bag over one shoulder. Gray got out of the car, looked around, checked the parking lot, then headed inside. Finally he returned, consulting his cell phone.

Curious, she tilted her head. "Why are you always looking at your phone? Checking messages?"

"Checking to see if anyone tampers with my vehicle. If anyone other than myself touches it before I disarm the vehicle, my phone pings."

Peyton swallowed hard. All these sophisticated devices

should have reassured her, but only reminded her of how seriously Gray took her stalker and thought him dangerous. He wasn't leaving anything to chance.

Hand at the small of her back, Gray herded her toward the aquarium building. Blue water lapped at the breakwater rocks along the causeway. A few seagulls flew overhead, while a pelican perched on the railing of the nearby marina, eyeing a fisherman cleaning his catch.

So serene. Quiet. Yet she and Brandy both knew how a perfect summer day along Florida's coast could turn gray with storm clouds in the space of hours, or worse, indigo with an approaching hurricane.

Peyton tried not to remember that day.

At the receptionist's booth, the teenager taking tickets looked bored as he glanced up from his cell phone. Must be a new volunteer.

Peyton smiled. "I'm Peyton Bradley, here to meet with Brandy Devine."

Her friend's name had always been a joke. Brandy said she bore no love of the alcoholic drink that she'd been named after. "But my dad did and so did my mom, because I was conceived after they'd consumed quite a bit," she always jested.

The bored teen rolled his eyes. "Yeah, I heard. Twenty dollars."

Peyton bit her lip, handed over the money. No big deal, and the facility probably needed the money, although her family's private foundation gave them funding. "Where is she?"

"Dunno. Around here someplace."

As she started to walk away, Gray followed. The teenager, who had seemed half-asleep, suddenly perked up.

"Hey that's a gun. You can't bring guns in here," he called out, sounding suddenly important.

Peyton waited for Gray to respond.

"Oh?" Gray edged up one charcoal black eyebrow. "You mean this?"

He removed the Sig Sauer at his waistband and held it with ease.

The boy gulped again. "Uh, uh, yeah. What are you, a cop?"

"I have an open-carry permit. Would you like to see my permit?" Gray was calm and polite, but steel edged his words.

The teenager gulped. "Um, no, that's okay."

By now she was holding back laughter. As they left the reception area and turned down the hallway leading to the tanks and exhibits, she finally laughed. "You scared the living daylights out of him. Maybe he was afraid you'd shoot the fish."

His mouth quirked a little. Only a little. "I'm sorry I disturbed his nap."

Peyton caught the clean, spicy scent of his cologne cutting through the briny air of the aquarium. This was a different side of the shadow, displaying humor and yet still very much on guard and alert.

Her curiosity rose. "Have you worked for SOS a long time?"

Instant shutdown. "Long enough." He gestured to the tanks. "Shall we? Where is your friend working?"

The aquarium was small, but offered plenty of educational exhibits. Brandy was in the back at the touch tank, talking to a child about the creatures in the saltwater tank.

Without looking up, Brandy called out, "Please wash your hands first before using the touch tank. We want to make certain the sea animals aren't contaminated by lotions you may be wearing."

Gray looked amused as he headed over to the sink. "I see dirty hands are more of a threat than a pistol," he said in a low voice.

"Around here, yes," she whispered. "Much more dangerous."

They dried their hands and approached the tank. Brandy was still absorbed in talking with a young child who used the step to peer into the saltwater tank.

"Don't lift up the animals. Just touch. Be careful." Brandy pointed to a sea urchin with shells adorning it. "Do you know why the urchin puts seashells on its outer structure?"

"Because it loves the bling," Peyton answered.

Brandy glanced up, saw her and her face lit up. "Peyton!"

Her friend came around the counter and hugged her, then gave Gray a twice-over. "Hi there."

Peyton introduced Brandy. "Gray, this is Brandy Devine. She used to work at the institute until she abandoned us for a better life on the island. Brandy, this is…"

Her bodyguard? It sounded so pretentious and Brandy was a curious soul. "Ah, Gray. My friend."

Satisfied she fulfilled the little social courtesies, she was dismayed at the wink Brandy gave her. "We talked on the phone and he already introduced himself a few minutes ago. Friend. Right. Nice to meet you… Peyton's friend."

Brandy smiled at him. "So have you known our Peyton long?"

Please don't tell her you work for my father, Peyton pleaded silently.

Gray merely shook Brandy's hand. "Pleasure. Are you the director here? What a fascinating tank."

Thank heavens Gray steered Brandy away from the conversational danger zone. Maybe he wasn't as bad as she'd thought.

Brandy flashed a radiant smile. "Excuse me a minute while I get someone to replace me at the tank."

After waving over another worker, Brandy joined them.

"Let's take a walk outside. My office is far too cramped and it's a gorgeous day. Unless you'd like a tour first?"

She glanced at Gray. "Would you like one?"

"Of course," Gray replied. "But we would prefer the meeting to be held inside, where there is more privacy. A conference room will suffice. Peyton, after you."

There it was again, the brush of his fingers against the small of her back as he steered her before him. It was a clear protective measure, but she couldn't help a shiver of awareness. The reaction bothered her. He was her body-guard and nothing more and she had work to do.

Brandy explained to Gray the various saltwater tanks and the sea creatures swimming inside. He seemed particularly fascinated by a jellyfish swimming upward, its nearly opaque body quivering with each upward movement.

"Jellyfish," he mused. "They sting."

"As a protective measure," Peyton quickly interjected. "Like most marine animals, they have a good defense system. They don't harm other animals, except to eat or protect themselves."

Something flickered in his gaze. "Unlike humans, whose sting can be far more detrimental."

Much as his response intrigued her, Peyton wisely didn't ask questions. By now she'd discerned he was all about her business, but shut down when she inquired about his personal life.

And speaking of personal lives… She adjusted the strap of her laptop bag and gave Brandy a meaningful look. "We need to talk."

Brandy's smile was too wide. "Sure. Gray, want to re-main here and look at the tanks? We're going to have a demonstration soon of feeding the fish."

"Where Peyton goes, I go."

Her friend didn't even bat an eyelash in surprise. "Okay. Follow me."

They headed to a small conference room where Brandy held educational seminars. Gray did a thorough check of the room, and studied the exits. He stood by the main exit after blocking the secondary exit with a chair.

Brandy raised her eyebrows, but said nothing. Peyton unzipped her laptop bag and removed a sheath of papers.

Gray didn't watch either of them. He stood a slight distance away, hovering in the background as if to give them some privacy. Yet she'd seen him spring into action if he felt she were endangered. The man struck with the swiftness of a cobra.

Brandy didn't look at the papers. "Is Gray your bodyguard?"

Ignoring the question, Peyton pointed to the legal documents. "You should have the lawyer who volunteers for the aquarium review these before signing them. Everything is what we discussed, but still, you need to have them reviewed."

"Peyton, what the hell is going on?"

She didn't want to play games, but she also didn't want Brandy worried. "This, Brandy. This is what's going on. My family's foundation is funding your facility for another year. I convinced the board of directors to add another twenty percent because the grant amount you requested isn't enough, not with rising cost of fish food and maintenance and cost of living…"

"Dammit, Peyton, is that man over there looking ready to shoot anything that would touch you a bodyguard! Are you in danger?"

"Brandy, he's with me as a precaution. And he's an executive protection agent. They don't call his type bodyguards anymore. Everything is okay…"

"No, it's not." Visibly shaken, her face pale, her friend shook her head. "Dennis is back. He's been back in town for four months now. You know what that means."

"Who is Dennis?" Gray stepped up to the table, his gaze sharpening as he studied Brandy.

Peyton went still, her mind racing. She'd known Brandy for almost as long as she'd known Michelle. The three of them had grown up together, played together, even dated together when they grew older. She trusted Brandy.

But her brother, Dennis, was another matter. She'd forgotten about Dennis when the police had asked her about suspects and past boyfriends.

Brandy answered for her. "Dennis is my brother. He was in jail for assault and battery."

Gray zoned in on her like a bloodhound scenting a trail. "Assault and battery of who?"

Peyton cringed as Brandy answered. "His girlfriend."

"Who is this Dennis to you, Peyton?"

What an interesting table. Real mahogany wood. Donated by a kind donor, but still, it was from a rainforest. She was glad the facility had replaced the picnic tables outside with environmentally friendly material, though she remembered the old wood tables outside near the causeway had some graffiti on them that made for great conversation, like the person who carved into the table "Big Rod Rules!" Who was Big Rod? Was it a fishing rod? What was the story behind the carving? So many stories…

"Peyton, answer me," Gray ordered.

His deep, stern tone indicated he would not tolerate silence. Peyton sighed, glanced at Brandy, saw the concern on her friend's face.

"Dennis was a little obsessed with dating me. It never went anywhere."

"Dennis might be my brother, but he's got a violent temper and he used it on Peyton once," Brandy burst out. "It's the reason why she never went out with him again."

A frown line appeared on Gray's face. "And you never thought to mention this to either the police detective working your case or to myself, Peyton?"

"What case?" Brandy pushed aside the papers. "Forget the grant. Peyton, tell me what is going on! Why do you need a bodyguard?"

Uncomfortable with all the attention, she looked at her friend. "I have a stalker. It started a little while ago. It's the reason why Dad hired Gray from a reputable agency. I made a deal with my parents that I would stay in town for the summer to do the nest counts and my work and allow a bodyguard, I mean, an executive protection agent, to tail me."

Saying the words and seeing the freaked-out expression on her friend's face made Peyton realize the gravity of her situation. She'd seen the shadow as a necessary nuisance, thinking only of her work and the inconvenience. Her overprotective family, well, she thought they were being overprotective. She never considered their worries or concerns for her safety.

It was selfish of me to not think of how this affects others, how they would worry.

Peyton gave Brandy a reassuring smile. "It's okay, Brandy. I have Gray here and he's vigilant…"

Brandy shook her head. "You should have told me. Dammit, Peyton, I don't like being kept in the dark. Not with my brother running around."

"I'm sure Dennis has other things to occupy himself rather than following me, such as checking in with his parole officer," she said dryly.

"Dennis is a control freak and he's obsessive." Brandy's

gaze looked almost accusatory as she glared at Peyton. "You should have told me what was going on."

"You should have told Peyton and myself what was going on," Gray said calmly. "Did you not think to inform your friend that your brother, an ex-con, was released?"

Brandy's mouth opened and closed. Her friend wasn't accustomed to being criticized.

"I'm sorry," she stammered to Peyton.

"I should have been more forthcoming." She slid her hand across the table to grip Brandy's. "I didn't want you to worry about me. You've had enough to deal with."

They both fell silent, thinking of today's anniversary. Brandy scrubbed her eyes. "As long as you're safe. That's what matters, Pey. I don't want to lose you, too."

Peyton squeezed her hand. "You won't lose me. I promise."

Brandy glanced at Gray, quiet, hovering but absolutely expressionless. "Whatever you need to know about my brother, ask. Peyton's my concern. Not him."

Removing his cell phone from a pocket, Gray sat at the table. "Where is he living now? With your parents?"

Brandy nodded. "It was a condition of his release, that he's with family. Not that I'm thrilled about it, but Mom and Dad assured me they would watch him, take care of him. He's also under court-ordered anger management classes."

Listening as Brandy rattled off all the details about Dennis, Peyton felt as if she'd lost touch with her good friend. Oh, she'd seen Brandy in social settings and in business, but everything had been superficial. Brandy wasn't a superficial friend. With a pang, Peyton realized she'd neglected her friend's needs and instead focused on her own.

And that was the ironic nature of her work. Marine biologists sometimes concentrated so much on the animals and environments they wanted to protect and preserve, they forgot about the people around them. People who also held the same concerns about protecting the environment.

Gray finished texting on his cell and glanced at her. Worry needled her. Was Dennis her stalker? He'd been free when the harassment began. He wasn't that far away, and during the day she suspected it was easy enough for him to slip the watchful eye of his parents. The Devines were indulgent parents who thought their children could do no wrong.

"One last thing. Does your brother own a gun? Do your parents possess any firearms in the house?"

Brandy blinked. "Dennis used to go hunting in the Everglades with Dad. He had a handgun, but my parents sold it after his arrest. All the guns in my parents' house are locked up."

Gray did not look reassured.

"I need to know everything about your relationship with Dennis," he told Peyton.

Peyton shrugged. "It wasn't much of a relationship. We went out a couple of times."

"Were you sexually intimate?"

The bombshell question made her flush to the roots of her hair. "What?"

"If you were, chances are more likely that he will seek that again, violently. Especially if you broke up with him."

Brandy seemed fascinated by the papers she now read. Peyton swallowed hard. "So now you're going to question my sex life?"

"Yes."

The blunt answer was oddly refreshing after all the dancing around she'd experienced with the police and her family. "The answer is no. We kissed and he wanted more, but the chemistry wasn't there. So I broke it off."

Gray leaned forward, intense. Purposeful. "But he did want more. What was his reaction when you broke up with him?"

A loud bang outside split the air. Brandy jumped and Peyton startled. Gray did not move a muscle. He rose gracefully from the table. "Stay here. Brandy, stay with her. I will be a moment."

"It was only a truck backfiring, I'm sure of it."

Her words were lost as Gray vanished. Brandy's hands trembled as she set down the legal forms.

"It's okay, hon, it was only a truck. Let's focus on the grant. Everything look good?"

"Yes. I'll have our lawyer look these over, as a formality. Thanks, Pey. You know my staff and I appreciate your family's foundation helping us out. Without your money, I doubt we could stay open."

"The foundation is happy to help." Peyton thought of the real reason she needed to be here today. "I'm asking Gray to drive me to the jetty. Do you want to come with us?"

Brandy shook her head. "No. I said my goodbyes three years ago and remembering this date is too…painful. I'll honor her in my own way."

Not wishing to pressure her friend, she nodded. "Would you like me to express your condolences to her parents when I call them later?"

"Yes. Although I did send them a card, as I always do."

She'd totally forgotten about Brandy's traditional card. One more thing she'd forgotten about. Peyton fiddled with the strap of her laptop. "Brandy, I'm sorry I haven't been a better friend these past few months. I can give you lots of excuses but none suffice."

Brandy's expression turned fierce. "Pey, you're one of the best friends I have. Don't apologize. But please, don't keep me in the dark from now on."

She nodded. "If you won't, I won't."

* * *

Some things were better left in the dark. At least for this moment. With Peyton's emotions running high, discerning that today was a solemn and painful anniversary, he decided against telling her the true source of the small explosion until later.

He'd let them draw their own conclusions as he'd returned to the conference room, suggesting to Brandy that she and Peyton check out the fish at the marina. He had wondered if some fool with leftover July Fourth munitions had decided to fish by tossing a firecracker into the water.

This was Florida, after all. All sorts of strange people made strange things happen.

Gray watched her walk to the marina with Brandy, a short enough distance where he could still watch her. With a covert move, he folded the note he'd found left on his windshield. Later, he would hand it over to the police.

The flat tire, that was another matter. He kicked it ruefully, noting the small round puncture hole. The acrid stench of gunpowder hung in the air.

No one had followed him here. He was expert at losing people. Someone knew they were headed to the aquarium. Someone with access to Peyton's schedule or someone who knew Brandy had a meeting with her.

It could have been Brandy's brother, Dennis. Or someone else.

But this moved Dennis high up on the suspect list. Brandy said her brother owned a gun and he had worked as a mechanic for luxury cars. Surely Dennis knew this vehicle couldn't be tampered with, but a bullet in the tire would surely slow him down.

He didn't believe in coincidences, and it seemed too coincidental they'd discussed Brandy's brother and this happened.

He changed the tire, glad he kept a premium spare in the trunk. Then he phoned SOS.

His friend and boss Jarrett answered right away. "Report."

"New development. I was tailed to Manatee Island as I drove Peyton here for a mandatory business meeting. Someone shot out my tire while Peyton was conducting her meeting. I'm leaving the evidence in the trunk for you to retrieve the bullet. There was also another note."

Gray took a deep breath. "This one read 'I'm coming for you and not even your grim reaper bodyguard will stop me.'"

"Well, you are a little grim, but that is excessive." Jarrett sighed. "Damn, I had hoped this was a case of an admirer gone cuckoo. Gunfire is another matter. You concerned he might try to take out Peyton?"

"Not with this kind of stalking. It's power and control and he's frustrated that I'm in the way of obtaining his target. He doesn't want to hurt her, at least not yet."

"He might try to take you out, Gray. Be careful."

"I always am," he replied.

A pause from Jarrett. "Does Peyton or her family know yet about your past? They might question why you took this assignment. I'm still wondering if you were the right choice for this job, Gray."

Muscles tensing, he began walking toward his charge. "I'm the only choice for this job and you know it."

"I'm putting a lot of faith in you, Gray. Don't prove me wrong."

He hung up, considering his options. The less the Bradley family, especially Peyton, knew about his past, the better. All they needed to know was he was dedicated to the job of protecting her.

His personal life was private. No one needed to know.

Chapter 5

Gray insisted on escorting Brandy and Peyton back inside the aquarium. He wondered if some fool with a firecracker had tossed it into the water. Such an offense was dangerous to the fishing industry, he'd told them, and here was this aquarium, dedicated to protecting marine life.

With that as his cover story, he questioned all the volunteers and staff working inside. Even the sleepy teen who'd taken their money had woken up with alert interest and insisted he had not seen or heard anything unusual. The few visitors they'd had were families with children.

Gray inquired about the whereabouts of Brandy's brother. She phoned her parents, who told her Dennis was on the dock, fishing.

When she insisted on speaking to him, surprise. He wasn't there. But the sedan they had given him was gone. Gray insisted on a description of the car and the license plate and texted them to the detective working the case.

Brandy hung up, looking worried again. "My parents said he probably went to the bait shop."

Or more likely, headed here to deliver a little bait of his own. Best they complete the task Peyton had on her agenda, and head back to her family's house.

At least on home turf, he could protect her better than here in the open.

When they left the aquarium, Brandy waving goodbye, he kept an eye out to see if anyone tailed them. It was a quiet day, only a few cars on the street. He kept his thoughts to himself, swirling in his head.

He had a car that seemed indestructible, and yet someone had found a way to disable it. It was painfully obvious he wasn't as prepared as he'd thought. Damn, he was exposed and that made Peyton vulnerable.

Gray hated feeling this way. Life was a crapshoot, but he'd tried his best to insulate himself against the unknown through discipline, control and being prepared.

That bullet in his tire flattened all his well-laid plans.

They parked at the local jetty. Peyton pointed to her laptop. "Can I leave this in the trunk?"

Thinking of the shot-out tire, he gestured. "It's safe inside the car. No one can break inside."

She unzipped the bag and removed a red silk rose and then handed it to him. "So you don't let anyone in your trunk? Don't want anyone to see the dead body in there?"

Gray's lips twitched. "No, I got rid of that last week."

"Oh." She considered. "Then you must have something else in there that's top-secret. Maybe a bazooka in there or other top-secret defensive weapons like 007's cars?"

"Yes," he said solemnly. "You've outed me. I'm exactly like James Bond. The car proves it. The martini and the penguin suit I save for later, along with the busty blondes and redheads and the drawl."

For a minute she didn't even smile. Then she grinned, shook her head. "I don't think so. By the way, I can't stand James Bond."

Clutching the red rose, she led the way to the boardwalk along the Indian River. Granite rocks piled up against the jetty bore plaques with names on them. They were memorial plaques, he realized.

Peyton stopped before one bronze plaque that looked fairly recent, not as weathered as the others. Silk pink and red roses wreathed it.

It said simply, "Michelle 'Shelly' Stevens, forever in our hearts."

Peyton took the red rose and set it into a container near the rock and stood in silence for a moment.

When she looked at him, her eyes were wet, like two blue glistening gemstones.

He didn't want to pry. Getting involved with an assignment was taboo in his line of work. But something inside him twisted at the sight of her distress.

"Your friend?" he asked in a soft voice.

Peyton nodded. "Today's the anniversary of her death three years ago. Hurricane May."

"The Category 3 that struck Florida," he recalled.

"Brandy, Shelly and I were good friends. We grew up together. She lived on the beach and didn't heed the evacuation order. Shelly was worried about the sea turtle nests that were vulnerable. She thought she had time and the hurricane would go further north. It dropped south instead. Direct hit. She went onto the beach to try to save the eggs, but the storm surge was too much. Her boyfriend insisted on remaining with her, tied a rope around her to prevent her from getting washed out to sea. They were both washed away. Kevin made it, but had a broken arm and collarbone.

He kept clinging to her, trying to save her. Shelly… She was dead when he finally got her to the surface."

She sat on a bench before the rocks, hugging her knees. Gray joined her. He knew about this kind of pain of losing someone close to you.

"Shelly wasn't afraid of anything. She always nudged me into taking it one step further, breaking the rules. We all were part of the turtle patrol growing up, volunteering to watch my parents' private beach for crawls and hatchlings. She was a real daredevil, the first one to zip-line, the first one to skydive and the first to get certified in scuba diving. After she died, I was devastated. That's when my parents, especially my father, put a halt to some things. They began worrying more."

"Because if something happened to Shelly, it could happen to you as well." He understood Mr. Bradley's reasoning.

Not that he agreed with it.

Peyton nodded. "He became overprotective after that. Shelly's dad and my dad were good friends, golf buddies. Dad saw what losing Shelly did to him… He became a ghost of himself. Never the same."

Losing a child would do that. Gray felt an unexpected lump in his throat as he remembered his own loss.

"You can't compare what happened to her to your own life," he said gently. "She risked her life during a dangerous storm."

Peyton wiped her eyes, the stubborn set of her jaw warning him he treaded on delicate territory.

"She would have done anything to save sea turtles. Even though it was illegal to touch the nest and the eggs, she was dedicated to turtles. I'm the same. So don't blame the victim."

Her lower lip wobbled. "There was enough of that already after the storm passed and people started pointing fingers. It doesn't matter. My best friend is gone and is never coming back. All those people on social media who kept insisting it was her fault for putting herself in danger and not evacuating…who didn't know her, her passion and sometimes, yes, foolish decisions. Strangers who blamed the victim instead of showing compassion. What is wrong with people?"

She stood and looked down at the memorial stone. "I don't get it, Shelly. How could you be dead? You were supposed to live until you were an old, gray-haired woman. We were supposed to get married together, have babies together, go on stupid cruises and be old ladies drinking vodka martinis as we drove our golf carts around the retirement village.

"Not this. This is stupid. Why did you die? You were so healthy. You were the one who jogged, who went to the doctor, who did everything right. Dammit, you ate organic. This wasn't supposed to happen to you. You were so generous, so giving, so filled with awesome life! Why did you have to die? Why do those who hate and thrive on the pain of others live and you died? I don't get it. It's not fair."

Gray knew about grief, the deep kind that punched in the gut and hollowed you from the inside out. With extreme gentleness, he put a hand on her trembling shoulder.

"Life is not fair," he said quietly. "It never is, Peyton. The best you can do is grieve, slowly accept and move through it. You will never get over her death because you don't. You get through it. You get through it one day at a time and if you can't take a day, you take it an hour at a time. And they teach you through their deaths. You learn. You learn to quit wasting time on people who waste your time. You learn to make your own happiness and live with intensity to honor their memories. You learn to grab every single precious goddamn moment you're given above ground and wring it out like a washcloth, and not waste a single second because you never know how long you'll have on this earth. No one does."

Two fat tears rolled down her cheeks. She made no attempt to brush them away. He couldn't stand seeing her cry and took an instinctive step forward, his arms open.

She went into his arms, quietly crying as he held her. Simple human contact. Touch. Nothing more. Nothing significant. But he felt her pain down to his bones.

He didn't want Peyton absorbed in grief. He released her as she fumbled for tissues in her pack. As she wiped her face, Peyton offered a lopsided smile. "I came prepared for this. I must look a mess."

"You look fine," he said gently. "Let's walk. You said this inlet is good for manatee sightings."

At the press of his fingers on her arm, she looked surprised. Then she looked at him, something in her watery gaze he couldn't quite read. *Damn, Gray, hold on. This is not in the rule book.*

Abruptly he released her and then they walked to the edge of the jetty. Peyton brightened as she pointed to three oblong gray blobs in the water. A fat rounded nose poked up through the surface, taking in air. Manatees.

"Look! It's a family. Mom, dad and baby!"

Busy scanning the area, he only nodded. Manatees didn't interest him as much as the twenty-something man in the faded ball cap who looked more interested in Peyton than the line he'd cast out.

Absorbed in the manatees, Peyton crouched down, peering into the water. Gray stiffened as Ball Cap abandoned his fishing pole and strolled toward them in an amicable manner. Was this the same person who shot his tire? His hand dropped to his sidearm. With his gaze on the man, and Peyton at his side, he waited. Watched.

The manatees provided his next move. They swam toward the jetty in Ball Cap's direction. But instead of following them, Ball Cap advanced toward Peyton, a look on his face of more than casual interest. Not studying the sea cows in the briny water as others did. No, his attention was focused on Peyton.

Gray let him get closer. His untucked shirt billowed around his waist, but Gray caught sight of a bulky object beneath the shirt.

Shoving Peyton backward, Gray pounced. In a fluid move, he tackled the man, throwing him down. He disarmed the man, taking the pistol and tucking it into his belt while training his own weapon on Ball Cap.

Ball Cap didn't resist, simply looked up at him.

"Overkill much?" Ball Cap drawled.

"Who are you?"

"Name is John Doe."

"Who's your handler?" Gray snapped.

The man's gaze went wide. "I work the same line of work as you do. Protecting her." He pointed to a shaken Peyton. "Look in my wallet and you'll see."

What the…?

Gray pulled the man's wallet free with one hand while training his weapon on him with his other hand. Sure enough, the business card read Acme Securities.

Glancing at a pale-faced Peyton, he gestured for her to come closer. "Recognize this jerk?"

She shook her head. Didn't think she would, but it was a good way to get her closer without drawing any additional attention to her.

Because this had already turned into a circus sideshow,

some people ceasing the filming of the manatees and now aiming their cell phones at him.

Later, he'd deal with that.

Losers.

Throwing the wallet back at the man and handing him back his weapon, he gestured. "Get the hell out of here."

The man stuffed his wallet back into his pocket, glancing at the gathering crowd.

Now to deal with the social media circus. Gray placed Peyton behind him, and whipped out his cell phone, taking video of the people taking video. He finished and dialed the number of a well-known former celebrity client, who answered on the first ring.

Gray put her on speaker and turned the volume up so the lookie-loos could hear.

"Hey there, sexy protector," Courtney drawled. "What's up?"

He raised his voice. "Need a favor. Can you upload this vid I'm sending to your Insta and TikTok accounts? You have what now? Two million followers?"

"Try five million," she answered, sounding amused.

"Upload the video with the message, 'And this is how you deal with nosy bystanders who think that videotaping anyone in public is their right to go viral. Look at all these faces. Are these the faces of people you want as your friends?'"

"What? Who are these people? Send me that vid right now."

He smiled. "Thanks, hon. Talk to you later."

After hanging up, he pressed Send and texted his client the video. People scattered and turned away. Some looked ashamed.

Gray took Peyton's arm, hustled her away from the gathering crowd.

"That was amazing," she murmured. "Great response back at the ones videotaping me on their cell phones."

He didn't reply. Not until they reached his vehicle and were safely inside did he breathe. Damn. Gray pulled out his cell phone and called his employer.

Jarrett answered on the first ring. "What's wrong?"

"Did you send backup when I did not request it?"

"What backup?"

"The man tailing Peyton whom I just tackled. He flashed a card that read Acme Security. He was tailing me. I checked everything out and this asshole shows up."

"Gray, listen to me…"

"Jarrett, if you don't trust me on this assignment, pull me," he said tightly. "But for God's sake, don't pull crap like that and hire others without notifying me. I could have shot your 'extra protection.'"

"He's not one of ours and I would never hire anyone without vetting them. Let me make a call, get back to you right away. Now I'm as pissed off as you are."

He hung up, raked a hand through his hair. Dammit, it was tough enough to guard Peyton without worrying he was being tailed as well.

She folded her hands into her lap, but was clearly shaken. "What's wrong?"

Nothing I can't handle. "Trying to figure out how many more men are on your case."

"And they didn't tell you? That's wrong."

He glanced at her. For the first time, they agreed on something.

His phone rang. Jarrett again. "I called the old man. Peyton's father, who contracted with us to hire you. It was him. He hired four extra security guards from another firm. He found out Peyton's schedule and arranged to have all of them there when she arrived. He knew she would go first to meet with Brandy, then to the jetty for the anniversary of her friend's death. Look for three others."

Gray closed his eyes. "Damn."

"Yeah. I'm pretty pissed off, Gray. Clients not communicating with us is a main reason they get into trouble. Listen, I'm ready to pull this assignment. You'll get full pay for it, but this crap hurts our rep and, worse, it hurts the client you've been charged to protect. You say the word, and I'm canceling the contract. Screw Bradley. I'll eat the cost. We can afford it."

Fingers tight around his phone, he looked at Peyton. Thought about how vulnerable she was. Made a decision. "No. I'll stick it out. But I'm giving Bradley a piece of my mind when we return to the house."

"Do it. He's going to have extra men every time Peyton ventures out in public. In fact, for tomorrow night, he's ordered four extra security guards. More rent-a-cop types."

Gray closed his eyes, swore.

Jarrett's voice softened. "I told him you were the best for this job. He said he had some misgivings."

His eyes flew open. "He did a check on me."

Silence gave him the answer.

Gray swore again. "I'll be in touch. Taking her home now."

Right now his rep was on the line. Sure it had been tarnished the past couple of years, but he didn't want any more screwups blackening it into oblivion.

Gray started the car. Glanced at her. "You okay?"

She nodded, hugging herself. "That was…intense. Does that man really work as a bodyguard?"

"Maybe not after today. He was supposed to be invisible. He was as invisible as a dump truck."

She moistened her soft, pink mouth. "Yes. He was rather scary."

Gray's gaze sharpened. "You scared of me?"

She relaxed ever so slightly. "No. It sounds strange, but even though I don't know you and my father thinks you need backup, I trust you to keep me safe."

After punching in the security code to start his car, he didn't know if her trust was a good thing. Or bad. He only knew one thing.

Her father had doubts about this assignment and his capacity to keep her safe. But Bradley didn't know Gray, didn't know his ruthless streak.

Once he promised to keep someone safe, he followed through on that promise.

Even if it came at a high personal cost to himself.

Chapter 6

Peyton had previously thought of the shadow as a necessary nuisance to doing her work. Seeing him in action, now she had a different opinion.

The way he'd tackled that man after Gray thought he was a threat to her showed his dedication. It burned into her brain that Gray took seriously every single potential threat to her safety.

And it burned her biscuits that her own father didn't trust him.

He stopped at a full-service station to purchase gas and have a mechanic tighten the lug nuts on one tire.

On the ride home, she kept the conversation light, talking about her work with sea turtles and her work in marine biology and conservation. Gray said little, seeming to focus on the road. But a telltale tic in his taut jaw indicated his true feelings. The man was incensed.

She didn't blame him. Who wanted to be second-guessed when you were doing your work? Peyton remembered a time when she first started at the institute and her supervisor sent another biologist to check her findings on new sea turtle nests. Necessary, but at least she'd been aware of it.

Not this business with Gray discovering by accident that someone else had been sent to guard her, someone in the shadows.

"You really know Courtney?" She flashed a peace sign. "That Courtney? The one-name celeb famous for her reality television series? Is she a friend?"

"Not a friend. Former high-profile client. She owed me a few favors."

"Your clients must be all high-profile."

Gray kept glancing in the rearview mirror. "Peyton, now that we're alone and have privacy, you need to know what happened. That wasn't a firecracker you heard earlier."

She swallowed hard. "It was a gunshot."

He blinked in apparent surprise. "Yes. Someone shot out my rear left tire. I did not want to tell you right there because of Brandy."

"Was there a note?"

"For me."

As he told her the contents, her stomach roiled. "How did this person find us? You said you were certain you weren't followed."

"I wasn't. But all it took was someone to know you had a meeting with Brandy. Look at what happened at the jetty. Who else knew you had a meeting with her?"

Peyton nibbled on her bottom lip. "Everyone, it seemed. Everyone at the institute, and the aquarium. And everyone Brandy knew…"

She looked at Gray as he zipped between cars. "Do you think it's Dennis?"

"Perhaps. I need to check on a few things. He does seem like a likely suspect."

Her cell rang. Peyton glanced at the caller ID. It was Martin Gauthier, the acting director of the institute.

"Hey. All okay there? Everything set for tomorrow's presentation?" she asked.

Martin hesitated. "Peyton, Adam and I were talking. We thought it would be best if you left the presentation up to us. We can handle it. You have your hands full with the grant proposal and preparing for the gala."

Her radar went on full alert. "What's wrong?"

"Nothing. We're only thinking of you. We can handle the kids here, do the Q&A and the tour and hand out the certificates afterward. They're all printed out and ready to go. That way you can take your time getting back, go over final plans for tomorrow night with your mother and the committee… You don't need to come into the institute. We've got it handled."

The note in his voice indicated something was up. She reined in her temper. "Talk to me. What happened? Why don't you want me there at the institute talking to the kids? Answer me!"

A few seconds of silence. Then in a small voice, Martin said, "Okay, didn't want to tell you because of everything going on with your life, but someone broke in last night and left a red rose floating in Molly's tank."

Her heart raced. The rare Kemp's ridley turtle was on loan to her hospital after being evacuated from a Gulf Coast hospital recently under a hurricane warning. "Is Molly okay?"

"Fine. We cleaned and flushed out the tank, put her in with Tiny, the new green turtle we got last week. They're happy together and…"

"What did the note say? There was a note." Her voice was sharp and Gray looked at her.

"Put him on speaker," Gray ordered.

She pressed the speaker button.

"Really, it wasn't anything…"

"Stop lying to me!" she yelled.

A small sigh. "It wasn't a note. Someone wrote on the mirror in the women's restroom that they were watching you. In lipstick. Almost looked like a kid's prank."

"Did you preserve the evidence? Or at least take a photo of it?" Gray asked in a calm, clear voice.

"Evidence? Who is this? Um, no. The cleaning people wiped it off before we opened. Um, sorry. We really didn't think anything of it, thought it was a joke…"

"It's no joke," Gray said tightly. "You know Peyton's being stalked and you thought this was a prank? Call the police immediately and file a report. Do it. I'll be there soon as Peyton and I return to town."

Peyton hung up to a blizzard of protests and apologies. Rage and grief filled her. Everyone had tried to baby her, stepping around the truth. She thought she could trust Martin, her supervisor and a friend, to be honest with her. Tell her everything concerning the institute, keep her informed. Now she found out Martin wanted to hide facts from her as much as her father had, and Brandy.

Was there anyone she could trust to tell her what was going on? Who knew how to communicate in clear, exact terms?

She glanced at Gray's tight-lipped face. There was her answer. Gray was one of the only people who told her what was really going on. He wasn't hiding anything from her.

Peyton struggled to contain her emotions. Slowly, she unclenched her fist and forced herself to relax.

"Breathe. You're too pale. Don't worry, I will go there when we return and find out what happened."

It's not that. "Thank you. Not for that, but being honest with me and telling me about the shot-out tire. Even if you waited, you at least were up-front with me. Too many people are coddling me and avoiding the truth."

His dark gaze remained level. "I find that being open and direct with my clients is usually the best way of co-operation. It's your life, Peyton. You should know what threats you face. Only then can you make clear decisions about the course of action to take. You are not a child."

She offered a wry smile. "Although I'm treated like one."

A frown touched his face. "This new development isn't a matter of withholding information to protect you. It does the exact opposite. Your stalker is now targeting you at your place of employment, in fact, inside your place of employment. I should have been notified. The police definitely should have been contacted if there was a break-in. Is this coworker of yours a few cards short of a full deck?"

He tapped his head. Peyton's mouth twisted. "No, he's protective, I guess, but more so, he's so into the animals he isn't as attuned to people. Like me at times. We get absorbed in our work and forget the others around us. Job hazard. We're good at making decisions regarding the marine life we try to save, and not as skilled at making people-centered decisions."

Ironic how she'd viewed Gray as an annoying necessity to keeping her job and fulfilling her duties at work, and now saw him as an ally. His attention to detail was far more reassuring than the casual dismissal of Martin with the red rose and lipstick-scrawled note.

Much as she hated asking, and dreaded the answer, she needed to know. "Gray, do you think I should skip the gala? Am I in that much danger that I should reconsider everything and stay at my parents' home in Nantucket and get away for a while?"

"At first when I took this assignment, I would have said yes, the best for you would be to leave and lie low. Now, I do not know. He's escalated, and a predator like this who escalates usually does not stop, even if his intended victim leaves the area."

Her heart raced as sweat beaded on her back. Not the answer she'd hoped for, but at least an honest assessment. "You mean he would follow me, wherever I went."

Gray studied her. "Yes. It is my belief, after dealing with cases like this, that he would indeed follow you wherever you went. This goes beyond casual and annoying interest. He is obsessed and obsessed stalkers do not relinquish their goals so easily."

"How can you be confident you think he would follow me?"

He changed lanes, slowed and then sped up. "Because I had it happen previously to someone I knew. And I let my guard down, let it slip."

Her stomach churned. Peyton had a bad feeling about his answer. "What happened to her? Was she safe?"

"No." His jaw turned to steel as he started the car. "As for what happened to her, you do not want to know."

Wasting no time, Peyton stormed into her father's study as soon as they returned to the house.

Inside his lavish office, her father worked at his laptop. He didn't look up as she dumped her computer case on the sofa and leaned on his desk, glaring at him.

"That was pretty damn low of you, Dad, and you know it."

"Now what did I do?" he asked, his gaze never leaving the computer screen.

"You hired extra security to tail me because you didn't trust Gray was enough." Peyton fought to keep her voice from shaking. "While we were at Manatee Island, Gray saw a man advancing toward me and tackled him, thinking the man was after me. He could have shot him!"

"Did he?" her father asked calmly, his gaze still on the screen. "Shoot him?"

Peyton stared. "No."

"No harm done, then."

Incredulous, she stood straight, seeing her father in a new and disturbing light. "I see. Forget the man's pride in his ability to do his job. Collateral damage, huh, Dad? Everyone who is not family is expendable, especially if you're employing them?"

Now he did look up. Sighed. Closed his laptop. "Peyton, my concern is for you and keeping you safe while police try to determine the identity of your stalker. Not Gray or his wounded ego."

"If you're so concerned about keeping me safe, then keep me in the loop. Tell me how many men you have following me! And why don't you trust Gray?"

He leaned back, the leather chair creaking slightly. "Why are you suddenly so defensive of him? You didn't want him on this case."

"I didn't want anyone. I hate being tailed as if I'm a suspect, hate having anyone follow me around. But at least Gray is professional and polite. And I know he's there." Peyton paused. She had a bad feeling about this.

"Exactly how many men have you employed to follow me around, Dad? The truth."

Her father looked out the window, then rubbed the back of his head. "Peyton…"

"How many?"

He sighed. "Four, in addition to Gray. I hired an independent security firm to back him up."

Hard to believe her own father had kept this from her. First Brandy hadn't told her about Dennis's release from prison. Now her own father had hired a battalion of bodyguards to protect her, not breathing a word of this to her.

Worse, not telling Gray. Only informing Gray's employer that he harbored doubts about her personal bodyguard.

"When were you going to tell me, Dad? Or Gray? Or were you?"

Her father gave her a level look. "I knew how you felt about all this protection, how it stifled you. I thought it best if they blended into the background and merely kept an eye on you wherever you went."

"You mean spied on me! And Gray, why can't you trust Gray? If you don't trust him, why hire him?"

He leaned forward, hands folded on his desk. "Because I did some background work and Gray is the best at what he does."

"Best at being a bodyguard? Because, Dad, if you don't trust him..."

His gaze sharpened. "Why all this interest suddenly in a man you didn't want around you?"

Peyton's head ached with everything she'd learned. "He's trying to keep me safe. Dad, what did you find out about Gray that made you wary of him, made you hire four others?"

"There's something about Gray I don't trust. Nothing that concerns you. It's best for you, Peyton. I know what's best for you."

"I know what's best for me, Dad. It's my life."

At the door, she turned around to face him. "Dad, I love you and Mom. But you can't keep treating me like I'm a child. Or fragile glass. I have to live my life and you need to keep me informed if you make decisions like that."

Her father gave her a sad smile. "Honey, you'll always be my little girl, no matter how old you are."

Peyton resisted the impulse to go and hug him. In the past she always had, but her instincts warned right now he would take affection as a sign she caved or had second thoughts. And in this she had to stay strong.

"Another thing. I think you owe Gray an apology."

Now her father morphed into the stern CEO. "No. I owe him nothing, only the fee his agency charges him. He's a contract employee, Peyton. Nothing more."

Harsh. Cold. She should have expected as much. Peyton turned and walked away, shutting the door behind her.

Gray wasn't around. She called him on her cell phone. "I have to go into work for a few hours."

"Good. I want to talk to your director."

"Meet me downstairs in ten minutes." She hung up.

Chapter 7

Work at the institute proved soothing and routine. Gray remained in the background. For once his presence was comforting and not distracting. He had a long talk with Martin, and after, Peyton saw her director looking a little paler, as if Gray's words had impact.

By the time they returned home, the sun had begun to sink lower in the sky. Peyton murmured thanks and went into her room to catch up on work.

Several donors had adopted sea turtles in the hospital and their names had to be plugged into the database so they could receive an adoption certificate, photo and thank-you letter. For an hour she quietly worked, then she went downstairs to the wine room. She selected a bottle of 2018 Pinot Noir from her favorite vineyard and uncorked it. Sighing with pleasure, she poured herself a glass and let the wine remain open on the kitchen counter. It would go well with the beef dinner the cook prepared.

Back upstairs, she kept working until hearing a buzzing noise outside.

Peyton went to her French doors and amusement filled her.

Gray was outside on her balcony, using a hedge trimmer to cut down all the vines on the trellis and then tossing them to the ground. Next he pulled at the trellis and sent it spiraling down.

She went outside. "Gardening isn't part of your job description."

"Consider me a jack-of-all-trades."

"Mom is going to be furious with you for ruining her prize flowers."

"Since your parents already have a low opinion of me, it doesn't matter. Your safety does."

Cringing, she realized how damaging her father's edict had been. "Gray, when you're finished, we need to talk."

He finished tossing down the plants.

Peyton drew in a breath. "I'm sorry about what my father did. On behalf of the family, I apologize for the way he handled this. It was not right, making you feel as if you couldn't do the job he hired you to complete."

Gray's expression remained blank.

"My feelings in this don't matter. I'm a professional, and what matters is getting the job done. I'm hired to protect you, Peyton, and if you want the extra detail because you don't trust my ability to do the job, level with me."

Such refreshing directness. A trait of his she was beginning to appreciate. "I trust you, Gray, and I know you will do what you must. I don't need an army following me."

Something flickered in his gaze and his mouth curved upward in the barest of smiles.

As she leaned over, Gray sprang forward, his hands around her waist. "Whoa. Watch it."

The warmth of his palms cut through her polo shirt. She turned to regard his face. Solemn, some unknown emotion swirling in his piercing brown gaze. Gray stepped back as if to give her space. Personal space was important. She'd grown up with everyone invading her space, not giving her enough room.

As his gaze locked to hers, he held open his palms as if to show he had nothing hidden. "Peyton, if you want to know my background, call Jarrett Adler right now and question him. What you need to know is that I am dedicated to the job at hand and I protect those under my charge. I take every assignment seriously."

She didn't dare look away or blink.

"I can only earn your trust. I hope you understand everything I am doing is to protect you. Even if it is something you disagree with or don't like. All I ask is that you communicate with me and be as honest with me as I am being with you."

The shadow was unlike any other man she'd ever met. He didn't play games or dance around the truth or try to win her favor. Direct. Honest.

He deserved the same from her.

She glanced at her wine. "I have to get back to work. I have a presentation to prepare tomorrow for a group of children at sea camp."

Gray nodded. "How many kids and what ages?"

"Twenty children, from six to ten years old." She flashed him an impish smile. "Very dangerous. Lots of questions."

"I'll bring my body armor and earmuffs."

She grinned again. "That will suffice. In the meantime, Caren is making an excellent beef dinner, if you want to eat."

"Thank you, but I have a few errands to run." He glanced

at his watch. "May I trust you to remain in the house and not leave until I return?"

Peyton picked up her wineglass with a wry grin. "As long as Mr. Noir keeps me company, I'll be here."

"May I?"

Handing him the glass, she wondered if he wanted to inspect it because he feared it might be poisoned. "It's a fine red and I selected it from my parents' wine room, so it's safe."

Gray sniffed the glass. "Excellent vintage… 2018. Russian River Valley, California."

Blinking in surprise, she nodded. "Mi Sueno winery. You have a terrific palate."

"I have some acquaintance with wine." Gray held the glass to the light. "You selected this on purpose?"

Peyton bit back a smile. "It's a favorite and my father's as well. I figured a glass or two at dinner would finally help him relax. Dad's an oenophile. He even invests in wine through an alcohol ETF. That's an exchange-traded fund. It's run by a firm out of New York called Mitchell Brothers Capital Management. It's an excellent fund."

Something flickered in his gaze as he handed the glass back to her. "Oh? Interesting."

"If you're interested, I can get information for you."

"Perhaps." He handed her back the glass. "I'll return by ten o'clock."

"Just in time to tuck me into bed." She winked at him.

He did not return her jocular smile. "Take care, Peyton."

She gestured to the French doors. "You can take the easy way back to your room through mine now that you've removed your emergency exit."

Now he did actually smile. "Did I?"

Astounded, she watched as he went outside, climbed over her balcony and like a spider, he found footholds in the bricks to maneuver downward. Gray swung over to the first-floor balcony directly below hers and then he peered upward.

"Now do you see how vulnerable you are?"

She swallowed. "I'll see you later."

He couldn't help the satisfied smile on his face as he headed back into the house. Peyton was independent and had a mind of her own. It was refreshing.

Gray went into the guest room assigned to him, splashed water on his face and stared into the mirror.

Seldom had he ever talked about Andrea's death. No need to mention it to Peyton. But it bothered him that Charles Bradley had hired him, and yet did not trust him with his daughter's welfare.

He thought about the trust she had started to place in him, her reaction on the jetty to him taking down John Doe after he thought the man threatened Peyton.

She was as incensed as him. Few clients, even the ones he'd liked, would care. They saw it as part of his job duties, nothing more.

Peyton seemed to understand his frustration.

He dried off with a towel and set out to find her father. Charles Bradley was in his study, the door partly open. Gray knocked, not to be polite, but as a warning.

Bradley barely glanced up as Gray entered. He sat in a leather armchair by a gooseneck lamp, reading over a financial magazine. A glass of ruby red wine sat on the table by the chair. Amused, Gray realized the wine was from the bottle Peyton had opened.

"I heard you met the extra protection I assigned to my daughter's case." Bradley did not look up from his magazine.

"I did."

"And you're here to complain about it. Well, she's my daughter and if I want to hire extra men to guard her, it's my prerogative."

"Your prerogative but don't interfere with me doing my job. That's what you paid me to do. If you wish to hire rent-a-cops, you need to inform both Jarrett and myself. It's for Peyton's safety."

Bradley bristled. "And if you can't do your job?"

Gray leashed his temper. "Do you know what could have happened today at the jetty? I saw a man intent on approaching Peyton. I had no idea who he was, nor his intentions. All I saw was a threat. What if your extra security drew out his gun? Fired at me? Hit your daughter?"

"That would never happen…"

"Why? Because he did carry a gun."

Bradley fell quiet. "It's not your concern how I spend my money."

Gray couldn't help his tight smile. "My concern is for your daughter. Not your money. Being her personal protector is more than muscle, Bradley. It means surveillance and checking out any possible threat ahead of time to avoid confrontations."

The man's gaze narrowed. "There's something about you I don't quite trust. But I hired you because Jarrett Adler, whose in-laws are good friends of ours, promised you're the best. Do you understand? If you let anything happen to Peyton, you will be held accountable."

So Peyton's father hadn't discovered Gray's murky past. Yet. Gray drew in a deep breath. "I understand. You need to understand I will work to the best of my ability to protect Peyton. No more interference. You can hire extra security if you wish, but I need to be informed of their presence and I need their names to run my own background check. In my area of work, most incidents can be avoided through investigating prior to the client making any kind of public appearance. Communication is important, Bradley."

Peyton's father waved a hand. "You can go now."

"Before I do, you need to know there was another threat."

He explained about the latest incident at the institute. Bradley paled. "It's getting worse. This maniac seems to be growing bolder. I have a bad feeling about this. You had better find this son of a bitch before I lose all faith in you."

Gray thought of the one he'd sworn to protect and failed. Never again. "I promise. I will do everything it takes. Even at the risk of my own life."

Chapter 8

The following morning Gray met her downstairs as usual, a paper bag in hand. When Peyton bounced out of the kitchen, ponytail swinging and coffee container in hand, she ground to a halt.

"The business look is back. You like wearing suits? It's a bit restrictive for a jack-of-all-trades like you."

"At times the occasion calls for it." Amused, he handed her the bag. "Here. You can eat it on the way to work."

Peyton set her coffee down on a spotless marble table and opened the bag, removing a takeaway container. Smells of fried eggs, onions, cheese and peppers filled the air. "Whoa. A cheese frittata. This smells amazing! Did Caren make this?"

"Cheddar, peppers, onions and roasted grape tomatoes. Caren did not make this. I did. You need to eat breakfast. Utensils and napkins are in the bag as well." He gestured to the coffee cup she carried. "You can't survive on caffeine alone."

"You cook?"

"I do much more than cook. Consider it job security when you're a jack-of-all-trades."

Gray led the way to the car. Last night he'd driven the punctured tire to a nearby parking lot where one of Jarrett's men had picked it up to bring to the police department to analyze the shell casing, and then he'd driven back to the house in time to check she was in her room, fast asleep.

This morning he needed her sharp and alert, not sleepy from lack of food. A client aware of her surroundings at all times was an asset.

At least that was what he tried telling himself as he drove along the beach to the institute.

Inside the institute, her attitude shifted to pure professional.

The bright yellow building, across the street from the gray sandy beach and the turquoise waters of the Atlantic, sat like a beacon on the roadway. Gray walked Peyton inside to the front desk, where two volunteers in powder blue logo shirts and khaki trousers greeted them. No admission was required, but donations were accepted. He took out his wallet and placed a few bills in the donation box while Peyton chattered with one of the volunteers.

The work Peyton did here was critically important. Conservation of marine species was a quiet passion of his, one he seldom shared with others.

Two large saltwater tanks were off to the side, inviting visitors to gaze at fish and crustaceans inside. A few benches lined the wall, most of them inscribed with names. He spotted Shelly's name on one bench.

He followed Peyton over to the gift shop, where she inspected the merchandise for sale.

"A lot of our income comes from grants, especially my family's foundation, and corporate sponsors and individual donations, but the gift shop helps to fund salaries and veterinary care. You'd be surprised how much it costs for laser surgery for a sea turtle."

Gray scanned the gift shop for threats. None except for an exuberant toddler shrieking with joy as he played with a life-size sea turtle on the floor. "Laser surgery? For what?"

"For one, treatment of fibropapillomatosis, commonly referred to as FP. It's a disease that affects sea turtles and causes tumors on the skin, eyes and mouth and even the internal organs. We have one turtle named Progress who was found entangled in a net a couple of weeks ago that had tumor growths on his mouth that were successfully removed by laser surgery. Here, you can read about our state of the art hospital and surgical unit."

Impressed, he took the brochure she handed him.

"We have a pharmacy, surgical suite, treatment room, even diagnostic equipment that includes digital X-rays. Every injured turtle we rescue is given X-rays to assess possible internal damage." Her expression grew troubled. "Sea turtles get pneumonia just as humans do. And they can swallow fish hooks, which comes with its own set of problems."

Peyton glanced at her cell phone. "I have a few minutes to show you around before the children arrive. Let's take a tour. Besides, I want to check on Molly."

He followed her to the outdoor courtyard where fifteen circular tanks sat beneath an archway of canvas canopies shading them from the sun. A white iron fence about four and a half feet tall kept visitors from getting too close to the tanks.

"We have fifteen ICU tanks that have their own water supply to prevent cross-contamination. FP is one reason alone for this. It's quite contagious." Peyton opened a gate to the Staff and Volunteers Only area and Gray followed her to one of the tanks.

A small sea turtle with an olive-brown shell swam around in circles. Peyton's expression brightened. It was like watching the sun come out after a long rainstorm.

"This is Molly, a juvenile Kemp's ridley. Hey, girl, how are you? You're looking good! Almost ready to return to the Gulf."

He understood her love for these beautiful, graceful creatures. "Kemp's ridley turtles are only found in the Gulf, correct?"

Appreciation shone in her eyes. "Yes. Few are found in Florida, most in Texas off Padre Island. Molly was found in the Gulf entangled in fishing line. She's nearly ready to be returned to the aquarium that rescued her. They will do the honors of releasing her back into the Gulf of Mexico. It's a big event when a rescued turtle is returned."

She gave the turtle a sad smile. "It's a little bittersweet as well. You come to care for them for days, weeks, sometimes even a few months. But you also realize that these are wild creatures who belong in the ocean or the Gulf, not in a tank."

"They are amazing to watch under the water," he murmured, recalling an experience last year.

Her eyes sparkled. "You scuba dive?"

"Sometimes. I was with a friend last summer and we took out his fishing boat for a dive trip. Saw a loggerhead while we were wreck diving off the Florida coast. My friend was more interested in the wreck, but I made him follow the turtle." He grinned, recalling how his dive buddy was not pleased. "I made up for it later by buying him a couple of beers. It was worth it."

She looked wistful. "I dive, but for work. It's been a long time since my family took the boat out. Everyone is too busy. If I knew someone who could drive the boat and knew boating regulations, I'd jump at the chance."

"When do you want to go? I have experience piloting boats."

Her doubtful look made him chuckle. "What kind? I'm not talking a kayak."

Gray considered, thinking of his home in the Keys and the sweet fishing boat he took out when he had time. "How about a forty-one-foot center console with a tuna tower? Mine has two three-hundred-and-fifty-horsepower out-boards."

Peyton looked impressed. "My family's boat is a center console. Maybe on my day off we can go? I haven't been diving in a while for fun, only work."

"We could do a reef trash cleanup while we dive."

"I didn't know you spoke my language. I never dive with-out doing one."

The look of respect she gave him made him aware of her as a woman, not a client. He didn't want to like her. Didn't have to like her. But damn, the more time they spent together, the more things he found out that he did enjoy about Peyton.

Gray slid back into professionalism. "It's safer on the water, anyway, away from your stalker. I would have to investigate the boat prior to taking it out, ensure it was in perfect working order…perhaps call in backup just in case someone follows us while we're diving."

She looked as if he'd handed her a candy bar and then snatched it back. Peyton shrugged. "Sure. Whatever. I have to get to work. The kids are arriving."

The moment between them was gone. He wasn't sure if he was glad of it, or disappointed.

No time left for touring the rest of the facility for she received a call that the children had arrived and were on their way to the courtyard. Peyton brightened as two camp counselors introduced themselves and the children joining her by the first tank. Peyton introduced herself.

Gray went through the gate and hovered nearby as if he were a visitor, watching and scanning the area for threats. A man lingered near the Children's Research Station, arousing his suspicions, but a woman and a child soon joined him.

Peyton began her presentation with the children safely ensconced behind the fence guarding the tanks. They could see the turtle swimming around, but not touch the tank or the water. She was good with the kids, involving them and asking them questions while driving home important lessons about preserving and protecting the marine environment.

"Where do sea turtles sleep at night?" she asked.

"A hotel," one child yelled out and they all giggled.

"Not unless it's in the ocean. Sea turtles do sleep at night. They're what we call diurnal, so that means they are active during daylight hours and sleep at night. They need air to breathe, but nature installed in them the ability to slow their heart rate and their breathing down so they can stay underwater for a long time. That way they can sleep, either under a rock or on the ocean floor, without needing to breathe air. This is called a 'diving response.'"

The children oohed and aahed as she pointed inside where a small turtle swam.

"This is Molly. She's a Kemp's ridley that got tangled in fishing line and one of her fins was severely damaged and then infected. Kemp's ridley turtles are what? Threatened?"

"Endangered," a child called out.

"Actually you're partly right. Kemp's ridley turtles are critically endangered. Unlike other sea turtles, they make their nests during the day and the babies hatch during the day, so they are more likely to be targeted by predators, even people. Molly was found in the Gulf of Mexico and brought here for safekeeping when a hurricane threatened the turtle hospital where she lived."

"What's the biggest sea turtle?" Gray asked.

The children's gazes shot over to him.

Peyton grinned. "Leatherback. If you see one coming onto the beach to lay eggs, it's like watching a truck rise from the ocean. Does anyone know how much a leatherback turtle can weigh?"

Nudging a young boy next to him, Gray pointed to the sign displaying the types of turtles and their weights. The child cried out, "More than a thousand pounds!"

Peyton gave him a mock scowl. "Hey, you cheated."

Gray grinned. "He read it for himself."

The boy gave him a fist bump, which Gray returned.

He leaned against the wall, watching with fascination as she lectured the children on the importance of saving sea turtles. Peyton launched into the dangers of plastic trash in the oceans and passed around a bin filled with trash, which the children handled and made faces over as they touched the objects.

Dedicated and committed, Peyton was different from any woman he'd ever known. Most of his family's business clients were high-powered and accustomed to having their orders obeyed. Few were as engaging as Peyton. Despite her family's wealth and her father's high profile, she was laid-back, friendly and approachable. The children liked her.

He was beginning to like her as well.

Feelings for a client weren't necessary. They could be dangerous.

Seeing Martin Gauthier hovering nearby, watching Peyton, Gray considered. He needed to talk to the administrator, but leaving Peyton alone wasn't a good idea.

He called Jace. "Need your help. Can you watch over Peyton while I check things out here at the institute?"

"Sure. I was going to take my bike out for a ride, anyway, so I'll be there soon."

When Jace arrived thirty minutes later, Peyton was taking the children on a tour. Gray glanced at his leather jacket.

"What kind of bicycle do you have?"

"Harley." Jace grinned, and went to join Peyton.

Gray sought out Gauthier, who was doing inventory in the gift shop.

"A word in private in your office," he said quietly.

Martin led him upstairs to a hallway, past a conference room and into a small, cluttered office filled with charts and a desk that seemed to overflow with papers. A glass globe featuring a swimming sea turtle held down the papers. Gray recognized the paperweight as the work of a famous local artist who specialized in marine life.

"I am sorry about neglecting to inform you and Peyton about the incident. I know she's under tremendous pressure with the gala tomorrow and did not wish to upset her."

Gray waited.

Martin grew a little paler. "If there is anything I can do to assist you, let me know. The police were here. They dusted the mirror and restroom, but found nothing of real use since the restroom is used by many visitors during the day."

"I need to see your security cameras."

Martin led him to another, much cleaner office where a bank of monitors showed the interior and exterior of the building. "We have a few, including one in the hallway leading to the offices. The main camera, in the lobby, shows entrances to both the men's and women's restrooms. I'll leave you here. I have a mound of paperwork."

He gave Gray the security code for playback.

Gray pulled up a chair and watched the footage. Nothing remarkable. If someone had broken into the institute simply to leave the rose and threatening message, they did it during operating hours.

He scrolled back to the previous evening. Just before closing, he saw it. Gray's gaze sharpened on the figure as it slipped into the women's restroom. In the wide-brimmed hat and shapeless coat, it was hard to discern if the person was male or female. The person did not leave the restroom until after the facility was closed.

Gray froze the image and went to Martin's office. "You need to see this."

"The image is time-stamped after closing. Whoever this is hid in your restroom. You need to send this over to the police," he told Martin after the administrator viewed the monitor.

"I can do that." Martin typed in a few commands. "Would you like a copy as well?"

"Yes. Send it to my cell."

After giving him the number, he studied Martin, wondering why the man had acted so cavalier about the incident. Clearly growing uneasy under Gray's scrutiny, Martin ran a finger around the collar of his polo shirt.

"Something else you should know. I didn't tell the detective. But there was a man here asking about Peyton. He wanted to know when she'd be here giving tours."

Gray had a bad feeling about this. But sensing Martin's unease, he wasn't going to grill him. The man already felt intimidated by Gray and pressuring him wouldn't get answers. He sat on the chair, leaned back, stretched out his legs as if he didn't care. "Oh yeah?"

He kept his voice deliberately casual.

It worked, for Martin relaxed slightly. "I think the guy was here to check out Peyton because he wants to hire her away from us. She's good at her job and another place had given her an offer… I found out about it through the grapevine. I don't want to lose her. She's the most dedicated…"

"What does this man look like?"

"Average height. He wore a business suit."

"I'd like to see if he was on the cameras. Like you, I don't want Peyton to leave her job here." *Mainly because I can track her here, not that I care about your needs.*

"Of course." The man glanced at the bank of security cameras. "Damn. He's here now. In the lobby. The bearded guy in the gray suit by the saltwater fish tanks. See?"

Gray raced from the office to the area outside where Peyton and another other marine biologist, Adam, were handing out certificates to the children. "Stay here," he warned her in a low voice. "Do not leave this area."

After telling Jace to watch her closely, Gray returned to the lobby.

A few people milled about, examining the saltwater tanks. Sure enough, a man of medium height, with dark curly hair and a faded gray business suit, examined with interest a poster identifying saltwater marine animals. He turned, went to the receptionist.

Gray overheard the man ask for Peyton Bradley. He took a photo of the visitor. Glancing through his phone, Gray realized this was his target.

Dennis Devine, Brandy's ex-con brother.

"Peyton is giving a tour to children right now, but if you care to wait," the receptionist told Dennis.

"It's really important I see her immediately," Dennis said in a raised voice.

The receptionist, a young, nervous woman, picked up a phone. "I'll page her."

Keeping his stride casual, Gray advanced. But seeing him, Dennis turned and headed for the entrance doors.

The man bolted.

Gray ran after him. But the intruder had a head start and climbed into a Mustang parked out front. Tires screeched as Gray made it to the parking lot. He took a photo of the license plate, texted it to his contact at the police department and returned to Peyton, who came to the lobby, followed by a clearly exasperated Jace.

Pale and a little shaken, she hugged herself. "I take it that was not an important visitor for me."

"No." He aimed her a stern look. "I told you to stay where you were."

"I thought you needed me. What happened?"

Gray nodded at Jace. "Thanks. I'll handle it from here."

He turned to Peyton. "Let's go to your office. Unless you have to return to the children."

"Adam has that under control." Peyton led him upstairs to an office outfitted with cubicles. Her desk was neat, stacked with file folders to one side and had a picture of herself with a loggerhead sea turtle.

He closed the door behind him. "Dennis was here just now. He's the one who paged you. He was also here the other day, looking for you. Your director thought he was trying to recruit you to work at another facility. That's why Martin didn't say anything to myself or the police."

Gray showed her the photo of Dennis. "He's our prime suspect, though Martin's behavior raised my suspicions."

Peyton rubbed her temples. "Martin is paranoid about anything changing right now. Not only did we lose our director earlier this year due to a slight scandal, our educational instructor quit recently to move back north and our programs have been sparse. The children's veterinary clinic, the lecture series, the reef conservation cleanup class for college students, all of that canceled until she can be replaced. I've tried to fill in the gaps and so has Adam and our two interns, but we're juggling enough as it is. Martin wants to keep operations flowing smoothly, but every day more things slip out of his control. I've been helping him with daily operations, so I can imagine he doesn't want me gone."

Stress radiated from her in waves. For the first time, he began to realize the depth of her predicament. Not only was she dealing with a stalker threatening her, but also the complications of trying to do her work while being short-staffed. Yet he'd never seen her complain. Peyton was re-sourceful and smart, and flexible.

"Since we are already spending so much time together, perhaps I can aid you in some of this work."

She gave him an amused look. "Ever necropsy a dead turtle? That isn't on my agenda right now, but I have a report to write for an upcoming conference. I also need to organize a deep-sea trip to track loggerheads because we're approaching the prime of their nesting season. Let's not talk about the nests on my family's beach that have produced less and less live hatchlings in the past year and the data I'm collecting for that problem. I don't know what is going on with that and I need to spend more time on the beach at night, watching the turtles nest and then doing an active count. Then there's the gala tomorrow night, which my mother thinks I should focus on instead of my work…"

"Slow down. You can't do it all." He put his hands on her shoulders and massaged her skin, hoping to ease her tension. "Prioritize. When is that report due?"

Her shoulders slumped. "The report isn't the problem, Gray. It's the nesting on my family's beach. That's the real trouble spot. Ever since sea turtles were put on the endangered species list in 1973, my grandmother stated her wishes to set that beach aside. Our family has taken pride in making sure that stretch of beach was safe for turtles, especially from May to October. We put up fences, no-trespassing signs and it was patrolled regularly. We had a success rate of eighty-five percent of live hatchlings. Now? Last year the only nest we had we got only ten hatchlings."

Gray frowned. "And there's nothing else going on at that beach?"

"No. Adam and Martin have been patrolling it regularly and report that all is quiet. If it continues this way, the beach will revert back to naked couples using the beach to have sex like they did ten years ago." She rolled her eyes.

Gray grinned. "Sounds like nature was driving them there as well."

A becoming tint of pink suffused her cheeks. "They'd have a hard time accessing that beach now."

"And with all that, the turtles still don't nest there?"

"I don't know. There were more false crawls this year, even though we're fairly early in the season. It's like the turtles that always nested on that beach don't like it anymore."

"How many eggs are usually in nests?"

"Loggerheads will lay about one hundred eggs per nest. They incubate about seventy days and after that, we'll dig up the nest until finding the egg chamber so we can count empty eggshells and unhatched eggs."

Peyton's mouth wobbled. "The nest from two weeks ago? All the unhatched eggs looked at stage three. They'd reached a good stage of embryonic development and then stopped. Adam and our interns concluded the heat in the nest was too high. But it's only June. It doesn't make sense."

Sometimes stress could make you overlook an obvious answer. "Peyton, what did you do with the unhatched eggs? Are there any still around?"

"We destroyed them. I did keep the shells from the hatchlings."

Later, he'd ask more about this. He knew something sounded odd about this.

Back at the house, Peyton turned her attention to the formal tomorrow night. A delivery service had dropped off dry cleaning. Gray picked up the hanger and examined it.

"Nothing suspicious," he told her, handing her the dress. "Except the price tag."

As she stared, he added with a slight smile, "That's a joke."

Peyton smoothed down the dry cleaning plastic over the navy blue dress. "It's not as expensive as some of the gowns I own. This is for tomorrow night's gala. Beaded appliqué tulle. I bought it because it's elegant, but subtle, and when you see some of the gowns tomorrow night, you'll understand why I need to blend into the background. Some of them will look like cotton candy exploded."

You can never blend in fully. You would stand out in any situation. That's what makes my job so difficult.

He wondered if the job was difficult because of Peyton's stubborn, independent personality or his increasing fascination with his client.

"If you need a tuxedo, I can arrange for one."

"No. However, there is something I need you to do." He glanced around. "In your bedroom."

Her silky brows rose, but she followed him upstairs to her bedroom, hung the dress on a hook in back of her walk-in closet door and then shut her bedroom door.

Gray removed the small case from his trouser pocket and opened it. On his index finger rested a small black device. "I need you to sew this inside your bra. It's a tracking chip."

Her gaze widened. "What?"

"Safety precaution." Damn he was not doing a good job with explanations. "If anything happens to you, I can track where you have gone."

"There's a GPS inside my cell phone…"

"It's not enough." He locked his gaze to hers. "I need to know where you are at all times, Peyton. After what happened, I know this asshole is escalating. I won't take chances."

Doubt shadowed her face. He continued. "This is intrusive, I admit. It's fully invading your privacy. I promise you, I will not abuse this. Only you and I will know you are wearing this. No one else."

She crossed the room, peered at the chip. "How does it work?"

"It uses satellites to triangulate your position to give me a real-time view of where you are at all times. This is a sophisticated chip, used mostly for people to track their personal property."

"Oh? So I'm personal property?"

Damn. He shook his head. "You are more valuable. Priceless. Irreplaceable."

Gray let her handle the chip and then pulled out his cell phone. "This one I've set up to track on my phone and my laptop, in case something happens to my phone."

"I'm surprised you don't want to inject me with one."

"There have been instances in doing that with criminals…" He pretended to consider.

Peyton saw his expression and rolled her eyes. "You have such a dry sense of humor it's hard to tell if you're joking. No. You're my personal protector, but this is too much. It's an invasion of my privacy."

Gray bit back a frustrated response. If he could lock her up, inside her room, until this bastard was caught, he would.

"Your privacy is already invaded. There are security cameras all over the house and I have an eye on you at all times. This is an added layer of protection."

"You would track my every movement!"

"Like you track sea turtles to keep them safe, and protect them as a species."

Her gaze glittered with fierce anger. "I am not a turtle."

"No, you're not. It would be far easier to keep a sea turtle safe."

Peyton grimaced. Then a calculating look came over her. She went over to a stately white provincial dresser, opened the top drawer. "You said to put it into my bra? Which bra?"

Frowning, he joined her and then stared. Rows of bras. Blue lace, pink, red polka dots, black… She picked up a red lace padded bra. "See what I mean? I like to change my undergarments depending upon my outerwear."

Heat suffused his face. He'd been in some awkward sitchs before with clients, indeed, some much more personal and intimate situations, but seeing all her undergarments made his imagination run wild. .

Professionalism was best because he kept envisioning her modeling all of them for him, her lush figure turning around, displaying the matching bra and panties as his blood heated… He was a man. A healthy man. Not dead.

But she was his client. Not one of his lovers.

Gray looked away, steeling himself. "You can select whatever one you wish. It's your clothing."

"No. It's too much to think about." She slammed the drawer shut. "Maybe after tomorrow night, I'll consider it. For now, forget it."

He was glad he had a backup plan.

"Peyton, you need to do as I say. You hired me to protect you."

She took a deep breath. "Look, I don't mean to be rude. I'm a little rattled by what happened at the institute and I have an ocean of work to do before tomorrow's gala. This is the most important night of the year for the institute. I have to make a good impression so we can receive the necessary funding for expansion. I have to be 'on' all night. I can't do that if I feel like my every single movement is followed."

"Then expect me to stick by your side with every single movement you make. Including following you into the restroom. If I must."

Her mouth parted, forming a little O of surprise. Gray took the chip from her, palming it. She had to know how serious he was about doing his job. Good thing he had a backup plan.

"Then let's compromise." From his pocket he removed a key fob. It was small, and looked decorative. "Put this on your keys. It's another tracking device."

Sighing, she nodded. "Fine. This is better."

Peyton took the fob from him. She eyed the closet door. "Besides, there's a slight technical issue with that plan for tomorrow night, anyway."

He folded his arms across his chest. "What?"

Her smile could make a strong man weak-kneed. "Regarding the bra. I'm not wearing one."

Imagination going wild, Gray closed his eyes to center himself. "I'll see you later, at dinner."

He barely bit back a curse as he headed out of her bedroom. He needed fresh air. Or a cold shower. Or both.

Chapter 9

The next day flew by in a flurry of activity. She spent time at the institute, going over the guest list with the public relations/education director and the committee members. In the afternoon, she and her mother supervised the decorating of the ballroom, the technical equipment for the presentation Peyton planned during dinner and the table arrangements and placement of the orchestra for dancing.

Then she and her mother went to get their hair styled at her mother's favorite hair salon. Through it all Gray stuck by her side, even at the salon. He sat in one of the chairs at the bank of hair dryers, sipping coffee,

Peyton sighed. He wasn't going to make her life easy.

The biggest glitch of the night happened when she returned home. Instead of her navy gown hanging pressed and ready in her closet, there was a red strapless satin designer gown and matching shoes. Peyton pressed two fingers to her temples, mindful of her upswept hair.

She marched into her mother's bedroom, where the good

doctor sat in her bra and panties in her dressing room, applying makeup in the mirror.

"Honey, get dressed or we'll be late."

"Mom, what happened to my gown? The blue gown. I'm not wearing red."

"I told Maria to prepare the red satin. You blend in too much with the blue. It's dull and ordinary and you, my darling Peyton, must not look dull and ordinary tonight. You're the star of the show."

I'm an employee. Not the star. She bit her lip, wondering if this was a battle she should fight. Her mother's eyes met hers in the mirror.

"Wear the red, Peyton. You'll look gorgeous and no man will take his eyes off you."

So that was it. Her mother was still interested in finding a life partner for her only daughter. Peyton sighed, turned on her heel and headed into her bedroom to get dressed.

If I ever get married, I'm wearing jeans. Take that, Mom.

She headed downstairs to the waiting limo. Gray stood at the foot of the stairs and gazed upward at her.

In elegant black tie, Gray looked as sophisticated as her parents' wealthy friends from the yacht club. He looked quite comfortable as well, which made her wonder if the man was accustomed to formal events.

Maybe, since he seemed to have guarded celebrities as well, and he knew how to blend in with his surroundings.

Her heart beat a little faster as he advanced, his gaze alighted with admiration.

"You look beautiful."

Why the compliment meant more coming from him, she didn't know. Maybe because Gray was honest and direct and did not bother with flattery.

Or perhaps it was something else. Certainly she felt more alive, aware, in his presence. He was the most interesting man she'd met in a long time, and yet she knew he was off-limits.

Soon as her stalker was found, he'd be out of her life. Disappointment filled her at the idea.

Peyton smoothed down the red satin. "Thank you. I'm supposed to look elegant and yet not command too much attention, but my mother insisted I wear this."

Her lips quirked as she nodded at Dr. Bradley, walking down the steps in a similar red satin gown. Gray smiled.

"Dr. Bradley, you could be Peyton's younger sister." Gray kissed her hand as her mother reached them.

To her amazement, her mother blushed. "Thank you."

Her father, always refined in his dinner dress, joined them. "Shall we? Peyton, you and Gray take the first limo. This way we are not all crowded. Wait for our car to pull up before getting out."

They went into the car, Gray checking out the interior first, and then helping her inside.

It was a short ride to the club, during which he said nothing. She noticed an earpiece on his right ear, similar to that she'd seen of Secret Service agents.

"Who's the radio contact?" She pointed to the earpiece.

Gray glanced at her. "Jace is attending with Jarrett and Lacey. He's helping me out. Jarrett and two other men from SOS were at the ballroom earlier, sweeping it."

When they pulled up in front of the yacht club, Peyton sighed. "My mother adores events like these. They make her happy."

Gray considered. "What makes you happy?"

Odd question considering the venue and the elegance surrounding them. Peyton settled on an honest answer. "Sea turtles and preserving the environment. And if I have to dress like this instead of my institute uniform of polo shirt and khakis, so be it. As long as it means we'll get the funding we need for expansion, I'm happy."

His own mouth quirked upward. "Why am I not surprised at your answer?"

Because you're getting to know me well, maybe even better than I know myself right now.

The evening promised glamour and glitz and the special touches her mother loved. Piper-Heidsieck Cuvee Brut Champagne. Caviar for nibbling, and lobster tail hors d'oeuvres. For those who preferred stronger drinks, cocktails at the bar in the corner.

Entertainment provided by her mother's favorite orchestra and a special guest singer, who sang sultry notes while couples took to the dance floor.

The club's exclusive ballroom, rented out for special occasions such as weddings and fundraising galas, provided a perfect venue for the turquoise green and blue of the ocean decor. An iced mermaid sculpture guarded a table of treats. A backdrop mural of sea turtles and fish swimming in blue ocean waters provided a perfect backdrop to the small orchestra playing onstage. Soft blue lighting made one feel immersed beneath the ocean waves. The ballroom's high vaulted ceilings, crystal chandlers and floor-to-ceiling windows added to the luxurious feel of the evening. Iridescent turquoise tablecloths covered every circular table, which had a centerpiece of colorful flowers and sea turtles. The stemware even featured etched sea turtles.

Peyton breathed a sigh of relief as they entered the ballroom after greeting the volunteers checking in guests at a table outside the doors. So much effort and planning had gone into this one night for a small but elite group of people.

Wearing their uniforms, Martin, Adam and a few other

staff from the institute were present and mingling with guests to answer questions. She went to the bar, ensuring the liquor was fully stocked and her father's golf partners would have their usual steady supply of bourbon. Next she greeted the orchestra and the committee members floating around the room like anxious jellyfish, ensuring all was going well. She ducked into the kitchen for a spot check on dinner. The five-course meal featured mushroom risotto, Atlantic salmon and filet mignon, as well as spinach polenta and glazed carrots.

She checked items at the silent auction table, pleased to see many bids far higher than anticipated. How fortunate she was to be born to a life of privilege and wealth, yet Peyton felt fully aware of her social responsibilities to charitable causes. Wealth meant little if one did not use it to aid others, her parents always dictated.

Maybe this is why I love working with sea turtles so much. I feel like I can give back something of what I was given. And they do not demand anything. There are no expectations with them, they simply want a peaceful, quiet beach on which to lay their eggs and a clean ocean, with plenty of food.

Through all her movements, Gray remained at her side. In the background, blending in, yet she was fully aware of his presence. When she finally sat for dinner, knowing she was expected to give a speech and a short presentation, he sat next to her. Touched at her mother's thoughtfulness in including him, as if he were a dinner date, she thought nothing of it.

She chatted with guests at her table, all new potential donors, who were eager to learn about beautiful sea creatures they might be persuaded to support. These donors alone could fund the new turtle hospital wing, and she knew she had to make a good impression. When Peyton paused to nibble at her meal, Gray smoothly took up the conversational reins.

"Yes, most of the sea turtles nesting on Florida's Atlantic Coast are loggerheads. However, I do recall a rare, extremely rare, leatherback turtle laying eggs on a public beach in Boca Raton one March. She was small, only about six hundred pounds. Quite a beautiful sight."

One of her avid donors leaned forward with a fascinated look. "*Only* six hundred pounds!"

Another rail-thin woman with bony shoulders laughed. "Six hundred pounds. I doubt anything weighs as much as that in Boca Raton. Is it even allowed?"

At the woman's teasing tone, Peyton held her breath. She wasn't certain how Gray would respond, despite his eloquent manners thus far.

Gray smiled and swirled his champagne. "I daresay she did not have access to a quality gym membership. But it was fascinating to watch her move on the sand."

He went on to hold them spellbound as he relayed how the massive turtle, so graceful in the water, struggled with her flippers to access the beach, ignoring the chattering beachgoers around her.

The bone-thin woman shook her head. "What drives them to go through all that, simply to dig a nest?"

Peyton's mouth opened and closed. Knowing her passion to ramble on about her favorite subject, she wisely decided to stay quiet and let Gray talk.

"It is impossible to disregard the natural instinct to reproduce," he murmured.

Innocent words, but they made her flush. Thankful for the low lighting, she sipped her champagne. Then a volunteer came to fetch her onstage. She excused herself to take the podium.

At the same time, Gray stood, nodding at their table

companions, and slipped away. She caught sight of him on the sidelines, eyeing the room. Discreetly blending in with the waitstaff, Jace and two other men in black tie also mingled. They must be Gray's extra security.

Knowing this crowd and their limited attention span, she kept her presentation short, stressing her thanks for their support of funding the new wing for the turtle hospital, and giving her usual emphasis on the dire need to protect the world's ocean habitats.

"Unfortunately, endangered sea turtles mistake plastic bags for their favorite food—jellyfish. Every year thousands of turtles die needlessly from either ingesting plastic waste or becoming entangled in marine debris. Let's all do our part and help save the turtles."

Applause sounded. Peyton paused, wanting to drive home a point. Seeing a familiar face in the crowd, she smiled.

"It's not easy with a busy lifestyle to remember to reduce our carbon and plastics footprint. I know many of you are doing a splendid job and all you can to save the planet for your children and grandchildren. Like Congressman Perez, who made it a point to swap out single-use plastic bottles of water for his staff and visitors with glassware. Sam, would you please stand up?"

A little flustered, but ever the smooth politician, the congressman stood to thundering applause, waving at the guests.

As he sat, Peyton added, "I know our favorite congressman has been instrumental in advancing protection for Florida's offshore waters, such as the recent Save Water bill. I'm so grateful to you, Sam, for all you do to protect and preserve our offshore waters."

More applause and the congressman beamed. The subtle push was a wink at the congressman, who still sat on the fence regarding that particular bill in the state legislature. Now all his high-powered and wealthy friends would ask him about it, and perhaps nudge the bill closer to becoming law.

She concluded her presentation and the MC invited guests to enjoy their desserts and the dance floor.

As she resumed her seat, gulping down her now-cold entrée, Peyton's mother brought over a young couple and made introductions. "Peyton, this is Mr. and Mrs. Jarrett Adler. Jarrett owns SOS Securities, as you know, and you've met Lacey before, when we entertained her parents, former Senator Alexander Stewart and his wife."

Abandoning her meal, Peyton stood and greeted the couple as her mother made small talk about Lacey's parents and then excused herself. Jarrett was younger than she expected, and blonde Lacey was pretty, with a radiant glow about her. She had not seen Lacey in several years and the woman looked happier than she had last time she and Peyton met.

"I wasn't certain if I would make it tonight." Lacey put a hand over the mound of her belly. "I'm due in another six weeks, but when we received the invitation, I had to attend. Anything that supports marine conservation is my cause."

"Your first baby?" she asked, smiling.

"We have Fleur, an older girl we adopted from Saint-Marc. She can't wait to be a big sister. We never thought this day would arrive. We didn't expect to be blessed this way." Jarrett's smile was soft as he gazed lovingly at his wife.

Peyton sensed a story there.

No time to ask about it, for Gray left his position near the stage and came toward her, along with Jace. He took her arm and escorted her to the Adlers' table as Jarrett settled his wife into a chair. "I have to get to work, honey, but you and Peyton can catch up," Jarrett told Lacey.

Then Jarrett's expression turned hard as he looked at Gray. "Let's walk."

Jace glanced at her, his normally cheerful expression turning serious. "I'll watch over Peyton."

The two men walked away, talking quietly, as Jace hovered near Peyton. Peyton made small talk as Lacey asked about the sea turtles and expressed genuine interest.

Suddenly Jace's cheerful demeanor changed and his eyes narrowed. Curious, Peyton turned to see a stunning blonde, her patrician features arranged in a wide smile as she spotted Lacey. The woman wore a sophisticated black ball gown and had a stride that announced she was not only familiar with gliding across a crowded room and commanding attention, but confident enough to ignore it. Like a queen before peasants.

A simple diamond pendant hung around her long neck. Lacey struggled to stand, but the woman motioned for her to sit.

"Lacey, you are positively glowing. I'm thrilled for you and Jarrett." The woman held out both hands, which Lacey squeezed.

"Kara!" Lacey glanced at her. "Peyton Bradley, this is Kara Wilmington, my friend. She owns an estate sale company and is a generous supporter of our women's shelter, and your sea turtles."

Kara had a genuine, friendly smile that belied her elegance. She shook Peyton's hand. "It's an honor to meet you. I've heard so many wonderful things about your work."

"Thank you." Peyton returned the smile.

Lacey turned to Jace. "Oh, Kara, this is Jace…"

"We've met," Jace cut in, his brows furrowing.

Kara recoiled a moment, but then recovered her smooth, polished expression. "Jason." A slight nod. "I'd say it was good to see you again, but I do hate lying."

"Funny," he drawled. "You didn't seem to mind lying last time we saw each other."

Ignoring him, the woman dropped a kiss on Lacey's forehead. "Let's try to do lunch before you have the baby. We can do it at your house. I'll bring whatever you wish."

Lacey nodded, putting a hand over her rounded belly. Peyton watched Kara walk away, but not before catching the wounded, almost vulnerable look on her face before it vanished.

"Who was that?" Peyton asked Jace.

He gazed after the woman a while before answering. "My ex-girlfriend."

When Jarrett and Gray returned, she excused herself to mingle among the guests, ignoring Gray. Rather, trying to ignore him. Peyton was too aware of how handsome and resplendent he appeared in black tie, his serious expression intriguing rather than foreboding. Gray's ability to charm seemed to win over guests. Yet she was always aware of him zeroing in on her like a laser, knowing where she was at all times. It was a bit unnerving.

If only Gray were old, practically bald and stooped, he'd be safer. She wouldn't feel like this—alive and aware of him, and herself, and the subtle attraction charging between them like a sizzling electrical current.

When he asked her to dance, her heart raced like a giddy schoolgirl's. Peyton slid into his arms as if she belonged there. No, she didn't. Their worlds were too far apart. Soon as her stalker was found, he'd be off on another assignment.

Like everything else he did, Gray was an expert dancer. She found herself easily following his lead as he guided her around the floor.

Much as she wanted to ask him what Jarrett had discussed, she refrained.

"How did you know about the leatherback in Boca?" she asked instead.

Gray expertly cut a turn. "I researched sea turtles, since they are a part of your life. My job isn't merely to protect you, Peyton. It's also to keep in tune to your world so I can do my job more effectively."

Disappointed, she had hoped for something more, perhaps a spark of real interest that would bond them together...which was ludicrous. He was her protector.

"They are fascinating creatures, elegant and graceful in the water," he continued. "I understand your fierce need for turtle conservation, and other marine species. Humans need to be more aware of the world around them, and stop ruining it. Or we ultimately will ruin ourselves."

Intrigued, she looked up at him. "I should have asked you to speak tonight."

His mouth twitched in a ghost of a smile. "You did an excellent job with your audience, though I fear many are more interested in the walnut cake and getting their photos in the society section than sea turtles."

"True. But why do you find sea turtles fascinating?"

He considered. "They humble me. They've been on this earth for thousands of years and will exist long after I'm gone. They are not arrogant or egotistical. They are driven by the basic instinct to survive, not by power or greed or cruelty, as some men are."

Her shadow was less robot-like and more human. Yet he never ceased at doing his job.

They swayed in time to the music. Peyton closed her eyes. Gray was a skilled dancer, the sensual sway of his hips and legs leading her across the floor. If he weren't her protector, she might even consider dating him, maybe even something deeper and more meaningful...

The music ended and his hooded gaze met hers. Heat suffused her face.

"You're blushing," he said softly.

"It's warm in here." She put her hands to her reddened face.

"Perhaps we should get some air."

Do you believe two people from different worlds can fall in love at first sight?

What an absurd thought. He'd asked her to dance not as a courtesy or as a man expressing interest in her as a woman, but as a bodyguard wishing to keep a close watch over her.

She declined politely. "I should return to my guests."

Gray paid no attention. His gaze snapped over to the congressman's table, where the man was coughing violently. "Follow me," Gray ordered.

He rushed over to the politician, who was struggling to breathe. Someone lifted him up and attempted the Heimlich maneuver. Gray stopped the man and looked at the congressman's face.

"He's not choking. It's an allergic reaction. Ma'am, do you carry an EpiPen on you?"

"There's one in his dinner jacket," his wife cried out.

Gray found the pen, tore off the man's jacket and rolled up his sleeve, expertly administering the shot. A minute later, the congressman began breathing easier.

Gray checked his pulse, nodded. "He's going to be fine, but I would go to the hospital just in case."

"Thank you," the congressman's wife said as paramedics came into the ballroom and attended to her husband. "You saved him... I am not good in an emergency and we're always so careful."

"What is your husband allergic to?" he asked.

"He's allergic to nuts."

Gray glanced at the cake. Peyton felt her stomach lurch.

Sitting on the congressman's plate was a slice of walnut cake.

The wife shook her head. "I don't understand. They served him the cake so I thought it was safe and didn't have nuts! I expressly noted on our response he is allergic to nuts. I didn't even look at the dessert offered on the program invitation."

"The kitchen staff probably made a mistake," Gray soothed. "I am glad the congressman is recovering."

Gray took her hand and steered her away from the table. "I suggest if you have something else to distract the crowd, present it now. I need to talk with Jarrett."

Shaken, she swallowed hard. "There's a video on hatchlings we planned to show after dessert as background to the dancing."

"Do it. Only announce to the crowd you're showing it. Then return to your table and your parents and do not leave their sight. Understand?"

She nodded. He gave her a brief smile, and squeezed her hand, and then vanished into the crowd.

The video on sea turtles nesting and the hatchlings boiling out of the sand served to draw attention away from the congressman's table. Peyton returned to her table to watch, her knees weak. If not for Gray, this evening could have gone terribly wrong.

How could the staff have served walnut cake to a man allergic to nuts?

Her mother looked anxious. "I was in the restroom when everything happened. I should check him out, he's our guest."

"Mom, Gray asked me to stay close to you, where you can both watch me. I don't know why, but please don't leave me."

Her father patted her hand. "Of course not, honey. We're right here."

Now was not the time to discuss the mishap of the mixed-up dessert. Peyton's head ached as she made small talk with her parents about the guests and their reactions to the decor and entertainment. The orchestra began playing again and several couples took to the dance floor.

Seeing Adam drift over, she plastered a smile on her face. Adam, like the other staff from her work, was dressed in a black polo shirt with the institute's logo and black trousers.

He held out his hand. "I know I'm only the help tonight, but may I have the pleasure of this dance, Peyton?"

Her mother looked over Adam and frowned. "A short one," Peyton told him. "I have to stick close to my parents."

They danced close to where her parents could still see her. Adam wasn't as skilled or as expert as Gray, but he managed. Peyton resorted to shop talk. He shook his head.

"Not tonight, please. I'd rather talk about you, Peyton. You're too serious. Anything I can do?"

She shook her head. "There's not much for me to talk about, Adam. Not here."

"It is a little stifling," he agreed.

She asked Adam for the time. He glanced at his watch and then grinned. "It's almost midnight. Why? Are you turning into a pumpkin or am I boring you?"

"Not you. But I wish I could get out of here. I haven't patrolled the beach in a long time."

He looked thoughtful. "You have a lot of other work, Peyton. Besides, that dress doesn't look like it would hold up to sand and surf."

Peyton smiled, but her mind drifted to the beach. She'd done her part, why should she remain? The twin pressures of family obligations and work weighted on her shoulders. Her work came first, so why couldn't her family understand that?

Because you're the girl and the baby of the family. Your parents' expectations are different for you.

Spying Roger, one of their interns, she stopped. "Something's wrong."

Adam turned.

The intern came over, bubbling with excitement. "Turtle sighting! Not a false crawl, either. I think it might even be a hawksbill! She's on the beach and digging, Pey!"

Forgetting about Gray's edict and her parents, Peyton wriggled out of Adam's embrace and fled to the bank of windows overlooking the sea. Too dark to tell, and the club had a natural barrier of sea grape trees to keep light from shining on the beach as to not confuse the turtles. Turtles used moonlight to guide them back to the water after laying their nests.

Chances were it was an ordinary loggerhead, not the rarer *Eretmochelys imbricate*, which seldom laid eggs on South Florida beaches, but she was itching to see for herself.

What if it were a hawksbill? Excitement brimmed inside her. This was her life, not socializing with wealthy patrons and sipping cocktails while bored old men stared at her.

A cool ocean breeze caressed her cheeks as she slipped outside. The familiar scent of brine and tangy salt filled her senses. Inside, she was the dutiful hostess, a smile affixed to her mouth, always aware of proper social etiquette. Here, she was free as the beautiful sea turtles swimming in the buoyant ocean.

This was her true calling. Her home.

Following close behind, Adam and the intern kept quiet as they made their way down the stone pathway leading to the beach. Peyton unlocked the iron gate and held it open for them, and stood at the top of the wooden stairs leading down to the sand. This stretch of sand was wider and had not suffered the erosion of beaches farther to the north and south. In addition, it was closed to all but members, who seldom frequented the beach at night.

For sea turtles, that made for prime nesting.

"You both go down and watch from a safe vantage point where she won't see you, closer to the dune," she whispered. "I'll be right down."

She removed her red satin heels, wishing she could remove the heavy satin gown as well. As her hand rested on the railing, and she was about to descend, strong fingers laced around her arm.

Peyton bit back a shriek.

"Where the hell are you going and why didn't you tell me?" he said in a deep voice.

Her bodyguard. She relaxed.

"Sea turtle nesting," she whispered. "I didn't want to send out a bulletin and have half the guests stumbling down here, scaring her off."

"I am not half the guests." He released her, withdrew his pistol. "I'm your protection and anyone can be out here, Peyton."

He handed her a flashlight. Annoyed, she glanced at him. "No flashlights on the beach. You'll confuse her."

Gray's fingers brushed hers, the contact brief but electrifying. He flipped a switch and the flashlight turned red. Peyton blinked. The man knew about turtles and how white light confused them in their nesting. Or he had researched what was necessary.

"We'll go together," he told her.

Glancing at the gun in his hand, she shook her head. "Is that necessary? I doubt the sea turtle is going to hurt me, Gray."

"It's not the sea turtle concerning me."

Knowing he had the upper hand, she sighed and descended the stairs with him. The sand was soft and warm beneath her bare feet as they skirted a clump of trees and walked closer to the shoreline. Spotting the loggerhead sea turtle lumbering onshore, Peyton hung back, as Adam and Roger remained a distance away, watching.

Gray holstered his gun. Together they watched the turtle digging in the soft sand. Peyton sighed with wonder.

"Look at her. She's amazing. All that effort to dig a nest, guided by years of instinct. I wish my mother understood my passion for saving sea turtles. But she's a renowned cardiac surgeon who saves lives with her skills."

"Don't underestimate the importance of your work, Peyton. You save lives as well, the lives of turtles, and in doing so, you're helping to preserve them for future generations," Gray pointed out.

Never had she quite thought about her career that way. It made her smile.

Peyton quietly watched the turtle dig her nest. "It's moments like this that I find meaningful. Ever since Shelly died, I've come to appreciate life's little treasures, the gifts I've been given. Oh, not my family's money. I know lots of people would envy me for the financial freedom they think I have. Moments like this that can't be bought or bartered. What you said to me at the jetty, Gray, you're so right. Every day we are above ground is a gift and we have to learn to take moments like this and cherish them while we have them."

"Nature gives us a rare gift in moments like this," he murmured. "The power of nature always amazed me."

She glanced at him. "Like a gorgeous sunset after a catastrophic hurricane at the beach."

The turtle finished digging a deep hole. Then she began

to deposit into the hole soft, leathery eggs the size of ping-pong balls.

"She's crying," Gray whispered, sounding amazed. "Is she in pain?"

Offering a wry grin, she shook her head. "It's a turtle's way of ridding her body of excess salt. That and the tears help flush sand from her eyes."

He reached over and wiped a tear from her own cheek. "You're crying as well."

Stricken he'd caught her with her guard down, Peyton tried to reel in all her tumbling emotions. "This is what's most important, Gray. Trying to save a species. Everything else is window dressing. I've been given a gift to under-stand science and sea turtles. It's my passion, not balls and teas and parties. Why can't my family support me?"

"Give them a chance. Talk to them. They may be more supportive if you communicate your needs more effec-tively with them."

As the female turtle lumbered her way back to the ocean, and then dived into the waves, Peyton cried harder. She leaned against him and he put his arms around her. It felt good to snuggle against him, breathe in the spicy scent of his cologne. Gray had no agenda. He wanted nothing from her, only to keep her safe.

He kissed her forehead and gently wiped away her tears with one thumb.

A rude circle of bright light broke them apart. Peyton squinted and put up her hand against the flashlight shin-ing in her face. "What's going on? No lights at the beach!"

"I've been looking for you everywhere." Her father's grim voice cut through the sounds of crashing surf. "I see you were otherwise occupied."

Wiping away her tears, Peyton felt as if she were four

years old again and caught sneaking cookies before dinner. "Dad…"

"Your mother needs you, Peyton. They're going to announce the winners of the silent auction and your presence is required. Clean up, honey, and join her."

Giving Gray an apologetic look, she ran to the stairs.

The game was up. Though the moonlight provided dim light on the beach, Gray didn't need to see Bradley's face. The man was breathing heavily, and his fists were bunched as if he wanted to punch Gray in the face.

"I know who you are. My sources finally found out and texted me a few minutes ago, Mitchell. Your real name is Grayson Mitchell, not Gray Wallace."

"My legal name is Grayson Mitchell. I apologize, sir, if my behavior seemed inappropriate." Gray didn't bother with explanations. Bradley wouldn't listen, anyway. He knew the man's type.

"Inappropriate?" Bradley snapped. "What's inappropriate is what you did in the past, Mitchell. I never should have let you near my little girl. What the hell was I thinking?"

Gray's anger rose up, but he leashed his temper. "You were thinking you wanted the best. I'm the best."

"You're several things I won't mention here for the sake of politeness. Did you think you could keep your past secret from me? I heard you were arrested and have a violent temper. I will take no chances with my daughter. I'm telling Jarrett Adler about you…"

"He knows."

Bradley snorted. "He knows? And he was foolish enough to hire you anyway?"

His blackened reputation had preceded him. Thanks to the rumor mill, he was losing this job. But he worried more about Peyton. She was far too vulnerable to her stalker.

"Whatever you think of me isn't important. What is important is that you let me stay with Peyton to keep her safe. This stalker is escalating. He's here tonight. I am certain of it. That wasn't an accident in the kitchen that the congressman received the walnut cake instead of the raspberry torte for dessert. Someone found out he was allergic to nuts and wanted to harm him, simply because Peyton expressed admiration for him."

Bradley made a gesture of dismissal. "That's nonsense. It was an accident. The kitchen staff were incompetent. And my wife and her committee carefully screened every single guest here."

"Your wife," Gray said between clenched teeth, "is an excellent heart surgeon. Not versed in matters of security."

"It doesn't matter, Mitchell. I want you gone."

He stared at him. "You're firing me?"

"Not just you, but the whole damn SOS agency. My company's security team will be on point now. Effective immediately, I'm terminating the agreement with SOS as is my right per the contract. Get your things out of my house and leave tonight."

Chapter 10

Once inside, Gray found his employer and told him what happened.

Jarrett looked grim. "I don't care about the money, Gray. But he's making a damn mistake."

"I know. We need to talk with her."

He signaled to Jarrett to follow him. They waited until Peyton finished her presentation onstage. When she headed to the bar for a drink, they cornered her.

"A word, Peyton," he said quietly. "We need to ask you some questions."

"All right. But can it wait until we get home? I'm leaving soon. My part in this evening is over and done with."

She looked weary and resigned, not the joyful and emotional woman on the beach who thrilled at watching a sea turtle.

"Ever had a sense that you were watched and followed, perhaps something that you dismissed as being paranoid?" Gray asked.

Peyton frowned. "No. Not really."

"No gifts left for you at work or home? Notes of admiration?"

"None. Nothing unusual until I started receiving those notes." Peyton's fingers curled. "When will this end?"

Jarrett and Gray exchanged glances.

"When he is caught...or..." Jarrett began.

Gray finished. "Or you are killed."

Jarrett shot his employee a warning glance as Peyton's mouth opened and closed. She looked around the room.

"He could be anywhere," she whispered. "Looking to kill me right now."

"Gray was being far too blunt," Jarrett said.

"No, I am not. Stay out of this, Jarrett. She's not a child. Peyton deserves the truth." Gray clasped her hand, warming her skin beneath his fingers. "I promised to be honest with you, Peyton. Tonight, while you were speaking onstage, my team and I scanned the room for anyone who looked at you with more than the typical interest."

"We both had the sense your stalker is here, tonight," Jarrett added.

"And now we know he was."

Blood drained from her face. "In this room?"

"He's escalating. There is someone out there who has a fantasy that you are his, and he will not stop until he reaches fulfillment. If he is here, he may feel you betrayed him tonight when you singled out the congressman."

Her mouth opened and closed. "But it was nothing, just acknowledging his contributions."

"Perhaps not with words, but your looking at him, your smile, your insistence on singling him out and talking with him after, if your stalker is here, he would feel hurt."

"You think someone gave him the walnut cake on purpose?" Peyton rubbed her temple.

Peyton was smart. She didn't need things spelled out for her. "Yes. Is there anyone you noticed paying you more attention than warranted?"

"No. I mean, this is a fundraiser my family sponsors, so naturally everyone wants to talk with me."

Gray nodded. "In the future, if you notice such a person, notify security immediately."

"What's with both of you? I know something is off. What is it you're not telling me?"

Glancing at Jarrett, who nodded, Gray said in a solemn voice, "This is the last night SOS will be providing protective services for you. I've been fired."

Peyton stared. "For hugging me on the beach? Dad overreacted."

"No." Gray compressed his lips.

"It doesn't matter," Jarrett cut in. "What matters is your future security, Peyton. If it comes down to it, you need to know how to protect yourself."

"Why would my father fire you? Is the threat gone?"

"Far from it," Jarrett answered, his jaw tight. "But your father terminated the contract. He hired another security firm to guard you."

Peyton looked hurt. "Why would he do that?"

Gray settled his hands on her shoulders, hating the fact he was leaving her in the hands of less competent people. "You'd have to ask him. But, Peyton, I promise you, I will not give up until your stalker is found. Even though I'm no longer under contract to your father."

He gazed around the ballroom. "I've been requested to pack my things tonight and leave. I'll drive you back to the house. But I am not leaving until I know my replacement is there."

Wisps of blond hair spilled from her intricate hairstyle.

Gray resisted the urge to tuck one behind her delicate ear. She looked forlorn and lost, as if he abandoned her.

"I thought of you as my shadow." She laughed, but there was no humor in it. "I guess I'm losing my shadow."

Gray gathered her hands into his. "No, you're not. Peyton, I promise you, I may not be on the job, but I will be your shadow."

At his wink, her eyes widened. "Oh."

"Remember the closet the other day?" he asked softly.

The smile she gave him filled him with relief. Gray squeezed her hands. "Say your goodbyes and let's go."

Gray accompanied her around the ballroom as she bid farewell to her guests. When they went outside, Jarrett was exiting Gray's Mercedes out front. Jarrett opened the door for her and then murmured to Gray, "Good luck."

When they were on their way back to the mansion, Peyton released a breath. "I thought we were going home in the limo."

"Too risky. I told Jarrett to arrange to bring my car here just in case."

He parked before the mansion and flipped on the interior lights. Gray turned to her, his chest tight. "Peyton, no matter what happens, I'm here for you. Call me. Any time of day or night."

Her gaze turned wide. "Gray, you're scaring me."

Grimly, he thought of what could happen to her. "I'm going to scare you even more." He turned out his hands, palms up, to show he had nothing to hide. "Before your parents get home or that new rent-a-cop your father hired, I need to show you a few tricks. Just in case, for your own protection."

It wouldn't take long for him to pack and toss his things into the car. He spent the next hour in the house showing her self-defense tricks and making her practice. Duct tape was best. Some used flex cuffs, but most amateurs resorted to duct tape.

When Peyton displayed an ability to break free, he relaxed. A little.

His cell rang. Jarrett, warning him the Bradleys were on their way home with the new security guard.

"New guy looks like Bradley hired him for the muscle, not the experience or skill set. Amateur," Jarrett scoffed. "Just as you thought."

Gray hung up.

A lump rose in his throat. The last time this happened, someone died.

Emotion welling up, Gray retreated to his room and tossed all his things into a duffel bag. He checked the driveway outside. A sleek black limo pulled up and disgorged the Bradleys. Behind the limo was a sedan, where a heavyset man lumbered out from behind the driver's wheel.

His replacement.

Still in his tuxedo, he paused at Peyton's doorway.

"Remember what I taught you. If you ever find yourself in trouble, don't yell 'Help.' People will ignore you. Always scream 'Fire.' That will get someone's attention. And I will be close, watching you."

Just not close enough.

She rose off her bed and ran to the door, flinging her arms around him, hugging him tight. "Please don't leave me."

Too emotional to speak, and liking the feel of her in his arms far too much, he smiled and tweaked her nose.

Then he was down the steps, his duffel slung over one shoulder. He ignored the Bradleys and the new security guard. Gray was out the door, the sounds of Peyton protesting in his ears.

Gray started his car and drove away, his chest tight, but he did not look back.

* * *

If her new bodyguard had arrived more than two weeks ago, she'd have been ecstatic. Large, balding and muscled, he acted more interested in checking his text messages than observing her every move.

His name was Ed. Nice enough, she supposed, but he lacked the polish and sophistication of her shadow. He did not wear a gun, for he said a good bodyguard didn't need a weapon.

Peyton went to work early Monday morning. Ed did not arrive at the institute until two hours later. So much for protecting her.

She embroiled herself in writing the report due later, then read it over and emailed it to Martin. Peyton stretched out her legs, staring at the laptop. Nearly eleven.

She missed Gray. Missed his dry sense of humor, his grim seriousness that was a reminder how he never stopped working to keep her safe.

Ed? If she were a text message, Peyton supposed she'd be safe enough.

Around noon, she left to meet her father for lunch. Ed drove her to the restaurant, but left when they arrived, with the excuse that her father probably didn't want him lingering nearby.

Gray would have not only lingered, he'd have checked out the restaurant ahead of time. He wouldn't have cared that her father grew annoyed with his presence.

Salvatore's was a small, intimate Italian restaurant with white tablecloths and excellent cuisine. Not her choice, but her father enjoyed the food and the attention the waitstaff showered on him. As the maître d' escorted her to the window table where her father sat, she startled.

Three tables away, nearly hidden by other diners, sat

her shadow. Gray glanced up from his phone, saw her and saluted.

Giving him a brief nod back, she turned her attention to greeting her father, who stood and kissed her on the cheek.

Peyton murmured an excuse about checking texts and texted Gray.

Thanks for being here.

I told you I'd be your shadow.

How did you find out about this lunch?

I have my sources. That and your father's secretary had already given me his schedule.

Gray added a smiley face after his text. Peyton grinned, ordered a salad and let her father talk. She'd been uptight about this lunch, knowing her father wanted to try to nudge her once more into quitting her job and moving back up north for the summer. The threat was still there. She didn't need reminding. But knowing Gray was there, watching out for her, made her relax.

Until halfway through her salad when the esteemed Charles W. Bradley, CEO of Bradley Industries, shocked her.

"I had to get rid of Gray, honey. With his shady past, who knows what he would have done to you."

Peyton's mouth opened. The fork fell from her fingers to the table with a muted clatter. "What shady past?"

"I sensed something off about him. I knew he had a reputation as an excellent executive protector, but I'd heard vague rumors…"

Rumors. Peyton picked up her fork. "Dad, didn't you

always tell me gossip was for nosy people with too much time on their hands?"

"This wasn't gossip!" Her father set down his fork carefully, as if controlling his temper. She knew what this meant.

"Gray was mixed up in some shady business. He was even arrested. His real last name is Mitchell, not Wallace. Whatever it is, I can't get to the heart of it yet, but I am not taking chances with your safety, honey."

She couldn't, no wouldn't, believe this. Still, the knowledge sickened her. Tiny doubts gnawed at her. Gray had been reticent about his personal life.

The man sitting a few tables away could tell her.

"You always prided yourself on the full truth. Not rumors."

Her father looked suddenly weary. "Peyton, as you go through life and get older, you'll discover the full truth is always laced with a good dose of opinion. I found out enough to make me fire him. He was involved in something shady. A crime that was covered up. More than that, I don't know."

Hope filled her. "Anyone can accuse someone of committing a crime. If there was no evidence…"

"Peyton, I don't need evidence to get rid of a man who might harm you."

Angered, she pushed away her salad. Gray had the wiry, tensile strength of an athlete and she'd sensed a lethal quality about him. But commit a crime?

"He must have had good reason," she snapped.

The dismissive gesture he made was one she recognized when her father was finished with a subject. "I heard the man has a vicious temper, Peyton, and I will not risk you around someone like that."

He didn't investigate further, she realized. He'd heard

something he didn't like, immediately judged Gray for it. Did not give the man a chance.

Glancing over at the subject of their conversation, she felt a tug of pity. Was Gray's life always like this? Doomed to public censure and getting fired from jobs because of a shady incident that no one bothered to ask him to explain?

Peyton was all too familiar with people judging her in haste, simply because her family was wealthy. They assumed she had everything handed to her or her family's money granted her privileges denied to others, such as a coveted job at the institute. It had taken hard work and dedication over the past two years to prove herself as a sea turtle biologist. Perhaps even double the work.

No use arguing with her father. But she had to say one thing in Gray's defense. "Dad, whatever you think about Gray, I know he's dedicated to the job he's assigned. You were the one chiding me to stop complaining about him being there, attached to me like a barnacle. There has to be another reason why you fired him. You're too smart of a businessman to let a nasty rumor make that drastic of a decision."

Seeing his gaze flick away as he drank his water, insight struck her. "It's the incident on the beach. You saw him hugging me and it bothered you."

"No, of course not. Don't be silly. Are you finished, honey? I have a one thirty meeting."

I'm not being silly. But that was it. You thought there was something more there. There wasn't.

Or was there? To be honest, she'd felt those sparks between herself and Gray, and wondered if they could turn to flames had the circumstances been different.

Peyton stood, kissed her father on the cheek. "Thanks for lunch. See you later."

Lingering outside the restaurant so Gray could watch

her through the window, she rapped on her new body-guard's window. When he rolled it down, she told him she was visiting a few stores within walking distance and he could wait.

At his nod, and rolling the window back up, she knew her father had made a grave error. Not only in dismissing Gray, but in hiring this Ed, who truly didn't know how to do the job.

She texted Gray. We need to talk. Meet me by the lingerie shop after my father leaves.

Using the guise of scrolling through her phone, Peyton waited until her father left the restaurant and then walked to the little shop with the lacy undergarments in the window.

"You need my advice on women's lingerie?" Gray asked with amusement.

Once more, he'd arrived as silently as fog. Normally she'd welcome his teasing. Not this time.

Peyton looked him straight on. "My father told me your last name is Mitchell, not Wallace, and you were involved in a crime. You were arrested. That was why he fired you."

Gray's expression flattened. It was like watching a favorite balloon deflate.

"And you want to know what the crime was."

"Gray…"

"You can fill in the blanks as you wish, like your father did. Like everyone else does. I don't owe you, or them, anything more."

She lifted her chin. "No, you don't. I wanted to give you a chance to tell your side of the story."

Dark, expressionless eyes regarded her. "I don't need that chance. Are you going shopping?"

All the joy in seeing him fled. "I have to get back to work."

He gave a curt nod. "I'll see you there, in the background, of course."

"You're still going to watch over me? After I accused you?"

"You did not accuse me. Your father did and I told you I wasn't abandoning you. Once I'm tasked with a duty, I follow through, Ms. Bradley."

No more first names. She understood, and it grieved her. The one person she trusted in this mess that intruded into her life and he distanced himself.

"Thank you, Mr. Mitchell."

Equally formal. Nothing of the warm intimacy they'd shared while watching the turtle on the beach.

Peyton headed to her car, aware of his gaze burning into her back, and feeling as if she'd lost a good friend.

She did not see Gray the rest of the afternoon. When the institute closed for the evening and she went to her car, followed by an indifferent Ed, she saw no sign of him.

Maybe Gray lied about being there to watch over her. Her parents were at a friend's house having dinner. No one else around but Ed, who'd discovered the joys of Caren's cooking, as well as snacking in the kitchen.

Peyton made herself a plate of food and ate alone in her room. After washing her dishes in the sink, she returned upstairs.

Ed was still downstairs, eating Caren's enchiladas.

After spending a couple of hours trying to lose herself in work, she closed her laptop lid. There was only one cure for the hurt she felt over Gray's abandonment.

The moon was waning and she itched to get out onto her beach to turtle watch. That night, Peyton made her plans reality.

She slathered on bug spray, loaded her backpack with her camera, notebooks and pen and wallet, along with

her keys. Then she grabbed her water bottle from the refrigerator and tucked it into the backpack's side pocket.
Peyton dressed in lightweight long pants, a long-sleeved
black shirt and her sneakers. Though the temperature had
dropped with sunset, it was still warm and muggy outside.

Ed could amuse himself with his phone. Or whatever
he wanted. She did not care, as long as he left her alone.

Her father's grim revelation about Gray's past had
shocked her. Yet deep down, she felt only sympathy for
her former protector. He had gone overseas as a SEAL to
serve his country, and possibly sacrifice his very life, and
then fell into trouble because of his violent temper.

Having been victim of the gossip mill before, she felt
sympathy for Gray. He seemed far too self-confident and
the discipline she'd glimpsed hinted at self-control, not a
man prone to a violent outburst.

Still, she wasn't certain. It no longer mattered. Gray
wasn't a part of her life anymore.

Slipping past Ed's open door, where he'd kicked off
his shoes and was watching a reality television show,
she started to make her way down the stairs when voices
alerted her. Peyton retreated to her bedroom and frowned.

The trellis! Gray had not gotten around to tearing all
of it down.

She went to the second floor and an empty bedroom
where the trellis still clung to the wall. Peyton went out
onto the balcony and, backpack over one shoulder, gained
a foothold. The trellis held. With a deep breath, she descended.

A few feet from the bottom, she jumped, gazed around.
No one saw her. Feeling absurdly giddy, she raced across
the lawn to the gate accessing the beach beyond. She unlocked the gate to access the private beach from the house.
This beach had only two entry points, and the steps leading

to the nearby street had a steel gate that always remained locked. Her family and the turtle patrol always accessed the beach from the house.

The waning moon glinted off the lacy waves washing onshore. A light breeze off the ocean cut through the humid, briny air. Her sneakers sank into the warm sand as she made her way farther from the house to the quieter stretch of beach where the turtles liked to nest. No lights here, and far away enough from any residences. Privacy.

Peyton selected a spot near the sea grape trees, snapped out her blanket on the sand and sat. A chain-link fence protected the beach from trespassers. She pulled out her 35mm camera and prepared to settle in for a few hours.

Patience was necessary when turtle watching. Some nights she'd remained here until nearly dawn without seeing a single turtle. It wasn't the height of the season yet, so her chances were still slim.

But a warm breeze blew off the ocean, chasing away the huge mosquitoes, and the sounds of the ocean rolling onshore soothed her frayed nerves. Hugging her knees, she stared at the water and the seemingly endless horizon. Being here always humbled her and made her own problems appear minute when she considered nature and the timeless cycle of life. Peyton felt part of something larger and more significant. Maybe that was why saving sea turtles had become her mission. Her mother saved lives.

You save lives as well, the lives of turtles, and in doing so, you're helping to preserve them for future generations.

Gray's words echoed in her mind. She missed him and his quiet observations, his wit and wisdom.

Peyton tried to push her former bodyguard out of her mind and focus on the ocean, for any disturbance in the waves. Suddenly she spotted movement. Excitement pulsed through her, as her heart raced. Lots of movement. Not daring to move in fear of scaring the turtle off, she strained to see what displaced the water.

Looking through the viewfinder of her camera, she focused, but darn, she'd forgotten her tripod in her eagerness to escape the house.

Grunting sounds of someone lumbering through the sand made her drop the camera on the blanket. A large figure loomed nearby, wheezing as if out of breath. For a moment she panicked, and then panic turned to sheer annoyance.

Ed, her bodyguard.

"What are you doing out here, Ms. Bradley? You're supposed to tell me if you leave the house," he said in a loud voice.

The man was as stealthy as a jackhammer. Peyton blew out a deep breath, thinking of how Gray's quiet movements had caught her off guard.

"I'm turtle watching."

"Oh?" He squinted at the ocean. "Don't see any."

"Quiet," she snapped. "There's a female ready to come ashore to nest. You'll scare her into a false crawl."

Ed stared at the water. "I don't think so."

She turned in the direction of his pointing finger and her blood went cold.

Ms. Peyton Bradley wasn't a difficult person to track. But her confrontation about his past made him question his decision to keep on the case.

Gray reasoned he could have simply turned around and headed home to New York. Summers here in Florida were hot and sticky, and he preferred the cooler climate. But he'd promised Peyton he'd be nearby to watch over her, even if she questioned his character.

Never again would he break a promise to a woman if he could help it.

He had to admit it rankled him that she had doubts, doubts her father had planted there. Yeah, wasn't nice to think that the woman he'd sworn to keep safe thought he was a violent criminal.

Deep down, he couldn't blame her father. If he had a daughter, hell, he'd be overly protective as well, especially considering the threats Peyton already faced.

Maybe he should quit and return to New York as his father wished. Settle down in the family business like his older brother.

But he'd agreed to this job and he owed Jarrett a favor. Once he committed to something, he didn't turn away.

You're stuck with me, Ms. Bradley. Like it or not.

He hovered around the perimeter of the Bradley estate, watching Peyton's room. Thanks to a little trick he'd pulled with the security cameras and putting the footage on a loop before he'd left, Gray knew he was mainly invisible. A test as well of the new security guy, to see if he noticed.

So far—no. New guy was sloppy.

Or lazy. Or both.

Gray glanced up at Peyton's room and then climbed the trellis to an empty bedroom. He went from balcony to balcony until reaching her bedroom and then, staying in the shadows, peered inside the well-lit room.

Empty.

She could be someplace else in the house, but his instinct warned Peyton had taken advantage of the lull in security to do what Peyton loved most—go turtle watching.

When his feet hit the ground, he jogged across the lawn to head to the beach.

A scream rang out. His blood pressure skyrocketed as he ran toward the private beach.

The gate prohibiting entry onto the beach was open. He slogged through the thick sand toward the screams. Seeing a figure lying prone on the shoreline, his blood ran cold. He ran toward it and ground to an abrupt halt.

The body of Peyton's current protector lay still, black blood staining the wet sand as he stared sightlessly at the night sky. Cursing, Gray looked around. No Peyton.

"Help! Please help! Fire!"

Peyton! There, coming from the stairs leading to the street.

He had to save her, get to her now. Gray pulled out his sidearm.

The steps leading from the beach to the street seemed miles away as he slogged through the heavy sand toward the sound of her terrified voice. Sand sucked at his boots as he ran, slowing his progress. Despite the burst of speed, despite every last ounce of his strength, he knew he couldn't reach her in time.

The last thing he heard before car doors slammed and her abductor drove away was Peyton, screaming for the rescue he could not give her.

Chapter 11

Her head throbbed. Peyton struggled to open her gluey eyelids. Everything seemed to swim in an ocean of gelatin. Muscles burned with strain, as if she'd run for miles.

Gradually she became aware of her surroundings. Lying lengthwise on the back seat of…a truck? She smelled old motor oil, grease and sweat.

Her hands and ankles were restrained. But loose enough. Whoever tied her up with duct tape had been in a hurry.

Or they thought she would remain unconscious. *You have the advantage.*

Voices sounded through the truck's open windows. Angry, raised voices in Spanish and then a man in high-pitched English yelling, "No. I'll take care of it!"

Broken English, sinister. "You will kill her?"

"She's my problem. I told you, I'll take care of this and you'll never see her again."

Her blood froze in her veins. Panic welled up, bubbling over and threatening to make her bolt. Calm down.

She heard Gray's voice in her mind. Gray, who wanted to protect her, who taught her a few tricks in case the worst happened.

Gray, who had not been there as the rag came over her mouth, rendering her unconscious as she was hustled off the beach. Remembering Ed, the security guard with her on the beach, she felt tears spring to her eyes. Too late Ed had spotted the ominous threat. He had walked closer to the shore to investigate, and paid dearly for his curiosity.

Gray would have hustled her away, his first priority getting her to safety. Peyton struggled with her emotions and against panic as she remembered the blood streaming from Ed's chest, his terrible gasps for air and then the stillness…

No one was going to rescue her. She had to save herself.

Peyton peered over the side of the seat. Had to act now, before they stopped arguing and decided to end her life. She managed to swing her arms over the side of the seat, and in the moonlight, spied two backpacks on the floor, one of them hers, and tools sticking out of a box on the floor.

Screwdrivers, a drill… The bit might suffice.

With extreme care, she brought her duct-taped wrists over the drill bit. Nothing. Tried again. Nothing. She was too weak.

You can do this, she heard Gray in her mind. *Focus.*

With all her might she drove the duct tape down on the drill bit, puncturing the tape. Tried again. Now there were two large holes in the tape. She went to attempt it one more time when the voices grew louder.

Her head fuzzy, she forced herself to lie still, her eyes closed, as the truck door opened and then slammed.

She heard a seat creak, as if the driver turned to investigate her.

Not daring to make a sound, she lay still.

The truck started and moved off. Whoever kidnapped her was driving her someplace to kill her and dump her body. As the truck bounced and rolled, and then sped up, she wasted no time.

Quietly she brought her legs upward and worked on the duct tape securing her wrists. But the position made it difficult and she didn't dare risk making any noise.

The vehicle lurched forward, as the driver ground the gears, as if he wasn't confident in mastering a stick shift. Listening, she heard traffic, car horns, saw streetlights passing by.

The truck picked up speed. They were on a local roadway. If she had any chance of people noticing her, now was the time. Peyton weighed her options. It meant the driver would see she had feigned unconsciousness if she dared to sit up and gesture for help.

Whoever had kidnapped her might do worse than shove a rag into her mouth filled with chloroform.

He might kill her.

As the thought spiraled through her mind, the driver turned, and she heard more traffic and car horns. They were on a major freeway headed north, I-95 perhaps.

Peyton remembered Gray's advice. Always be aware of your surroundings. Stay alert. She must have dozed off for the next thing she knew, they were slowing down. The truck stopped. She held her breath, wondering if she should run for it, but the driver rolled down his window and seemed to punch numbers into a keypad, then sped up. Peyton raised her head a little and saw pine trees passing by. They drove up and down a small hill and a winding curve.

He stopped again, his door opening. The driver cursed and slammed the door. She heard the crunch of footsteps on something…pine cones, maybe. Peyton dared to sit up.

Her kidnapper was at the locked gate that looked to be an entrance to a sandy road. Peyton looked around. Scrub and pine trees… She knew this place. It was a large state park, where she'd enjoyed canoeing with friends.

The driver cursed loudly again as he fumbled with the locked gate. She looked down, brought her wrists once more onto the screwdriver to puncture the duct tape. Footsteps alerted her to her abductor's return.

Peyton forced herself to lie still as he drove forward once more, then he got out and apparently locked the gate.

They drove for a few minutes over a bumpy road that felt like oyster shells. Finally the truck halted and the driver shut off the ignition. The loud tick-tick-ticking of the engine sounded like an ominous metronome.

Fight, she heard Gray's voice in her mind. *Fight with everything you've got if he captures you. Use teeth. Fingers, your nails can scratch, do whatever it takes.*

But Peyton sensed until she left the truck, the element of surprise remained her advantage. Her ankles were still bound and her head was still foggy.

Her door opened and Peyton forced herself to go limp as her captor lifted her into his arms. She smelled humid air, pine trees and sour sweat.

Good. I hope I'm too heavy for you and you get a hernia.

Keeping her eyes shut was hard when she wanted to open them and wriggle free. As he carried her inside a structure, and then closed the door, Peyton used all her willpower not to move. She felt herself sink down into something soft.

A sofa, perhaps.

Or a bed.

"So beautiful," he muttered. "So damn beautiful."

A shudder raced through her as he traced a line over

her cheek. Then her abductor walked off, seeming to pace the wood floor.

Peyton strained to hear as he made a phone call. She knew this voice, and equal parts of dread and alarm raced down her spine.

This was her stalker? Her kidnapper?

Then fury overtook her. How dare he!

"Got it. Don't worry about her. I'll take care of her tonight. Too risky to do it now. Besides, I have to meet someone for a couple of hours real soon or I'll be under suspicion. I want…"

His voice trailed off as he went outside.

I'll take care of her.

No doubt he meant kill her.

Peyton opened her eyes. Fury faded, replaced by fear once more. Tied up, helpless, unable to escape. No lights inside this structure. No, it was a small cabin. A crude table, with two chairs, a kitchenette to one side…a coffee table in front of her. No magazines. Raising her head, she was able to look out the window by the table at the darkness beyond. Too dark. The only place in the area without ambient light from nearby communities or businesses…

The woods. A large state park, perhaps.

What would Gray do?

Only you can rescue yourself, Peyton. You can't rely on anyone else.

Gray would encourage her to rely on her instincts and get free from her captor. Use anything at her disposal to fight back.

You're a fighter. It's in you.

Keeping his voice in her head helped her center her scattered thoughts, push away the terror choking and immobilizing her. Gorge rose in her throat as she remembered the horrible price Ed paid for her abduction.

Footsteps sounded. She shut her eyes again and lay still as he plodded over to her, sitting on the sofa next to her. Fear skidded down her spine like spiders on bare skin, but she pretended to remain unconscious.

She wanted to retch as he traced a line down her left cheek. The movement would be sensual and welcomed in a lover.

Was that what he wanted? Her stalker kidnapped her because he loved her in his sick and twisted mind?

When he tore at her blouse, and his hands went elsewhere, she screamed.

Mistake. Their gazes locked. Anger dawned there.

Peyton opened her mouth to scream again when she caught the glint of light on a metal object in his hand.

Then pain exploded in her head and grayness rushed up, turning everything to black.

She woke later, how much later, she did not know. But glancing around, she saw she was alone. Her head ached and there was something sticky in her hair at the top of her scalp…

Who was she?

Why was she here?

She tried to remember, but her mind felt like someone scrubbed it clean. All she knew was a tremendous sense of heightened danger.

No one around… Where was she? Some kind of cabin, with a dim oil lamp glowing on a table set beneath a window. Pitch-black outside.

As she tried to sit up, she realized something prevented her from moving much. Raising her hands to touch the wetness on her hair, she stopped. Horror filled her as she glanced down at her wrists. Bound with…what? Sticky, strong, some kind of tape.

Duct tape. That much she remembered.

The same tape wrapped around her ankles. The urge to relieve herself was strong. Whoever had done this to her hadn't considered her personal needs.

But as she examined her wrists again, she saw holes poked in the tape. *Did I do that?*

Swinging her legs around, she managed to sit up, feet on the ground. She listened, heard only the sounds of insects through the opened window, the soft call of an owl in the distance. Nothing human.

A sense of dread shadowed everything. She hopped over to the kitchenette, looking for something to tear off the tape from her wrists.

Something flickered in her mind. A tall man, talking in a deep voice. She held her hands above her head and slammed them down. Once. Twice. The tape broke.

Free! Quickly she worked at tearing off the tape from her ankles. Looking around wildly at the cabin, she spied two black backpacks. First, she found a bathroom and attended to her needs. The face in the mirror as she washed her hands was a stranger's face.

Who am I?

Next, she grabbed a bottle of water from one backpack and drank half the contents. Unzipping the pack, she found several items in it, including a wallet. Opening the wallet, she saw a driver's license with her photo on it.

Peyton Bradley.

I'm Peyton Bradley.

There was an address on the driver's license. Somewhat relieved she had a name, an identity and a place to call home where someone surely must be worried about her absence, she looked around for a phone.

No phone in the backpack. Nothing but a paper booklet, a few pens, a camera and bug spray, a jacket and keys.

Had to get out of here, flee. Now. Whoever had done this could return any minute. Finish the job. Hurt her, even kill her.

She hunted through the kitchenette, found another bottle of water in the refrigerator, and then stuffed it into the pack. Slinging the pack over her shoulders, Peyton opened the door and fled into the night, praying she could find help.

Before her kidnapper found her.

Chapter 12

Gray hated being right, especially when it came to risking someone else's life.

Leaning against the wall, he watched through the one-way glass showing the police station's interrogation room. Dennis Devine sat at a rectangular table. Across from him, Detective Dave Sims, the lead detective on Peyton's stalker case, and Jason Beckett. Jace had worked in the Human Trafficking Task Force and was here as a courtesy after Sims called him in.

Devine had turned himself in to police after the BOLO was issued after Peyton vanished. Gray studied Devine in the hot seat as the two lawmen grilled him. He was the prime suspect in Peyton's abduction.

Gray had heard a truck drive off and backfire during Peyton's abduction. He'd wasted precious moments when the truck he'd followed got away while he'd been stopped by the local police, who grilled him about the screams heard on the beach.

All he could do was follow the location of the GPS tracker on Peyton's keys. It had pinged a location going north on the interstate and then stopped. Police were headed in that direction.

Sims had gone through video footage of a ten-mile radius of traffic cams near the Bradleys' private beach. Footage showed a late-model red pickup speed through the intersection closest to the beach.

Gray doubted Devine abducted Peyton. He knew the drill with eliminating suspects. First you started with family and friends who could have taken Peyton. However, in this case, since she had a stalker, that possibility was slim.

"I didn't do anything." Dennis squirmed in the chair. "I wasn't threatening Peyton. I was trying to meet with her to apologize."

"Apologize for what?" Detective Sims demanded.

"Apologize for being a jerk to her, and losing my temper. Spending all that time in prison made me realize I needed to get my life together. I went to a program that teaches you to amend for past mistakes."

Dennis looked at the window. "One of the actions you need to take is to apologize to anyone you hurt in the past. But Peyton is so hard to see, and her family is so guarded… I didn't want this to be a big deal! Just a few moments alone with her."

"Alone with her so you could hurt her again?" the detective grilled.

Insight struck Gray. He opened the door to the room. "It's not him. He wasn't present at the fundraising gala when the congressman was deliberately poisoned."

Jace nodded. "Gray is right. He's also not lying. He has none of the tells of a liar. Guy is innocent. Cut him loose, Sims. You're focusing on the wrong man."

When Devine was released to the custody of his parents, Jace asked Brandy to stay behind. He motioned to Gray and Detective Sims and led her into a quiet room.

Gray leaned on the desk, his gaze boring into Brandy's. "Brandy, you're her good friend. Can you think of anyone who would want to hurt Peyton? Who was obsessed with her? Any former boyfriends or even someone in her past who admired her and she rejected?"

Tears shimmered in the woman's eyes. "No. I really can't. Please, shouldn't you be out searching for her?"

Sims hesitated. "We have police out looking for her, and we're waiting on a phone call about the ransom."

Jace and Gray exchanged glances. "You're not going to get a call. This isn't a kidnapping for money, Detective. Or sex trafficking. There's another motive here," Jace told him.

"Until we figure out that motive, we're stuck," Sims mused.

"The motive is more than stalking and an admirer." Gray felt certain of this.

"Please, do something," Brandy begged.

Gray had enough. "I'm going after her. I need to see if it went on the interstate and in what direction."

"What good would that do?" Brandy cried out. "She could be anywhere."

Gray steeled his spine and looked Peyton's friend straight in the eye. "I will find her."

Nothing more, only that quiet assurance. He would find her, and find her before the worst happened. He glanced at his gold watch. "She's been missing for six hours. Her cell phone was on the beach. But her backpack was gone and I had the GPS tracker I slipped into her pack ping up to ten miles before I lost the signal. I need to see that traffic cam footage now."

Less than an hour later, he was in his car headed north on I-95. Gray hoped and prayed the GPS signal would pick up again. Fortunately the battery in the tracker had a long life. However, it wasn't waterproof. If Peyton's backpack was submerged…

Couldn't think like that. He had to focus on the best possible outcome. Peyton wasn't Andrea, his ex-fiancée. He would not be too late to save her.

Detective Sims and four patrol units followed him on the interstate. Suddenly the tracker began to ping a signal.

Gray followed.

He drove off an exit ramp along local roadways until reaching US Highway 1, then turned north.

The entrance to the state park was closed, but he called the emergency number on the gate. When a ranger pulled up to the gate, Gray explained what he needed. The ranger had not seen a late-model red truck that day. There were security cameras at the station, though.

It would take too long to go through the footage.

"I need a map of the park, including any camping spots, including primitive camping, and cabins."

The ranger handed him a map. "These are all the places for rent."

He shook his head. "What about ranger cabins?"

The man frowned. "Those aren't for rent."

Even better. "Any not occupied recently? I'm talking about an area where few people would hike."

Instinct told him her abductor wanted privacy. He didn't want to entertain the reason why Peyton's kidnapper desired privacy.

"There's a primitive cabin deep in the northern section, but it's only used by rangers and environmentalists studying the wildlife in the area. It's dark and has no exterior lighting."

A perfect place to bring a kidnap victim. "Give me the latitude and longitude."

He jotted it down on the map, and the combination the ranger gave him to unlock the gate prohibiting entry onto the cabin road. Gray drove off, letting the uniforms and Sims deal with the park ranger and the security tapes as he followed the tracking signal.

Halfway through the massive acreage, the signal faltered. Cursing, he pulled over, thought fast. It might be interference from the satellite signal.

His thoughts immediately went dark. What if Peyton was dead? Her backpack tossed aside and her abductor had already left with her?

Stop it. She's alive. She has to be. You promised to be her shadow.

Putting his car into gear again, he drove forward,

The signal pinged again, this time much weaker.

Gray pulled off the road, used his phone and a map app to plug in the latitude and longitude of the research cabin. Sure enough, the signal came from the direction of the cabin. He turned off onto a dirt road, came to a gate barring entrance.

Examining the locked gate, he snapped on latex gloves and used the combination the ranger had given him. Gray called Sims and explained his location.

The police would dust for prints on the gate, but he doubted they would find any.

About a mile north of the main road, his headlights picked out the one-story cabin. Hewn from rough wood, with a small space allotted for parking, it was far from any public hiking trails or utility access. Gun and flashlight drawn, he went inside.

The cabin was deserted, but he spotted lengths of silver duct tape on the rough wooden floor. Outside, he found a personalized water bottle with a sea turtle logo on it.

Peyton's. The emblem was from the Marine Institute.

She'd left him a clue, but if her kidnapper found her before Gray did…

Time to hunt.

He'd dressed appropriately, in lightweight dark trousers, a long-sleeved navy shirt and boots. Eyeing the thick palmetto scrub, Gray knew Peyton had to be here, somewhere. The scrub was too thick for the average person to navigate.

But a desperate woman, fleeing her captor?

Gray headed into the brush, following a narrow trail through the thick scrub. Less than a mile from the cabin, the circle of flashlight spotted her by a tree.

She screamed, crab-crawling away from him, her blue eyes wide, caked blood on her forehead and temple. Ugly red scratches covered her bare arms.

"Peyton, it's me. Gray."

Shaking, she kept backing away, headed for a large, dangerous fire ant nest. Had to calm her down or she'd bolt, injure herself further. He didn't know why she didn't recognize him, but that didn't matter now. Gray gambled. After setting down the flashlight on the ground, he held out his hands, palms to the sky, in the same gesture of trust he'd shown her days ago.

"Peyton, I'm not going to hurt you. I'm here to help you. Trust me. I'm your shadow."

She stopped, staring at him with a woebegone look. He picked up the flashlight and was at her side in four steps, lifting her into his arms as the ants began crawling toward her. Those nasty stings could trigger an allergic reaction.

"Are you allergic to fire ants?" he asked.

"I, I, don't know. I don't know anything!"

In a few steps, he lifted her into his arms and carried her to safety.

Gray held her tight against him as she wrapped her arms around his neck. Heart pounding, he jogged down the narrow pathway to the cabin, where two patrol units had parked next to his Mercedes. Sims turned, saw him, his relief palpable.

"I doubt he's coming back. Not now." Sims's expression tightened. "But we'll find this son of a bitch."

"She doesn't know who she is. She doesn't remember anything," he said grimly.

Including the very man who kidnapped her, and was still out there, wanting to harm her.

Or worse.

Chapter 13

The backpack police found inside the cabin told a grim story. Inside the bag they found more duct tape, rope, a knife and a tube of lubricant.

"Looks like the bastard planned this well," Jace said, his voice filled with anger. "If you hadn't planted that GPS tracker in her bag, he would have gotten away with it."

He gave Gray an approving nod. "I wish more guys were as proactive as you are, Gray."

They stood outside Peyton's hospital room with the sheriff, Detective Sims and four other deputies. She'd been admitted into a private room. Peyton's worried family milled in the hallway as the medical staff attended to her. Brandy Devine, Peyton's friend, had joined the family.

Gray's sole concern was Peyton. No one had allowed him to see her after she'd been transported to the hospital.

Jace nodded at Sims, and then shook Gray's hand. "I have to see Jarrett about something. But if you need me, call."

Watching the other man walk off, Gray felt a sense of

isolation. Jace understood Gray's obsession with ensuring nothing happened to Peyton. Jace had been in the trenches, knew combat, knew how life could deal you one blow after another and you did all you could to keep those under your care safe in an unsafe world.

The doctor emerged from the room. Her parents, brother—Marc—and Brandy rushed over to him. Dr. Bradley clutched a stuffed sea turtle, a toy he recognized from Peyton's room.

Good job, Doc. Perhaps the toy might jog her daughter's memory.

"How is she?" Bradley asked, his voice husky. "How's my little girl? Is she any better?"

The doctor did not offer a reassuring smile. "Peyton still has no memory. She's suffering from retrograde amnesia as a result of the blow to her head and the emotional trauma. How soon she will regain her memory remains unknown."

Bradley scoffed as her mother paled. "She'll eventually know us. We're her parents," he declared.

"Charles, we were with her for an hour and she has no recollection," his wife pointed out.

"Then I'll try again." Bradley headed for the room.

"I wouldn't advise..." The doctor's voice trailed off as her parents sailed into Peyton's room, followed by Detective Sims.

Brandy tugged at his arm. He glanced at her.

"Please, help her. I know Peyton's father can be overprotective, but I saw how you were with Peyton. Please help my friend."

Gray nodded. "I'll do what I can."

"I have to go home now...to my own parents. We're all trying to work together to support Dennis. He is trying to get his life back together."

"I know," he said gently.

He knew what it was like as well, once you made a mistake and tried to move forward.

Gray lingered in the doorway of the hospital room as Brandy left. Had to see for himself how Peyton fared. His heart lurched. She looked so tiny in the bed, her blond hair tangled and dirty, her expression confused.

He'd ridden with her in the ambulance as EMTs worked on her, assuring her she was safe and he wouldn't let any harm come to her. But now everything was out of his hands.

Bradley approached the bed with the worried confidence of a father. He leaned over, smiling. "Hi, honey. It's us. Mom and Dad again. You're going to be fine, honey. You remember us. Of course you do, Peyton."

"Charles, you shouldn't pressure her," Dr. Bradley began.

"No. I don't remember you!" Her eyes wild, she shrank back in her bed.

He felt sorry for Charles Bradley, who looked devastated.

"Honey, we only want what's best for you." Dr. Bradley reached for her hand.

Peyton pulled away. Then she did the most extraordinary thing. She spotted him and reached out as a drowning person would grasp for a life ring.

"Gray! Please help me!"

He sprang to her bedside and sat in a chair as she grabbed his hand. "I don't know any of these people, Gray, but I trust you. I don't know why, but I do."

Her mother began to cry as her father made a strangled sound. *Guess they don't like the idea of me being the only one you trust, sweetheart.*

"Peyton, before this happened, I promised to be honest with you." His gaze flicked to her worried parents. "I promised to be your shadow and protect you. Will you keep trusting me?"

She pressed two fingers to her temples. "At this point,

you seem to be the only one I can trust...a little. What do you want from me? Are you going to keep insisting I know you?"

Professional training kicked in. "No. But I will try to jog a few memories. If you feel tired or upset, we'll stop. Deal?"

She nodded. Gray squeezed her hand. He beckoned to her mother and pointed to the toy and then the hospital bed.

Dr. Bradley placed it on Peyton's bed.

"I told you in the ambulance, Peyton. You're safe now. You're here and you're safe. Can you recall anything? A name? A voice?" he asked in a deep, soothing voice.

Licking her lips, she shook her head. Then she looked at the stuffed sea turtle.

Gray picked it up. "This is yours, Peyton. You love sea turtles. You're dedicated to saving them."

Turning the toy over in her hands, her gaze lit up.

"Sea turtles... Fletcher Richardson," she whispered.

Her entire family looked bewildered. "Fletcher did this?" her father asked, frowning. "The man has to be seventy years old!"

Relief filled him. He smiled at her. "You did great. You love turtles. Green sea turtle. Status?"

Her brows knitted. "Endangered. *Chelonia mydas.*"

Encouraged, he made a dismissive gesture at her family as they began chattering. Gray focused solely on her as he recited the rest of the sea turtles, and she responded with the correct scientific name and the turtle's status.

Peyton rubbed her forehead. "Fletcher Richardson, why do I remember his name?"

"You were his friend," Gray pointed out.

Sims scribbled something in his notebook. "We'll find him, bring him in for questioning."

Suddenly her gaze sharpened. She clutched the bedcovers, her fingers tightening on the sheets. "He won't talk to you."

"Why?" Sims grilled. "What does he know? Who is he to you?"

The detective's raised voice and crowding Peyton only further agitated her. "I don't know! I don't know. Leave me alone!"

The doctor stepped forward. "That's enough for now. Let her rest."

Pushing back the chair, he started to stand when she cried out, "Don't leave me."

"I'll be right outside, Peyton," he promised.

She glared at her parents. "I don't know who you are. I want him to stay. Only him."

In the hallway, her family had the same shell-shocked expressions they wore upon finding out Peyton had amnesia.

He was in Peyton's corner. Perhaps the only one who remained there without pressing her to remember her identity.

"She trusts you, Mr. Wallace. Only you." The doctor swept her family with a sympathetic look. "Time will tell if Peyton regains her memory."

As the doctor walked away, Gray felt a pang of regret. He'd saved her, but without a suspect, the police had nothing to find her kidnapper.

"She doesn't have time," he stated bluntly. "Whoever did this is still out there and she's in danger every moment she doesn't recall who he is."

"And I know how to care for my daughter, so back off. Thank you for rescuing her. Your job is done now," Bradley said with a dismissive gesture.

No, it's not.

"My job is not finished. Peyton trusts me." Gray folded his arms across his chest.

"I don't understand why she'd remember you. Or trust you," Bradley said, clearly agitated. "Your past tells me you can't be trusted. I don't need to spell it out for you."

"Charles, please," Dr. Bradley said softly. "Let it go and stop insulting the man. He's the only one who managed to break through with Peyton."

For what it was worth, Gray's feelings didn't matter. Peyton's did. He'd promised to be her shadow, her protector. Not going to back down now. Peyton was scared, feeling alone in a world suddenly foreign to her.

She needed an anchor and he was it. He nodded at the sheriff.

"You need to put a deputy here around the clock to guard her. We don't know if her kidnapper will return to complete his work."

"Already on it." The sheriff glanced at Peyton's parents. "If she recalls anything else, let me or Detective Sims know."

Gray formulated a plan. "I'll stay with her at the hospital. She trusts me. With an armed deputy in her room, will that satisfy you, Bradley? That way if I try anything, the deputy can shoot me."

"Stop the sarcasm," Bradley grated out.

"I'm not sarcastic. I'm serious. I promised Peyton I'd be there for her until this bastard is caught."

The man seemed to consider. "Very well. Until she's released from the hospital."

No obstacle there. He'd find a way to remain close to Peyton at the house. For all the money Bradley spent on a security system, it was not impenetrable.

Sims walked off to take a phone call. Gray liked the detective, but he was green when it came to stalking cases. Quiet, friendly Sea Grape Beach wasn't a haven for criminals on the level of Peyton's stalker.

Dr. Bradley's phone rang. Blood drained from her face as she listened, and then she hung up.

"That was our maid. Deputies are at our house. Someone broke in, ransacked Peyton's room, Charles." Dr. Bradley's voice broke. "All the pillows were slashed and her belongings scattered."

Bradley cursed. "Marc, go to the house. Find out what the hell is going on."

As Peyton's brother left, her parents peered into Peyton's room.

"This is horrible. Whoever did this wants our daughter, he came back and bypassed the security system. We can't bring Peyton home, Charles." Dr. Bradley paced, clearly agitated.

"No, we can't."

"I highly advise all of you to stay with friends or a hotel until you hire extra, and competent, security. Whoever did this could return, and put all of you in danger." The sheriff gave Peyton's father a stern look. "I'm on this, Charles. But you have to listen to me. I'll escort both of you back to the house to pack a few things. You can't stay there."

Her father paced, then seemed to come to a decision. "I'll do whatever I must for her. But can I trust you?"

Dr. Bradley confronted her husband. "Charles, he rescued her. Whoever is after her is determined to find her again and hurt her. If there's the slightest chance he can help her remember her stalker and get him arrested, I'll take it. I've let you handle this your way. From now on, we'll handle it mine. I'm the medical professional in this family and Gray made more progress with her in ten minutes than you made in two hours."

Bradley's shoulders sagged. Suddenly he seemed older than his fifty-five years. "I don't have a choice."

"Not if you want to gamble again with Peyton's life," Gray stated.

Harsh, but necessary words. Sometimes hardheaded über-businessmen like Bradley needed to know all the stakes up-front.

Bradley exhaled. "Fine. But there's something I don't understand. Why would she mention Fletcher Richardson? What does he have to do with this?"

"He may have nothing to do with Peyton's abduction. Or everything. What's important is that she recalled his name, which is significant. It's a clue."

Sims palmed his cell phone. "Leave this to me. We'll find Richardson, extradite him over county lines and bring him in for questioning."

Gray didn't agree with the detective's methods. "Have you managed to find him yet? You said you checked out all the men in Peyton's past. He was friends with her."

The detective frowned. "Richardson moved to Venice, Florida, after leaving the island, but vanished off the radar after that. We've checked credit card receipts, phone records. Nothing. We'll find him."

"He's in Clearwater," Gray said bluntly. "My sources already checked. Richardson is ex-military, like me."

Sims seemed less confident. "Then we'll head there."

"If Richardson realizes he's wanted for questioning, he'll run again. Right now he's the only lead you have," Gray pointed out.

Sims mulled it over, nodded. "All right. What's your plan?"

"When Peyton gets released from here, I'll take her with me on the road to find Richardson, if she agrees. SOS has a safe house near Clearwater. And perhaps visiting the aquarium will jog her memory."

Both her parents looked alarmed. "Is that a good idea?"

Dr. Bradley asked. "Why not take her back to the institute where she works first?"

He gave her a level look. "Because whoever did this is local and may even be at the institute as we speak. Was it a good idea to fire me based on conjecture without finding out exactly what did happen in my past? Did anything happen to Peyton under my watch?"

As they shook their heads, he continued, clamping down on his anger. "And now a man is dead, a man who wasn't fully briefed or prepared to deal with this level of stalking."

Her parents fell silent.

"We either do this my way, or I walk."

Bradley's jaw dropped. "You said you promised to protect her."

"I promised to keep her safe, but I can't do that, nor can I risk any more lives, if you interfere with my plan. One man is already dead."

He turned to Sims. "Soon as I find Richardson, I will notify you and your department, and then the local authorities."

Sims's gaze darkened. "I can't say I like this idea of yours, Gray, but if her parents agree, and Peyton does, there's not much I can do."

"You can find out who broke into the Bradley mansion. Richardson is tougher. He's an old spec ops soldier. Trust me, when they vanish into thin air, they can."

He knew because he had done it himself.

And he planned to do it once more, only this time with Peyton at his side.

Two days later, Peyton stood outside his car as he loaded her suitcase into the trunk. Next he opened the passenger door for her. She did not climb in, but stared at the seat.

Such a loss of control she must feel. If he didn't reassure her now, he'd lose her.

Gray stepped back. "I get it. You're scared. You want to know why this is happening to you. I don't know. I do know this. Your 'why' has to focus on why you recalled Fletcher's name and whatever memories you can recover on this trip. It's going to take a giant leap of faith to get into this car with me after the shock you've had, Peyton. If you can't make that giant leap, then take a small one.

"At any time you want me to stop, turn around and take you back to where your family is staying, say the word and I will. You're in charge. Not me."

Big blue eyes beseeched him. "Promise?"

Gray thought of a promise he'd made and hadn't been able to keep, despite all his fierce efforts. "I promise. I'm your shadow and as your shadow, you're calling the shots."

Sweat trickled down the small of his back to the waistband of his trousers. Peyton climbed into the car, fastened her seat belt.

He let her close her own door. After punching in the security code and starting the car, Gray regarded his passenger.

"Where to?"

Peyton drew in a breath. "I'm a little hungry."

"There's a decent Thai place not far from here."

"Do I like Thai food?"

"With spicy peanut sauce, yeah."

She gave him her first real smile since he'd found her. "I'll take your word for it."

She felt lost in a fog of uncertainty, but this Gray Wallace seemed a lighthouse in a thick mist. Literally she put her life into his hands. He'd promised honesty with her and said she could trust him.

Did she have any other choice? Lying in a hospital bed hadn't made her memory return and now she couldn't even return home because whoever abducted her had threatened that safe stronghold. Her parents had brought people from the Marine Institute to visit her in the hospital and those visitors hadn't triggered any memories, either. Not Martin, the acting director; Adam, who said he was a close friend; and a couple of interns. She didn't remember anyone. Didn't trust anyone, except Gray.

At least the restaurant he'd chosen was perfect. Eating Thai food hadn't freed any recollections, but the meal was tasty. Best, the service was discreet and efficient. Fortified, they'd returned to the road.

He'd made one stop, to purchase a prepaid cell phone for her. Gray called it a burner phone. No one could trace it if it wasn't switched on. He seemed to know a lot about things like this.

Peyton closed her eyes as he drove, unsure of why Gray seemed familiar. Try as she might, she couldn't recall details about him. But something deep inside urged her to listen to this man.

That gesture he'd made of opening his palms had triggered a faint memory. She knew this as surely as she'd remembered the scientific names of sea turtles.

Letting herself drift off to sleep, she tried to remember. Anything. Everything. Recalled…nothing.

All that played through her mind was a series of images of sea turtles and an older man's face. The name. Fletcher Richardson.

Her eyes flew open. "Who is this Fletcher Richardson and why are we going to Clearwater Beach to find him?" she asked.

"Richardson is your friend and the fact you remembered his name and no one else's is significant. He may have something to do with your abduction. He was spotted on a boat near the Clearwater Marine Aquarium." Gray's gaze flicked to her. "You've been there before. Perhaps visiting will trigger another memory."

She rubbed her temple, a headache blossoming there. "Are you telling my parents where you're taking me?"

"Not the exact address. They need to trust that you're safe with me."

Her mind still felt fogged. Was she safe with Gray Wallace? She remembered him as being protective and something about him sparked deeper emotions, an attraction she couldn't quite trust.

But though her mother seemed fine with Gray, her father didn't like him and regarded Gray with near hostility, so what did that mean?

As if reading her mind, he nodded. "I told you, you're in charge, Peyton. Any time you wish to return to your parents, tell me and I'll turn around. I can find Richardson on my own."

"He won't talk to you. Or the police." She wasn't certain how she knew this, but she did.

"Maybe. Don't worry about that. Do you wish to continue?"

Giving her a choice had eased a little of her fears. "Let's keep going. Tell me something… Why is it dangerous to tell my parents our location?"

"Because not only is this a safe house owned by SOS, your parents might accidentally tell someone else and word can travel to your kidnapper. SOS is the security company employing me, the company your father originally hired to provide you with executive-level protection."

Gray's expression tightened. "Whoever did this, Peyton, he knows you. This was not a stranger abduction, but done by someone you've interacted with in your past. Or your present. Until you recall who it is, you're in constant danger. So try to relax, and get some rest."

Rest. All she'd done for the past few days was rest. Peyton sighed and settled back into the seat, hoping she'd made the right decision to go with Gray.

The drive was smooth and Peyton finally slept. When she awoke, looking groggy and a little panicked, the car was on a residential road. Gray pulled into the driveway of a small, one-story turquoise-and-white house, knowing she must feel disoriented.

He shut off the engine. "This is SOS's safe house, part of their underground railroad for women fleeing abusive spouses or partners."

He unlocked the door using the keyless entry code and wheeled their suitcases inside. Peyton followed him. She looked too pale, acted too quiet. He appreciated the trust she placed in him, but this silence unnerved him, as if she had given up hope of regaining her memory.

And her life.

The door opened to a small living room, with a colorful turquoise and dark brown floor. A sofa and easy chair were arranged around a teak coffee table. Nearby, a china cabinet contained board and card games. The wall television had been removed after they'd discovered one of their SOS clients spent all her time searching for news stories about her disappearance.

This was supposed to be a safe house, not a place to frazzle the nerves.

The living room opened to a kitchen with granite counters, stainless steel appliances and a window overlooking the backyard. A dining area off the kitchen had plenty of windows for natural lighting, and the back door opened to a small screened porch.

He took Peyton's hand and inspected the rest of the house. Laundry room and master bedroom and bathroom, with another side entrance off the laundry room. Frowning, he tested the lock. Jarrett had mentioned a key was outside in case of emergencies. He opened the door, found the key and pocketed it.

Peyton remained standing in the laundry room, not the least interested in her surroundings.

She needed food, water and, most of all, she needed to relax. But he wasn't going to see to her needs until he first became assured of her safety. His standards were higher when it came to guarding Peyton.

Because he'd already screwed up once, he didn't intend to do it again.

Taking her hand again, he explored the rest of the house, the two bedrooms off the living room and the bathroom. Attic access. He considered, told Peyton to stay put and found a ladder in the closet. He opened the access, peered inside the small crawl space. Empty. He noticed a latch on the outside door and secured it before storing the ladder.

Finally they went into the backyard. The white plastic fence was high enough to avoid prying eyes. A shed off the deck was locked. Jarrett had told him gardening tools and the lawnmower were stored inside.

Gardening shears made formidable weapons in the wrong hands.

But the lock was sturdy and the shed solid, without a window, so for now he was satisfied. He glanced around the deck at the metal patio furniture and the turquoise cushions. A bistro table with two chairs beneath the shade of a bottlebrush tree made a picturesque spot for morning tea or coffee.

Peyton said nothing, showed no signs of interest or disinterest as he led her back inside. He saw a lock on the inside of the screen door. Good. Wouldn't stop someone from breaking inside, but would slow them down.

Sometimes those few extra minutes were a precious resource when you needed to escape a threat.

Peyton went to the table and sat, staring at the corner display of seashells and air plants. A turquoise-and-white sailboat carving sat on one white shelf. The accessories were placed to be homey and pretty, but he weighed everything as a potential threat. The seashell with the pointed ends could poke out an eye.

He joined her at the table. Lacey had decorated in a beach and nautical theme, so the light over the table was a glass globe with rope netting. Even the doors were painted powder blue with white accents.

Jarrett had spent a lot of money on this house. Sometimes the agency rented it out as a vacation home to alleviate suspicion, while putting money back into the nonprofit's coffers.

Jarrett had assured him everything had been checked out and cleaned prior to their arrival. Still… He couldn't take any chances.

The beach was a five-minute walk across the street.

In the backyard, sea grape trees and ferns lined the white fence, affording pretty landscaping and privacy.

Peyton glanced at him. "Why can't I remember anything except sea turtles? Will I ever get my memory back?"

I hope so because, sweetheart, if you don't, every minute your mind is a blank slate of the past means you're in danger.

He'd brought her here in hopes of jogging her memory, but this house wouldn't do anything. The beach, and the aquarium, might do it.

Peyton's parents said she'd interned at the aquarium and spent time on the beach. Her grandmother had owned a beach house in Treasure Island and Peyton had spent summers there, fascinated by the turtles crawling onto the sand to lay their eggs. She'd shunned the family's cooler summer home in Nantucket in favor of staying with her grandmother.

Peyton hugged herself, much too pale for his liking. "Nice house. The colors are soothing."

Gray's mouth curved upward. "Jarrett's wife, Lacey, designed the house to make the women staying here with their children feel reassured and relaxed. It used to belong to Lacey's family."

"And people stay here for free?"

"It's a house SOS provides to women and children to give them a safe place to stay until we establish their new identities and send them to new lives away from their abusive partners. All the ones who stayed here have beachcombed and put a seashell into the jar. That's the only payment SOS requires."

She pulled a shell out of the jar, fingering it. "I like the idea. Maybe we should visit the beach and add to the collection."

"Later." He glanced at his watch. "It was a long drive and I have a few things to do before dinner. Why don't you settle in and relax."

"I'm tired of relaxing." Her chin lifted in that stubborn gesture he'd come to recognize. "I want to find this Fletcher person who's supposed to be important to me."

Impatience. He understood. "We can't rush into this, Peyton. Not without jeopardizing your security. I have to make some calls."

"Fine. Make your calls." She flounced down on the sofa, scrolling through the burner phone. "This place have Wi-Fi?"

"Yes, but don't use the internet on that phone. You can be traced." He found the card with the code and a tablet he'd brought and handed both to her. Gray palmed his own cell phone.

Time to test the waters of recognition. Now that she was distracted, it might work. "I have a few questions for you, Peyton."

She didn't look up from the tablet. "What?"

"Who are you?"

"Dumb question. I don't know!"

"Who are your parents?"

"Charles and Amelia Bradley, I guess. So they say."

"Your siblings?"

"Marc and Tricia. Marc told me Tricia lives in California."

"Who is Fletcher Richardson?"

"A friend. He told me how to watch for high tides early in the nesting season because leatherbacks usually nest above the high-tide levels. He found that out in his travels."

Her fingers loosened their death grip on the phone as she looked up, eyes wide with surprise. "I know him. I know…but…"

Mouth wobbling, she looked confused and upset once more. "Why can't I remember more?"

"You're trying too hard. It's why you need to relax."

Scowling, she rubbed her temples. "Is the interrogation over with now?"

"For now. I asked you those questions as a way of triggering automatic, honest responses."

"You think I was lying about not remembering him before?"

He met her gaze, square-on. "No. But I do believe you had trauma that blocked your memory, and it wasn't only the injury you sustained. This is one reason why I wanted to take you on this trip, Peyton. Not only to protect you from whoever wishes you dead, or to find this mysterious Fletcher, but to trigger memories."

Gray looked around the room. "This is a good place to recall memories. It's private. Quiet. Tomorrow we'll visit the aquarium."

He removed his cell phone, glanced at it. "Why don't you get some rest before dinner? I'll be out back. Stay here. Don't go outside."

"Yes, sir."

Her sullen tone reminded him of when they'd first met. Sighing, he headed into the backyard to check messages. The house was perfect for his purposes.

The neighborhood was quiet, filled mainly with retirees or snowbirds. Best of all everyone minded their own business. No one asked questions. No one held loud parties or caused much trouble.

The house was perfect for them to stay hidden while he figured out a strategy. Gray didn't want to take chances.

He'd already taken enough chances with Peyton.

Gray dialed Jarrett's number. His friend answered on the first ring. "Gray. You get there safely? Everything okay?"

"We're here. I did a quick Q and A and she remembers Fletcher. He's key to all this, Jarrett. Find anything on him yet?"

"Not much, other than the sighting at the marine aquarium. He's been lying low since leaving the Bradleys' employ. Jace is still checking. He found evidence of Richardson's vice. Gambling."

Gray considered. "If he gambled, he may have borrowed money from someone who wanted it back and left to save his skin."

"Detective Sims is running background checks on everyone associated with Peyton going back as far as elementary school. Nothing of use yet."

"If things change, let me know." He hung up, pondering.

Richardson was key to all of this, he felt certain. But why he was involved in Peyton's kidnapping, he didn't know.

All he did know was they needed to find Richardson soon, before Peyton's kidnapper found her.

Chapter 14

She needed fresh air. Sunshine. Peyton went outside as Gray roved the backyard, talking on the phone. Seeing her at the door, he hung up and regarded her with a wary look.

Breathing deep, she lifted her face to the warm Florida sun. The air was sullen and still, thick with summer humidity, the distant scent of brine threaded through smells of gardenias and someone's backyard grilling.

Compared with the antiseptic, bleached odors of the hospital, it was heaven.

"I'm tired of being inside. I want to visit the beach."

Consulting his watch, he gave an approving nod. "I have an errand to run, but when I return, we'll have enough time to walk to the beach before dinner."

She rolled her eyes. "Does everything revolve around dinner at this place?"

A guarded look came over him. "It does when I'm taking you out to eat and trying to avoid the crowds. There's a hole-in-the-wall seafood place a short walk from here. I know you like scallops and shrimp."

Good thing he knew, because she wasn't sure she did. Peyton shrugged to hide her discomfort. She hated this loss of control over her life, whatever life she'd had. "Fine."

They returned inside, Gray giving her abandoned suitcase a long look. "You should unpack while I'm gone. Settle in."

I'll never feel settled in. Not here or anywhere until I remember who I am!

Knowing this was a safe house reassured her a little more.

You're taking a big chance with this man. What if he had something to do with your kidnapping?

Gray took the handle of her suitcase. "Which bedroom do you want?"

"We're not sleeping together?"

Instantly she felt her face turn red. Gray's mouth twitched. "You'll have your own bedroom, Peyton. But I'll be close by."

Why had she said that? Something about this man did attract her. Her hormones were working overtime around him. For heaven's sake, she'd been traumatized but she wasn't dead. The thought almost made her laugh.

She went to take the suitcase from him. "I can do it."

Their fingers brushed. Standing so close she could smell the faint, spicy scent of his aftershave, she became fully aware of him as a man, not a stranger. He'd worn dark clothing in the hospital, but was now dressed in khaki board shorts and a plain navy T-shirt that fitted his trim upper body.

The man looked athletic, with the wiry muscles of a long-distance runner. A shiver ran through her as she recalled how terrified she'd been in the woods, and then he appeared, lifting her into his arms and carrying her to a waiting ambulance.

But what if he pretended to rescue her, only to get her alone now, away from her family and law enforcement? Her hand gripped the suitcase handle. She looked at the door, a ready escape. They were miles from anything or anyone she knew, not that she remembered any of it.

Was she safe with him?

He seemed to read her emotions. "Do you want to stay here, Peyton?"

Peyton breathed deep, inhaling his scent. She glanced up at his face.

Solemn, oh-so-serious. Not smiling. Did he ever really smile? Laugh? She reached up, touched the scar on his left cheek.

"Where did you get this?" she asked.

For a moment, he hesitated. Then he drew in a breath. "Iraq. In combat."

"You're military?"

"Ex-military. Navy SEAL. It's how I became acquainted with Jarrett Adler. We served together." Gray's voice sharpened. "Some people find it ugly. Others think it's a damn mark of honor, like a medal."

Peyton traced the scar, not finding it ugly or repulsive, nor a mark of honor as some would. It seemed a part of him as much as his raven hair, the deep brown eyes and his thin mouth that didn't seem acquainted with laughter.

Essentially Gray Wallace.

Could she trust him? He'd told her any time they could return to her parents.

I need to find out who I am, and who wanted me dead.

Gray's eyes closed under her gentle strokes. Suddenly they flew open, his dark gaze sharpening. He pushed her hand away.

"What do you want, Peyton? Stay or go?"

Sensing his barricades go up, she stepped back, equally formal. "I have to go through with this. Find out who I am. If this is the way to do it, I'm staying."

She wheeled the suitcase into the smaller corner bedroom. Peyton sat on the bed as Gray watched. Awareness of him, his lean frame, his serious, oh-so-serious look, flared. He was sexy and here, alone with him in this house, made her imagination dance with possibilities.

He glanced down again at his watch.

"I have to run out for a little while. But while I'm gone, take this. I purchased it while you were still in the hospital."

All her sexual interest vanished like a small fire under a bucket of cold water. Peyton grimaced at the black pistol he'd placed into her hand.

"It's small enough for your grip, but will suffice if someone threatens you."

Her heart raced as she handled the weapon. A dim memory tugged at the edges of her mind. She'd handled guns before, but this was different.

This was home defense, not sporting events.

"I don't know if I'm ready to shoot someone." She set the gun down on the bed.

Gray's dark brows scrunched. "If it comes down to shooting someone to save your life, you'll be ready."

"I can't do it. Kill someone?"

Gray sat on the bed, picked up the pistol. "Sweetheart, you never know what you're ready for until you face the situation. Knowing you're armed and this is with you while I'm gone gives me a little peace of mind."

Warming at his use of the endearment, Peyton looked doubtfully at the gun. He handed it back to her.

"You point the barrel at whomever you want to shoot."

Glancing up, she saw his faint, teasing smile. Peyton sighed. "All right. Give me the basics."

After a few minutes, he seemed satisfied. She slid the gun into the nightstand drawer.

"I'll lock the door when I leave. Stay here. The yard is gated and the privacy fence is high enough but don't let your guard down. Meaning, don't fall asleep out there."

As he started to walk away, she called out, "Gray. What if I accidentally shoot you?"

Something flickered across his face before he answered. "You won't have reason to, Peyton."

She watched him leave, her head pounding, uncertain if she had made the right decision in coming here with Gray.

She thought she could trust him in this sea of uncertainty.

Damn, she hoped she was correct.

Gray wasn't gone long. He returned and didn't say where he'd been.

Eager to get to the beach, she didn't ask. But his mysterious phone calls and leaving her alone made her wonder what he was hiding from her.

The house was two blocks from the main road, with a pedestrian accessway to cross the street and stop traffic. The smell of salt carried on the breeze, and her shoulders eased from the tension felt the entire drive over. Peyton brightened as they accessed the walkway and then stepped onto the soft white sand.

"Sugar sand. Gulf of Mexico and the west coast beaches are different from the Atlantic and the east coast," she said almost absently.

Gray nodded. "As are the nesting turtles."

"Loggerheads nest on the east coast beaches." Her head

throbbed a little. She squinted in the bright sunlight as she removed her sunglasses to peer up at him.

He was tall, wiry and so serious. Even dressed in khaki board shorts and a forest green polo shirt, he had the formal, stiff posture of a military man. She frowned. Where had she seen that before? Did she know anyone in the military?

"Let's walk."

They headed north on the shoreline. Beachgoers were packing up colorful umbrellas and shaking free towels of the finely grained sand. A few people remained, splashing in the warm surf.

Gray pointed to a small area of sand with pink plastic tape roped around wooden stakes. She squinted at the sign. Sea turtle nest.

"There's quite a few on this beach. I can make out four of them," he pointed out. "I wonder why they're so close to the seawall and the homes. You'd think the turtles would lay eggs closer to the water."

"Sand's softer there," she said, frowning. "Hard-packed closer to the Gulf. Sea turtles use their flippers to dig nests so they need a softer sand."

Unsure of why she'd remembered that when she hadn't been able to remember her own parents, Peyton approached the nest, careful to keep her distance.

Gray joined her. "What kind of turtles are these?"

She squatted down, touched the warning tape. "On this coast, hawksbill or green turtles maybe. Loggerheads are more commonly found in the Atlantic."

"You remember." He sounded pleased. "Have you ever seen them lay their eggs on the west coast?"

His conversational tone, not as grilling as previously, triggered more memories. She loved sea turtles and that love came from somewhere…

An elderly woman, wearing a pink floppy hat, always clad in white. White linen trousers, a flowing white shirt. Barefoot. Her paper-thin hand clutching a child-like one as they trudged along the beach and then sat on the warm sand.

"Wait, honey. You need to be patient to see them. They're not always on this beach but seeing them is a gift."

"A gift like the kind Mommy and Daddy buy me, Grandma?"

"No, sweetheart. You can't purchase this kind of gift. It's a gift of nature, much more precious than anything money can buy."

"Nana Victoria. My father's mother." Peyton pressed a finger to her temple. "I was a little girl. Adored my nana. She took me to the beach to watch for the Kemp's ridley turtles. I spent three summers with her at her beach home while Mom was busy with her practice and Dad was expanding the family business overseas.

"I loved those summers here and watching for Kemp's ridley turtles nesting. They're the most endangered sea turtle because they dig their nests in the middle of the day and people see this and steal the eggs. The hatchlings hatch in the middle of the day as well, unlike the other turtles that hatch at night. Nana told me we had to protect them because they were becoming rare."

Gray sat on the sand, his long legs stretched out. "Tell me about her. She sounds like a true environmentalist."

"Long before environmental science became popular, she was protecting the sea turtles. Nana was a huge advocate of conservation and sea turtles. She's the one who insisted the house on the east coast remain in the family, along with the land. She was protecting nests and hatchlings long before I even thought about becoming a sea turtle biologist…"

Her voice trailed off. Peyton sat on the sand, hugged her knees, staring into the Gulf. The beach. The beach by her family's luxurious oceanfront mansion, the beach her grandmother put into a trust to ensure no one would ever build on it. Memories flickered like candlelight.

Why was that beach so important? The police told her she'd been kidnapped from the beach. But why there? Something kept flickering in the back of her mind, telling her it was pertinent to everything happening to her.

"Turtles nested there on that stretch of sand. It was safe," she murmured, trying to pull free the memory. It kept sticking like taffy.

"What is it?" he asked softly.

Troubled, she glanced at him, his look of concern. She didn't want to answer him, but knew each loose memory was a threat that could be tugged to unravel the rest.

Perhaps the most important one—why she'd been targeted by the stalker who surely abducted her. Sweat beaded her temple, though not from the still-warm sun.

Peyton glanced at him. "If I remember everything, what's going to happen to me? I'm scared. I'm scared to know exactly who did that to me and why they did it. What if I'm a bad person and said or did something to deserve it?"

His expression tightened. Gray grasped her hand, his grip strong and yet gentle. "Peyton, I assure you, you did nothing wrong. What happened to you was not your fault. Yes, we are sure whoever did this is someone you know. Stranger abductions are rare. But you did nothing to provoke this. Now, did you remember something important?"

Images of a moonlit beach faded. "I'm a marine biologist. Sea turtle biologist. I remembered. I got my master's in marine biology from the University of West Florida…

I wanted to stay in Florida at school in this area because of Nana. And then…"

She pressed two fingers to her temples. "I was half-way through my master's when Nana got sick. She died."

Her mouth wobbled. "But she'd insisted on me staying in school because she knew it was my dream, and she wanted someone in her family to carry on her work in protecting marine animals. She deeded her home to me."

"So you could continue to live here while you went to school. And keep watch for the turtles."

"Yes." Peyton nodded slowly. "I remember telling my nana I was going to be a sea turtle biologist, but didn't want her help or her money's influence in finding a job. When I got a job, it had to be on my own merits."

Gray looked satisfied. "That doesn't surprise me. You always seemed to be that kind of person."

"What kind of person is that?"

"Someone who forges her own path instead of living off her family's achievements. A person who deeply cares about the environment more than she cares about money."

His quiet statement reassured her a little. Every small bit of information she remembered fed her self-confidence.

Peyton hugged her knees tighter. "It's odd, not knowing who I am and then regaining some of these memories. The ones of Nana are good, but still hurt because I missed her so damn much when she died. She taught me a lot about turtles, even when I was young. I guess I got my love for marine biology from her. She never had any formal education when it came to science, but she had natural instincts."

"Instincts she passed along to her granddaughter." Gray stood, brushed sand off his long legs. "Come. The restaurant isn't far. We can walk to it from here."

She gave a doubtful glance at her wrinkled shorts and crumpled pink shirt. "Like this?"

"It's casual."

"I don't know if Nana would approve." Peyton gave a wistful sigh. "Another thing I recall is she always presented herself as a lady. Even when on the beach."

"I think your nana would be fine with how you look," he said. "And proud of you now, with everything you've accomplished."

A lump formed in her throat. "I hope so. She was so strong and wise. I wish she could be here now, to tell me what I should do."

He pointed to her chest. "She's still with you, Peyton. In there. In your heart. And there she'll always remain."

A sweet sentiment. Still, as they headed for the restaurant, she hoped he had nothing in his past to prove her trust in him wrong.

Sleep proved elusive later for Gray.

He lay in one of the two twin beds next to Peyton's bedroom, his feet dangling off the edge. The main bedroom held a king-size bed suitable for his height, but was on the house's other side. He needed to sleep closer to Peyton.

She'd enjoyed the dinner at the oyster shack, devouring the sea scallops with pleasure, sticking to water and rejecting his offer of a glass of wine. He knew she liked wine, but wouldn't press her. Perhaps that memory would return later, along with more-significant ones.

Punching the pillow, his restlessness increased. Being in close proximity to her was sorely tempting. Couldn't deny the attraction between them, the feelings she aroused in him when she'd touched his scar. Peyton was smart, funny, passionate and, now, utterly lost. It was his job to help restore her memory and protect her.

Not dive into a relationship with her. Yet she affected him like no other woman had. Her ready smile, sweet laughter and trim figure, and her long blond hair that had him imagining gripping it in his fist as they made love…

Groaning, he tried to think of other things. Peyton had a zealous dedication to her job. That same dedication he recognized in himself.

Since Andrea's death two years ago, dating had been a low priority. He'd finally gotten his life together, thought about what his future held and where he was headed, and then Jarrett had called in a favor for one last assignment.

Protect Peyton Bradley, only daughter of a wealthy CEO.

"Soon as this assignment is over, I'll cut you loose and you can go forward," Jarrett had promised.

Go forward…where? Return to New York and his family? Settle in Florida? He still had a home in the Keys inherited from a great-uncle who shared his love of boating and fishing. Could return there, work remotely in the family business.

Gray felt as lost as Peyton did, except he remained in full control of his memories.

Peyton threw a huge wrench into the well-oiled machinery of his plans. Much as he hated to admit it, he harbored feelings for her. He would not, could not, move forward with his life until he felt satisfied she was safe and ready to move forward with hers.

He finally began to drift into sleep, as thoughts continued to dance around his mind.

Peyton's situation remained precarious. She was vulnerable in a way Andrea had been, except Peyton had more street smarts when it came to men. Breaking it off with Devine when she recognized the signs of an abusive partner. She was single-minded and perhaps had blinders on with her work, not with men.

Andrea died because she fell for the wrong person.

Peyton would not die because she'd chosen the wrong profession.

Gray bolted upright. There was the connection. Had to be. Her work with sea turtles. What if her stalker hadn't chosen her out of lovesick dedication, but something to do with her job?

Rolling over, he grabbed his cell phone and texted Detective Sims, questioning if he'd found anything suspicious in the background checks on all staff of the Marine Institute.

Sims texted back immediately.

Guess I'm not the only one fighting insomnia.

The usual suspects—two employees with large student debts but no records. One thing popped up on the radar. Martin Gauthier, the acting director of the Marine Institute.

Guy has a record of B&E at his former employer. Tried to steal the employee file on a woman named Cheryl Moore. Moore accused Gauthier of sexual harassment and he got fired.

Gray rubbed his eyes. Gauthier had been cavalier about the breaking and entering at the Marine Institute and the message written in lipstick for Peyton.

He's on my radar as well, he typed back. How did this get buried?

Charges were dropped. Questioned the former director at Peyton's job and he said Martin came with glowing recommendations from a few places. Now we're tracking down the woman who accused Gauthier of sexual harassment. She's moved out of the state.

Gray knew all about dropping charges and making accusations vanish. His father had hustled and used his considerable influence to expunge Gray's arrest record regarding Andrea, but rumors persisted.

Check to see if Gauthier had or has any connection to Fletcher Richardson. He's key in all this.

How's Peyton? Any recollections? Sims texted.

Making progress. I'll be in touch.

He set the phone down and stared at the ceiling. Gauthier had moved up on the suspect list. Perhaps his interest in Peyton hadn't been fear she'd leave the job, but something deeper.

For now, all he could do was keep her safe, and hope they'd have answers soon.

Chapter 15

Peyton opted to eat breakfast outside on the screened-in porch the next morning. A lopsided ceiling fan spun lazily, stirring the already sullen air. She wore plain black yoga pants, a sleep shirt with flamingos and Olukai fluffy slippers. Though the slippers were warm, they comforted her in this strange place.

She chewed the cereal Gray had found in the cabinet. Kids' cereal, but it also proved comforting, as if she'd eaten the same sugary substance when she was a child.

Last night she'd had dreams that left her restless and aching. No memories, only sensual dreams of the man in the next room. It didn't help that she'd fallen asleep wondering if he slept naked.

At least her dreams hadn't been threaded with tormenting images of the mysterious man who wanted her dead, or the ugly gun Gray insisted on keeping in her nightstand.

The kitchen door opened and Gray stepped onto the porch. Serious as usual, dressed in pressed tan trousers and a white cotton shirt with the sleeves rolled up to display strong forearms dusted with dark hair. Peyton swallowed her gulp of cereal, staring at his arms. She never knew arms could be so sexy, the tensile muscles and sinew flexing as he reached up to turn down the wobbling ceiling fan.

He caught her staring, and his mouth quirked upward. Embarrassed, she turned her attention back to breakfast, but her appetite had fled.

"What's on the agenda for today? Another beach visit?"

"The Clearwater Aquarium. The aquarium does valuable conservation work with sea turtles, but they're famous for Winter."

"The tailless dolphin featured in that movie," she mused.

Gray smiled. "You remember Winter."

"A little." She set her bowl down on a side table. "I feel drips of memory returning, but nothing solid."

"What about your dreams? Sometimes our memories are prominent in our dreams."

Peyton felt her face flush further. "Uh, no."

He sat across from her in a white wicker chair. "Do you remember what you dreamed about last night? Tell me."

I dreamed about you being naked in bed with me and it was oh so delicious...

"You," she blurted out.

Well, she was being honest. Gray didn't look surprised. In fact, he nodded, as if it seemed normal. Natural.

Peyton looked away, rubbing her hands. A faint memory blinked on and off like a faulty light bulb. Sexual interest…attraction but something else overriding that. Someone who wanted her sexually, made advances but his overarching goal was far different.

"Can you be attracted to someone you want to kill?"

His normally cool facade shattered. For the first time, he seemed uncomfortable as he drew back, scowled. "Where did that come from? Where the hell are you headed with this, Peyton?"

She rubbed her arms, trying to keep her composure.

"I was thinking about who took me and why. You told me I had a stalker before someone abducted me and that's why you were hired—to protect me. Well, if my stalker desired me, why would he want to kill me as well?"

His relief palpable, Gray's expression smoothed out. "Many reasons. Sometimes stalkers erupt in anger, sometimes they wish their victims dead so no one else will have them."

She shook her head. "He didn't want me dead because he feared someone else having me. He had to kill me because they wanted me dead."

Stunned, she shook her head. "How did I know that?"

"What else? Who wanted you dead? Was your stalker following orders? Wanted a ransom for you?"

Frustration overcame her as she tried to wrench the memory free. "I don't know! Stop badgering me."

"Okay. Relax."

"Relax. That's all you've ordered me to do since we arrived. How can I relax? I'm regaining bits of memory, but not knowing who I am…"

"That's why we're here. I'm trying to help you recall, Peyton. I know it's upsetting, but you have to work with me, trust me…"

"It's not easy," she shot back. "What memories are buried deep inside me? It's more than disconcerting. Everyone has secrets to hide. I don't know what mine are and I'm sure I don't want to share them."

Gray blinked, his jaw tensing as if she'd hit a raw nerve. Peyton suspected she had.

"What about your secrets, Gray? Would you want to share them with me? You promised to be honest with me.

It's one reason I trusted you enough to go with you on this journey."

Instead of answering, he glanced at the bits of cereal floating in the bowl of milk. "Finish, ah, your breakfast. Or whatever that is. I have a few calls to make and then we'll leave for the aquarium."

Emboldened and needing to lift the intensity of the moment, she lifted the cereal bowl like an offering. "This is the finest breakfast food known to kiddom, I'll have you know. It's fortified with essential vitamins and minerals."

Humor reflected in his gaze. "If you insist it doesn't look like something found floating on the beach at low tide..."

He headed into the house, his playful mood gone, the serious Gray returned.

Because what she'd remembered was pretty damn serious, and much grimmer than sugar-laden soggy breakfast cereal.

He wanted to uncover her past, her memories, and with them Gray knew he'd expose secrets Peyton may want hidden. He didn't want to share any of his, especially the biggest one of all.

He knew all about keeping secrets. It had nothing to do with his background as a SEAL. Yeah, he was tight-lipped regarding his past career, even missions no longer considered classified.

His tightly guarded privacy related more to his personal life over the past two years. Gray had built up layers around himself, a fortress of barricades few people ever penetrated. Better that way. Being vulnerable was not in his résumé, thank you very much. Gray promised to be honest with Peyton. But honesty didn't mean exposing himself and burdening her with his own troubled past.

Dressed in a casual purple T-shirt and denim shorts, Peyton said nothing on the drive to the aquarium. He'd filled the silence in the car with music from his iPhone, because music seemed better than small talk. Or answers he wasn't ready to give.

He paid for their tickets and herded her outside to the giant sea tank where fish and other marine animals swam freely. There was an exhibit dedicated to Winter, who sadly had died a couple of years ago.

The staff worker had told Jace she'd seen Fletcher Richardson on a small boat in the bay. The employee knew it was Richardson because up until a few weeks ago, the man was always at the aquarium. Then suddenly, he quit without explanation.

Right around the time Peyton's stalker had shown up.

Gray was certain the two events were connected.

Since the entrance was on the third floor, he guided her outside to the dolphin terrace to view the enormous tank containing dolphins and other marine life. Peyton looked disinterested.

The turtle bayou was on level two, so he suggested that they visit that area next. Peyton trudged down the stairs, seemingly listless. Her shoulders sagged. What happened? He needed to find out.

A volunteer was giving a presentation at the turtle cove, so they bypassed the turtle bayou to stand at the railing. A couple of sea turtles swam around the tank as visitors peered down.

Gray leaned over the railing and pointed to a turtle. "Is that a hawksbill?"

Peyton rolled her eyes. "Green sea turtle. *Chelonia mydas.* Hawksbills have beautiful speckled brown carapaces. They were hunted for them, used in making eyeglasses and jewelry. It's illegal to possess tortoiseshell items, even as antiques, because authorities are trying to cut back on the trade. Hawksbills' scientific name is *Eretmochelys imbricata*. Omnivores. Their diet consists of seagrass, barnacles, crustaceans, but their favorite food is sea sponges."

Giving an approving nod, he flashed a brief smile.

"You baited me into remembering."

"I did. It worked." He couldn't help but feel satisfied.

Peyton rubbed her temples.

"You've been quiet for a long time now, except for that recital of facts about sea turtles. Are you feeling well?"

"I'm feeling fine, except I should go home." Her blue eyes suddenly flashed anger. "Alone. I don't like how you're manipulating me."

Gray felt a tug of worry. "Let's not talk here."

He led her over to a quieter corner, away from the fascinated tourists. "What's wrong?"

"Nothing. Everything. This." She spread her hands out. "I'm taking a huge leap of faith in you, Gray. You promised to be honest with me. Why are you making all these phone calls and running errands without me? As if you're hiding something? For all I know, maybe you're the one who arranged all this and abducted me."

Accusing him of trying to hurt her? What the hell? Gray's temper rose. Taking a deep breath, he strove for patience. Understanding. Had to view the sitch from her eyes. He could almost smell the fear rolling off her in waves, as surely as he scented the brine from the turtle tank.

"Peyton, everything I'm doing is for your benefit."

Her chin lifted and he saw a challenge in her eyes. "For my benefit? I lost my memory, not my ability to make decisions for myself. If you want me to share everything with you, you need to do the same."

When was too much information too much? An info

dump that might scare her or cause her to shut down all the progress they've made? Gray made a snap decision. Settling his hands on her slender shoulders, he locked his gaze to hers.

"The phone calls I made were to Jarrett at SOS and the detective in charge of finding your kidnapper. I shared information with him, as I promised I would. I didn't call him in your presence because I didn't want you worried about information overload."

She gave him a cool, level look. "Let me worry about information overload, Gray."

He began to see it her way. In shielding her from case updates, he was overprotecting her. "I apologize. You're not a child. I will keep you updated from this moment on."

"My gray matter can handle it fine. Better than I could handle your gray matter if you had sinister ulterior motives about me."

Gray's mouth twitched. "My gray matter? Pun intended?"

"Of course."

"I've heard worse. And sinister? You make me sound like a villain out of a gothic horror movie."

"Another cherished habit from my childhood," she murmured. Peyton frowned. "I seem to recall things more from my younger days. Why's that?"

"Less stressful, happier times."

"Will you let me make my own decisions about what I can handle and what I can't?" She tilted her head at him.

"Yes. Providing those decisions don't endanger you. Your safety, and the recovery of your memory, is my prime concern."

He took her hand in a firm, yet gentle, grasp. The dynamic in their relationship had changed, and he felt relieved about it. His responsibility wasn't to encase Peyton in layers of cotton to guard her from the outside world.

In asserting herself and her needs, she had begun to show her true personality.

The same personality that fought to live and escaped her captor. Peyton wasn't a doe-eyed naive woman who needed a man to tell her what to do and how to live.

Perhaps a breakthrough wouldn't be far off.

He only wished his former fiancée had half of Peyton's grit. Maybe she'd still be alive today. Did it matter? Gray had played the game of "What if" long enough to know it was a moot point.

"Let's go downstairs. The employee who spotted Fletcher is on the boat tour today." He gave her a pointed look. "Unless you do want to return home alone. I'll help you make the arrangements."

Deliberately he loosened his grip. If she wanted to cut loose, now was the moment. Instead her fingers curled around his.

Humbled by the trust she'd placed in him, he vowed to be worthy of it. Gray led her downstairs to the ramp inside where people were disembarking from the latest cruise on the water. When he spotted the employee whose picture Jace had sent him, he called out.

"Carol Walker? I'm Gray Wallace and this is Peyton. Jace told you to expect us."

The woman, in her early twenties, smiled. "Yes. Jace said you're the one who needs to know about Fletcher."

"Do you have a recent photo of him?"

Carol scrolled through her phone, and pulled up a photo. "He was amazing. Knew so much about turtles."

Peyton looked at the picture, her eyes clouded with concern. "That's him. I remember him now. He looks so much older than last year. What happened to him?"

"I haven't seen him in about a week. He came almost every day and had a membership. He had excellent knowledge of the marine life in Florida, the kind of knowledge you can tell he got from experience, and not from a book."

"Do you know why he stopped visiting?" Peyton asked.

She shook her head. "No, but we got the sense he felt uneasy around all these people. It was odd because he seemed fine with the visitors during the busy season, and then one day he started acting a little paranoid."

Gray exchanged glances with Peyton. "Paranoid in what way?"

"It was during the afternoon feeding at the tank. He was talking to a few visitors and suddenly he went pale, as if he were going to pass out. When I went to see if he needed medical attention, he walked away, muttering something about someone following him here. Someone he'd wanted to leave behind.

"I thought maybe it was a girlfriend he'd broken up with. But the only ones around were families and a man."

Gray's attention sharpened. "What did the man look like? Tall? Short? Pale? Tanned? Dark hair or light?"

She frowned. "Black hair, like yours. Tanned skin, as if he spent a lot of time outside. Kind of tall, a little skinny. I remember thinking he looked…I don't know…hungry? He kept looking at Fletcher, as if he wanted to ask him something. He worried me because he made Fletcher uneasy."

Clearly Carol had affection for Fletcher, as Peyton had. Gray pressed further. "Any idea where Fletcher went? Or if he's still in the area? Do you have his phone number or know anyone he could be staying with?"

Carol shrugged, but not before he caught a flash of worry in her gaze. The woman started to walk away. "No idea. Why are you so interested in him anyway?"

Holding her hands out, Peyton blocked her way. "He's not in trouble. But he could be in danger, if we don't find him. Please. Tell us what you know. Fletcher's a good guy.

He taught me a lot about the ocean and tides and turtles. He helped me. I want to do the same for him."

Carol hesitated a moment, and then searched Peyton's expression. Finally she nodded. "He is a good man and I wouldn't want him in trouble. I had the feeling he was running from police or something. Or trying to, anyway. If you think you can help him…"

"I can."

"Okay. He rented a room on the mainland, in Largo, but it was only temporary. He said soon as he came into a little money, which he was expecting soon, he was headed to the Keys."

A good lead, but not defined enough. "Which key?"

Ignoring him, Carol gave Peyton a beseeching look. "Promise you'll help him and won't turn him over to the police?"

"I won't," Peyton said.

I'm not making the same promise.

"He intended to stay at a friend's house in Islamorada. The friend winters down here and wanted Fletcher to house-sit for the summer, take care of the place during storm season. Name's Sinclair. That's all I know."

Peyton gave her first real smile of the day. "Thank you. Thank you for trusting me."

"Please, let me know if you find him. I hope he's okay."

They exchanged cell phone numbers. As Carol walked away, Gray scanned the surrounding crowds. Even here, Peyton could be in trouble. If someone had been after Fletcher for the same reason her stalker targeted Peyton, she wasn't safe.

"Let's go." He took her arm.

"Hey! I thought you were letting me make my own decisions. What if I want to stay? You're not in charge anymore, remember?"

"I am when your safety is a concern. Remember?"

Once they were in his car, the doors locked, and he pulled out onto the road, Gray could breathe.

"You saw something back there?" she asked, her eyes wide.

Gray shook his head. "No, but I wasn't taking chances. Not knowing Richardson had been followed by whoever targeted him back at your parents' house."

"Good thing Carol was honest with us."

"She wasn't very forthcoming. Except with you." He glanced at her. "You two connected."

"You're too serious. Like a cop interrogating a suspect." Peyton gave him a teasing look. "I'm much easier to talk to."

"I am not serious."

"Right. And it snows in Florida."

"Sometimes it does," he muttered. "Let's get back to the house so I can check out this new lead."

Heading east, he focused on driving on the causeway. Gray accessed a main road, then turned south on US-19 ALT to head back to the house. They had a bigger problem than finding Fletcher Richardson. Someone else wanted to find him as well. Someone who'd scared him into running.

She started to speak when suddenly a black sedan, windows tinted, pulled up beside them on the passenger side right-turning lane. A sizable dent had crushed part of the front left bumper. All his internal warning censors signaled danger as he glanced over, felt something threatening in the way they paralleled the car.

Suddenly the sedan slammed into them. Gray jerked the wheel to the left, narrowly missing hitting the car in the lane next to him.

"Hang on," he muttered.

Accelerating, he zipped in and out of traffic, eyeing the rearview mirror. He took a few side streets and then pulled into the parking lot of a grocery store, parking in an area in the back so the car was partly hidden by tractor trailers. Gray kept the motor running, and kept looking in the mirror.

"That was crazy." She shivered. "What kind of jerk doesn't look in the next lane when he's wanting to pass you?"

"The kind who wants to run you off the road so he can shoot you," Gray said calmly.

Blood drained from her face. "He had a gun?"

"Saw something on the driver's side that could have been a handgun. Wasn't taking any chances of getting closer to check it out. Whoever it was did that on purpose."

"He was after me," Peyton said slowly.

"Yes. I'm sure of it. You're not safe here anymore. We have to leave and move on to another location."

The sunny day, filled with so much promise, suddenly turned dark and ominous.

"Do you think they're following us?"

"Maybe. They're probably searching, and I'm good at losing anyone tailing me. But I'm not taking chances." Jaw tight, he dialed a number, glanced at her. "Jarrett? Need a favor."

Quickly he explained what happened on the return to the house. Gray pressed a button and bluetoothed the call to the car's speakers.

"Could have been an angry, impatient driver. Plenty of those in Florida, but I don't like it. Pack up and leave right now. I'll have someone there soon to keep you secure. Can you hold out until then?" Jarrett asked.

Gray glanced at her. "I don't want to compromise your safe house, Jarrett. You need it for SOS. If someone is tailing us, and I'm damn certain they are, they'll find the location if I drive straight there."

A brief pause. Then Jarrett said slowly, "You have a point. But the house isn't as important as your safety and Peyton's."

Making up his mind, Gray kept heading south. "I'm taking Peyton to another location. Have your guy pack up everything in the house belonging to us and meet us there. Better yet, send Jace if you can. I trust him. Our leaving won't compromise your house and it'll give me time to lose these yahoos. I'll text you the address."

He hung up and pulled out of the parking lot. But as he got to the main road, the same black sedan with tinted windows came into view in the side mirror. Peyton shuddered.

"How did they find us?"

Not answering, he jerked the wheel to the right and pulled off the road as the sedan passed, then the driver realized his mistake and went to make a U-turn. Gray pulled out again and sped up. Soon the car was left far behind in traffic.

He dialed Jarrett again, rattled off the license plate number and hung up. Dammit. He thought they hadn't been followed, and couldn't figure out how the hell someone had found them.

Gray glanced at her. "I'm heading east, not going to take I-75 south. I-4 to Orlando, we'll find a rest stop there and a place to eat, and then the turnpike south to find a hotel room there for the night. Drive will take about an hour."

It was unnerving knowing they had been followed. Unnerving to think the safe house was no longer safe. Neither was she.

All she could do was trust Gray knew what he was doing. Trust that he would keep good on his promise to keep her safe.

Trying to calm her nerves, she thought about all she'd

remembered about sea turtles. Gray bluetoothed music from his phone and the quiet strains of violin and piano soothed her. But as they turned onto the exit for the turnpike south, Gray cursed. Peyton glanced in the mirror and saw the same black sedan following them.

"I don't understand! You almost broke all the speed limits. We lost them back near Tampa. How could they find us again?"

"They're pretty damn good. Too good. It's as if they knew where we're headed at all times..." Gray frowned. "I'm pulling off into the next service area."

He pulled into the lane leading to a busy service area off the turnpike filled with tourists visiting Orlando and all the theme parks. Gray parked the car next to a mother buckling a toddler into a car seat. "Come on. You need to visit the women's restroom."

"I don't..." But he was already out the door, opening her door and helping her out of the car.

Gray herded her into the building. People streamed in and out of the service plaza, some stopping to eat at a busy food court or peruse items at a gift shop.

He kept guiding her toward the women's restroom. Several heads turned as they hurried into the restroom. Some mouths dropped open.

"Hey, you can't be in here," protested a startled middle-aged woman wearing a T-shirt advertising a popular theme park.

"Sorry. Urgent need," he shot back.

Hustling Peyton into a handicapped stall, he shut the door.

More bewildered than embarrassed, Peyton folded her arms. "Please tell me there's a reason for this."

"Yes. Get undressed. You're being tracked."

Now it was her turn for her jaw to drop. "What? I don't... What?"

"Strip down to your bra and panties," he said in a low voice, then turned away from her. "Do it!"

Biting her lip, she timidly slipped out of her clothes. Handed them to him. He made an impatient sound as he grabbed the soft cotton shirt and shorts. His fingers were brisk, and he paid her nakedness no attention as he examined the articles.

He felt the denim shorts and frowned. Next he removed a penknife from his jeans and cut into the shorts. Shock filled her as he pulled out a small black square no larger than a quarter. He turned back to show her.

Gaze grim, he nodded. "Knew they had to be tracking you somehow. It's a GPS tracking device. Probably with real-time tracking that provides a constant data connection."

She took the device from him, staring at it. "I can't believe this."

"I have questions, but not here." His gaze flicked to her breasts and she saw his eyes widen, now with simple lustful interest.

Peyton felt her nipples perk up beneath his caressing gaze. Then he looked away, a muscle in his jaw twitching as if he struggled for control.

Taking a deep breath, he plucked the device from her palm. "Get dressed and let's get out of here."

Peyton pointed to the device. "You should flush that thing. Get rid of it."

"I've a better idea." He pocketed the tracking device. "I'll dispose of it outside."

She gave him a doubtful look. "How are we getting out of here without raising suspicion?"

"We won't."

"They'll think your urgent need was sex with me."

"Maybe it was," he joked.

But Gray's gaze smoldered as he gazed at her mouth. A muscle throbbed in his temple as if he was considering sex with her right here, right now.

"Maybe I wouldn't mind," she whispered, reaching out to touch his hand, feel the tensile male strength in those hands.

Calloused hands that possessed enormous strength, but would feel gentle as he stroked her naked body, arousing her to put her pleasure before his own.

Drawing in another breath, he shook his head. "Not here. Not my style and you deserve much better. If we made love, I'd treat you to soft sheets, a terrific bottle of wine and all night long. Not a five-minute quickie in a rest stop."

Peyton tilted her head, daring to say what she felt. "If? Or when?"

Gray ran a finger down her cheek. "I'd like to think so, eventually. I'm not denying there's something between us, Peyton. You can't deny it, either."

She wanted more than acknowledgment. She wanted to follow through on the sparks jumping between them.

As he kept studying her mouth, she leaned forward, pressing her palms flat against his chest, and lifted her face to his.

Gray's mouth descended upon her lips. Rough at first, as if fueled by desperate need, then he gentled the kiss, framing her face with his hands. He kissed her deep, as if taking in all her anguish, all her need, and funneling it into himself. Wrapping her fingers around his wrists, she surrendered to the moment, tasting him, smelling the faint, spicy fragrance of his aftershave and his own unique male scent, feeling his mouth possess hers with quiet authority.

With a groan, he released her, bent his head to hers. Gave a short laugh. "This is really lousy timing."

"Yes. But we have a few moments." Her mouth felt swollen, her heart happy, even with everything that had happened.

His kiss had been a beacon in the ever-present fog shrouding her, a light of pleasure and hope directing her forward. She wanted to run toward that light, ignite herself with passion instead of this damn feeling of being lost all the time.

Gray tipped her chin up, his dark gaze tender and yet heated. "Not here. Not now. Because what I have planned for you in bed isn't going to take a little while. I'm a demanding guy. With you, I want you awake and ready for the entire night."

Peyton felt her entire body tighten with anticipation. Sounded great to her. A long night in bed with him was worth the wait.

"We need to get out of here." Ever efficient, he glanced around, ran a hand over his short hair.

"And get rid of that…thing…tracking me." Peyton shuddered. "Let's do this."

Gray opened the door and they walked out together to more than a few staring faces.

"Was it good for you, honey?" he drawled, glancing at Peyton.

Her cheeks flaming, she shrugged. "For a quickie, you're not half-bad."

Gray chuckled as they hurried out of the restroom. He stopped at the gift shop to purchase chewing gum.

Handing her the gum and the hateful device, he instructed her to chew a piece. "When I get to the vehicle I select, put the device onto the gum and stick it on the car where it can't be easily spotted."

Once outside, he headed to the northbound parking lot. Pointing out their car was parked in the southbound lot was moot, for she knew him well enough by now. He had a plan. Maybe his plans weren't always aligned with what she thought was best, but he had more experience in being a shadow. She trusted him.

People streamed in and out of the building, and the northbound lot was equally busy as the southbound. Gray headed for a Florida Highway Patrol officer's vehicle. Alarm filled her. Going to the police now was not a good idea...

Gray hung back, studied the officer leaning against his vehicle, sipping from a soft drink can. A smile of approval touched his expression as he looked at the man's forearm. Semper Fi was inked there. Gray hurried forward, Peyton trailing behind, still chewing. He called out to the officer.

"Hi. Sorry to bother you, but my girlfriend and I wondered if you ran into any accidents coming south. Got an app for traffic, but always trust humans more than these damn apps."

The officer shook his head. Gray pointed to the tattoo on the man's forearm. "Jarhead? See any action?"

A flicker of recognition. "Yeah. First Battalion, Second Marine Regiment in Afghanistan in 2014. You served?"

"Navy. Special ops. I was there in 2014. Might have seen you."

Now the officer's face broke into a smile. "SEAL?"

Gray gave a modest shrug. They began discussing combat missions as Peyton hung back, inching toward the car's bumper. She took the device, stuck it into the chewing gum and slid it just beneath the back door handle.

Peyton poked Gray in the back. "Honey, we really need to hit the road if we want to make Mama's house by nightfall."

"Sure, sweetheart." Gray stuck out a hand for the trooper

to shake. "Great talking with you, Sam. Name's Grayson Mitchell. Stay safe on the road, bud."

The trooper echoed the sentiment and then climbed into his vehicle. He took off as she and Gray watched.

"I get the whole buddy thing with ex-military, but is it wise to give a fake name?" she asked.

A shadow crossed his face. "It's my real name. Figured he would look me up to see if I was being truthful or an outright liar. He's going to ask around, might as well know my real name."

Confusion filled her as they headed for the southbound parking lot. "Your real name is Grayson Mitchell? Why the alias?"

He didn't answer until they were inside his car, driving south. Finally he did. "I'd rather not tell you now, Peyton. Let's focus on you and getting you away from these bastards who are intent on tracking you."

It made her wonder what he hid. What secrets did Gray hide? She had his real name now; she could google it. But he was right. Other things mattered more now.

Still, it made her uneasy, like discovering a snake hiding in a gorgeous blue trumpet vine on a trellis...

Trellis! "You were on my balcony, cutting my mom's flowers and removing the trellis so no one could climb up into my room at home." Peyton felt the first real surge of hope since this morning. "I remember!"

He flashed her a quick smile. "Good. I don't want to know how you remembered. The important thing is your memory is returning, even if only bits and pieces."

"Where are we going now? The Keys to find Fletcher?"

"Too risky. Besides, it's getting late and we need to stop for the night."

A flicker of alarm surged. "Late? Gray, it's barely past one."

"I know how to tell time, Peyton."

His impatient tone quieted her. Peyton twisted her hands in her lap. All she had on her was a purse with her driver's license and a little money. Not even a credit card to her name. Her parents must have removed them from her wallet.

After they'd been on the road for a while, he asked her if she was hungry. Peyton nodded. Gray pulled off the turnpike and headed for a well-known restaurant.

Over dinner, she nibbled at her food, falling into melancholy. Around them couples and families talked, ate, laughed.

Four women in their midtwenties, wearing dresses and carrying drinks, laughed as they headed for an empty table. They looked to be having an amazing time, four friends out for the evening.

Was she like this? Had good friends she went out with for dinner, friends she could not remember? Conversations she could not recall? Laughter she could not remember?

"I'm a stranger in a strange land," she murmured, setting down her glass. "Do I even belong here?"

Peyton didn't think he could hear her, but Gray leaned forward, touched her hand. "You belong here, Peyton. You will get your memory back. You're starting to recall more things."

But the question of who she was seemed to be one that wouldn't be easily answered. "I don't feel like I belong anywhere right now."

Then the answer came to her with remarkable clarity. "Except with you. I feel like I belong with you."

Gray blinked, sipped his drink, but said nothing. It wasn't a rejection, but not exactly assuring, either.

"Gray, if I hadn't lost my memory, if I was still…Peyton…and the threat against me was gone, would I be the kind of woman you'd date? A woman you'd want to get to know better?"

She knew her answer. She not only felt safe with him. Gray was helping her to rediscover herself, the true Peyton. In a way, she had a second chance few were granted. She could know what she really wanted out of life, what mattered most to her because she had no expectations to cloud her way.

He finally looked at her, his dark gaze unfathomable. "I promised to be honest with you, Peyton, long before you lost your memory. I will not lie to you now. The answer is yes. You are exactly the kind of woman I'd want to date and get to know better. Intriguing, thoughtful, with a wicked sense of humor and a sincerity few people in my circle have."

The declaration warmed her.

Gray signaled for the check.

After he pulled into the parking lot of an oceanfront hotel in Vero Beach, and they walked into the lobby, her anxiety lessened. Cool air caressed her sweaty cheeks, and the elegant surroundings with their trendy, South Beach style were a welcome balm after the fright on the road and the news about Fletcher. Peyton felt the tension slide off her. This was the kind of hotel she needed for a good night's rest. Perhaps a swim in the pool, a massage, a drink in the bar before falling blissfully asleep on Egyptian cotton sheets…

You owe me, Peyton. You're gonna pay for all of it in bed and then I'll decide if you live or die.

Peyton rubbed her temples.

"What's wrong?"

This memory scared her, but instinct warned against sharing it with Gray. She didn't know if her captor said it. What if Gray uttered that threat? He admitted to using an alias.

"Nothing. Um, we have no clothing. I was thinking about a massage or a swim."

Removing a credit card from his wallet, Gray inquired at the desk about a room for one night. They did have a room, but only a king-size bed. Gray didn't hesitate. "We'll take it."

He slid the card across the gleaming counter. She caught sight of the name on the card before the receptionist picked it up.

Gray Jones.

If his legal name was Grayson Mitchell, how did he have a card with an alias? Peyton rubbed her temples again.

Should she trust him? All she had to go on were some fluttering memories and her instincts.

Who was this man? Was she truly safe with him?

Chapter 16

Peyton had been unusually quiet since they checked into the room. She hadn't asked why they were traveling as husband and wife.

Too quiet. She kept looking at the king-size bed, then at him.

"I had to book a single room for us in order to look as if we are a married couple. You are now officially Mrs. Peyton Jones."

"I don't get it. Another precaution? And if so, why keep my first name?"

"Because keeping your first name is easier and you will respond more naturally to it. It takes a while to assume another identity and we don't have adequate time to train you."

"How many identities do you have? Your name is Gray Wallace, and then you told me Grayson Mitchell is your real name and you used a credit card with Gray Jones." Her voice dropped. "Who are you?"

Sighing, he rubbed his chin and the bristles there. Could

use a shave. "My real name is Grayson Mitchell. I have a couple of identities used for security work, just in case."

He gave her a pointed look. "In case I'm with a client whose identity needs protecting as well."

Peyton kept staring at the bed. "We're sleeping together?"

He felt a twinge of something other than professionalism at the thought. One of major challenges of the forced proximity with Peyton was turning off his lust for her.

"I can take the sofa."

Gray swept the hotel room for listening devices and video cameras. Always the first thing he did upon entering a hotel room. Peyton sat at the bistro table by the sliding glass doors overlooking the ocean. Tense as iron, she had lost the carefree spirit he admired.

What happened?

Gray realized she'd lost trust in him. Damn. It must have happened when he told the highway patrol officer his real name and she discovered he'd used an alias all this time.

He checked his cell phone for Jace's update. At least two hours away. Gray made a snap decision.

"Let's go shopping."

Peyton eyed him as if he'd suggested skinny-dipping in the outdoor pool. Not that he'd mind…

"Shopping? For what? Bullets? Spy stuff? More secret agent James Bond gadgets?"

Ah, sarcasm. Better than the silence. "For new clothing for you."

"I thought my clothing was arriving soon with your sidekick."

Here we go. "I instructed Jace to dump your clothing. Everything."

Her mouth opened and closed. Gray cringed, expecting her to shriek, wail, anything. Instead she got quiet again. Damn.

After picking up a bottle of water from the counter and uncapping it, Gray sat on the bed next to the table. "Peyton, I'm not taking chances. Whoever planted that tracking device could have planted others in your clothing. It's best to buy all new things. I'm sorry, sweetheart, if those clothes meant anything to you."

A half-hearted shrug. "Guess it doesn't matter. I don't remember any of that clothing anyway, whether it was sentimental or not. It felt like a stranger's clothing."

She glanced out the sliding glass doors at the turquoise ocean. "I do recall one thing… Did I call you James Bond before?"

"Yes." He gave a wry smile. "Among other things."

"Guess I didn't like you much before. Too bad you're not giving me a lot of reason to like me now, either."

Ouch. But that wasn't important. *You don't have to like me, Peyton. Only trust that everything I do is to protect you and help you regain your memories.*

"How about this memory… Did you tell anyone about my idea of putting a tracking device in your clothing?" Gray chugged his water.

Peyton shook her head. "I don't recall. Why?"

He palmed the bottle. "Your director, Martin, might have done this, Peyton. Maybe you gave him the idea if you were talking with others at work. You have showers and lockers for changing because of the scuba dives you do for the institute as part of your work. The police went through your locker after you were abducted. Easy enough for Martin to grab your clothing while you showered and insert the tracker to monitor your every movement. That type of tracker is waterproof. You can even launder it and you'd never know it was there."

"Maybe someone else did it."

Gray looked at his cell phone. "Let's go. We need to be

back in two hours and I don't know what kind of shopper you are."

They spent an hour at a local shopping mall. Peyton was brisk and efficient in selecting clothing. Most women he'd shopped with were not as methodical. They combed the racks, spent a leisurely time examining each article of clothing. She was military efficient.

So efficient he managed to let his guard down while she was in the dressing room. Instead of hovering outside the room, he walked onto the clothing floor to call Jarrett for an update.

When he hung up ten minutes later, he returned to the dressing room. "Peyton? Find anything?"

No answer. Suspicion flared. He squatted down.

Empty. Cursing, he opened the door. The new clothing hung neatly on hooks.

Can't have gotten far. He began asking around. A woman examining bathing suits had seen her heading for the exit leading into the mall. But the woman didn't meet his gaze when talking to him.

She lied.

Where could Peyton have gone? Scared of him, most likely, wanting to get away from him, she might have looked for public transportation. She had some money...

Heart racing, hoping she hadn't gotten far, he ran outside to the bus stop. The bus was pulling away. Gray cursed, started to head to his car when he spotted a lone figure sitting on the bus shelter bench.

Casually he walked over and joined her. Her blond head hung down in abject misery. He wanted to pull her into his arms, assure her everything would be fine.

Gray did not. He waited for his cue.

Raising her head, she glanced at him, eyes filled with tears. His stomach roiled.

Tears he'd put there because she was so afraid of him she'd bolted.

"I had to get away. And then I realized, you'd find me anyway."

Chest tight, he waited.

"I don't even know where I was going. Stupid, huh? I have no clue who I am or where I'm headed. I'm tethered to you because I have no money. Nowhere to go."

He took her hand, encouraged she did not pull away.

"I'll always find you. Not because I'm stalking you or intend you harm, Peyton. I'll find you because I'm damn good at finding people and I'm even better at protecting them. More than that, sweetheart. I'll find you because I worry about you out here, alone."

He ran a finger down her cheek. "This kind of reckless running away endangers you. I told you, if you want to return to your parents, give the word. I'll make the call now and your father will be here in less than two hours."

Watching her, he tensed. Now was the moment. If she doubted him, she'd phone her father. Maybe Peyton didn't remember her parents, but they were her parents.

He had been a total stranger, once and now again.

Pushing a hand through her long hair, she nodded. "I'll return with you, on one condition. Level with me. Why do you use an alias? What are you hiding? When you don't tell me what's going on, Gray, it makes me suspicious. Scared."

Gray took a deep breath. "I use Gray Wallace because I got into trouble two years ago and people research my real name, like your father did."

Her eyes rounded, but she didn't draw away from him, only searched his face. "What kind of trouble?"

"The kind that gets you arrested." His chest felt hollow. "I had a violent outburst, Peyton."

"Did you get convicted?"

"No. The charges were dropped. I was cleared, but people still talk." His throat closed up. "I was innocent. That's all I can tell you for now."

Silence draped over them for a few moments, as if she digested the importance of what he'd shared. Few women had known about his past. Those who found out usually ran in the other direction.

Like Peyton had.

He felt something soft and warm encase his hand and looked down to see her palm atop his. Gray's gaze met hers.

"I believe you."

Three simple words that meant everything. Something deep inside him let go, as if he'd waited for this moment. Too emotional to talk, he nodded, squeezed her hand.

Peyton placed her other hand over his, as if trying to anchor herself. Or him.

"I don't need you to rescue me anymore, Gray. I need your help to find my way." She thought a moment, her pretty face scrunched into a frown. "Like a human GPS. You don't expect the GPS to drive you to the destination. Only tell you how to get there."

A sudden breeze stirred her long blond hair, cooled the sweat on his forehead. Gray thought about how everything in nature seemed timed for a reason. Sea turtles nested in the thick of summer heat so the warm sand would incubate the eggs. Like the turtles, Peyton had a homing instinct where to go and what to do. Except her instinct had been temporarily obstructed by memory loss.

He was no knight in a shining Italian-tailored suit. Hell, some days his best weapons against evil were his wits, instincts and training. Gray didn't want Peyton to think he was brushing aside all her concerns and galloping in to save her. He wanted her to save herself.

Gray studied their linked hands. "Do you know how

much I admire you for everything you've done, everything you stand for?"

Confusion clouded her expression. She drew her hands away from him. "I don't understand."

"You have strong convictions and aren't willing to compromise. Not for the sake of your own personal benefit, but for others. The ocean and marine life. The planet. Not many people harbor such passion in life, Peyton. Your parents do, and your mother saves lives with her work as a cardiac surgeon. But you… You're quietly saving lives in a different, equally important way."

He leaned forward, capturing her gaze, knowing he had to make a point or he'd lose her again.

"I'm not about to take over your life, only help you find your way back to it. So yeah, consider me your human GPS. You do realize a GPS can help you change direction?"

For a moment she looked fragile and vulnerable, doubts filling her expression. "What if I head in the wrong direction? Into a dead end? I feel like all I've done since losing my memory is wander in circles. How will I remember what I wanted in life?"

"You're tough. You know what you want. It's buried—" he tapped his head "—up here. But it's there. You will remember what you've lost and pursue your dreams again. Soon as we catch this son of a bitch who put you in this position."

Gray's jaw tightened. "And that SOB isn't me. Far from it, Peyton."

Her lower lip wobbled. "Will you find him?"

"I'll do everything in my power to find him, sweetheart. The police are hard at work on your case as well." He stood.

They returned inside to finish her shopping. It did not take long and soon they were back in the Mercedes. Gray felt as if he'd crossed an important threshold with Peyton.

When they arrived back in the room, strain was evident on her face.

"How about a massage?" he suggested. "You can have alone time while I meet with Jace."

The way she lit up it was as if he'd handed her the world. "Can I? Is it safe enough?"

Mindful of her need for control, he nodded at the phone. "Go ahead. No one knows you're here. Remember, you're Peyton Jones, here with your husband on a short trip."

As she left for her massage, he met Jace in the lobby.

Jace rolled the suitcases over to him. Blue gaze steady, he was all business. "Yours, and I bought a new suitcase for Peyton, along with basic women's stuff, as you asked. Toothbrush, hairbrush, things like that. Wasn't sure about cosmetics."

"She doesn't wear any. At least not recently."

The FBI agent nodded. "I put a gift in your suitcase from Jarrett. Mi Sueno Pinot Noir 2018. He knows how you like it."

Gray managed a smile. "Thanks." Then he considered. "Wait… I gave him a bottle of that as congratulations on Lacey's pregnancy."

Jace grinned. "Jarrett gave up drinking when his wife got pregnant. Besides, his taste runs more to beer."

Gray chuckled and then indicated the lounge. Inside the quiet bar area with its neon blue lights and soft jazz playing in the background, they found quiet seats near the bar. Gray ordered a whiskey and soda for himself, while Jace stuck to iced tea.

Jace handed him an envelope. "Here. Everything you requested."

Gray pocketed the items. "And Richardson? What did you find out?"

"Fletcher Richardson was more than an old salty vet

who liked to roam. Remember that gambling problem I mentioned?" Jace handed him a sheaf of papers.

They fell silent as the waiter brought their drinks. Gray studied the papers in the dim light. Richardson was in deep, all right. Six figures to a well-known loan shark in Miami who insisted on timely payments, if you didn't like your face rearranged.

Gray's concern doubled. "That explains why he was on the run, but why would he leave Bradley's employ? The family was fond of him, and Peyton considered him a good friend. She could have easily loaned him the money, or given it to him outright."

Jace sipped his iced tea. "No details I could find, but I believe Richardson was doing something shady to help repay his loan. Fell in with the wrong people in trying to get out of the wrong sitch."

"It makes sense. Peyton saw something she shouldn't have. I'm certain of it."

Jace set down his tea. "What do you want me to do? Track him down?"

Gray thought a moment. "Ask Jarrett to track him. You've already done enough and you're on vacation."

"I was on vacation." The man's expression hardened. "This is more important. It burns me that someone wanted to hurt her. I can't get the Bureau officially involved, but if you need my help, I'm here."

"Find his home address but do not approach. He will open to Peyton, no one else. A man running scared when cornered will lash out. Don't jeopardize yourself, or him."

"Easy enough. I'll track him through cyberspace." Jace stood, shook his hand. "You need me, you know how to find me."

"Thanks." He meant it.

Gray glanced at his watch. Peyton was still getting her

massage. He thought about joining her, but she need private time and, relaxed, maybe her memory would return.

I know a better way to get her to relax.

He shifted in his seat, thinking about it. Ever since he took this assignment, he'd been professional. Aloof at times. Necessary for the job and to be impartial. But now that he'd managed to relax a little, he had time. Time to think about Peyton and that kiss in the women's room. Her mouth, all soft and sweet, pressed against his, her breasts tight against his chest. Couldn't think, couldn't breathe, only let his body take over and his cock strain eagerly against his shorts.

It was like a switch had been turned on, allowing his hormones to finally claim what his mind had resisted since the day he rang the doorbell at the Bradley house and Peyton answered, all long blond hair flowing past her shoulders, her incredible blue gaze locked to his, her figure curvy and outlined in a sundress with big orange flowers. It had taken him a minute to recover his composure and stop staring. But man, he'd had his share of women and Peyton Bradley was different. It wasn't her beauty or her self-confidence or the smile lighting up her pretty face that day.

It was the way she'd leaned forward toward him, as if she'd felt the same, her eyes widening and her breath hitching…a moment of pure connection neither of them ever felt before. Even with Andrea, yeah the sex was terrific and he'd loved her, but in a distant, selfish kind of manner. He hadn't felt anything like that first moment he'd seen Peyton.

Peyton made him want to toss aside all his personal concerns and do whatever he could to make her happy. See that smile again. It was like he'd lived in an inky-black prison cell since Andrea's murder and suddenly he was free, out in the blinding, warm sunshine.

Yet she was a client, and his cool, calm professionalism took over. He hadn't been a SEAL without knowing how to shove aside feelings and bodily needs. The same training worked well with his past few assignments for Jarrett.

Until this moment, when he finally could breathe a little, knowing they weren't being tailed and she was safe. Upstairs. In a hotel room with one bed. Peyton, whose kiss could slay all his resolve and shatter his cool exterior with her heat. He ached to touch her soft skin, run his hands over her body and tangle with her between the Egyptian cotton sheets.

He shouldn't leave her alone for long. It was time to surrender to this wild sexual attraction binding them together in an invisible rope of hormones. Gray gulped down his drink and, taking the suitcases, headed for the elevator. He soldiered on, ready to meet his fate in the bedroom.

Peyton stretched out on the king-size bed, languid with bliss. The Swedish massage had only been thirty minutes, but it worked out all the kinks in her tensed muscles. Add a hot wax for a finishing touch and all the ugliness of the past few days had peeled off with the wax.

The room key clicked and Gray walked inside, wheeling two suitcases. He set them in a corner and dropped an envelope on the table.

Eyes half-closed, she watched him.

Forget falling asleep. Gray tugged off his T-shirt, showing tanned muscles along his back, along with a few nicks. Battle scars, she guessed. As he turned, her lady parts began paying real attention. His stomach was flat, ribbed with muscle, and his chest had a sprinkling of black hair stretching from one small brown nipple to another. Just enough to tantalize.

Peyton's breath hitched as he caught sight of her staring

at him. He did not smile, but caught her gaze with his own, the heat smoldering in his dark eyes. She sat up, knowing her nipples clearly showed through the thin cotton shirt.

He glanced at them, a muscle ticking in his cheek. Gray inhaled a deep breath as he opened a suitcase and removed a shirt and tugged it on. Disappointment filled her. She liked him with his shirt off.

"How was the massage?"

"Perfect. Relaxing." Peyton gave a long stretch, knowing he watched her like a hungry man at a buffet.

She wanted him, and by his reaction, the need was mutual. But instead of joining her on the bed, he went to the table and picked up the envelope.

"New IDs for you. Mrs. Peyton Jones. Driver's license, two credit cards. You have your own money now."

Peyton climbed out of bed and fingered the twenty fifty-dollar bills. The cash and cards spilled from her fingers. "You did this for me?"

Gray's steady gaze met hers. "Money gives you freedom and independence. I don't want you to lose yours, Peyton. You said you feel tethered to me by lack of money. I want you tethered to me in a different way…by finally giving in to this thing between us, this attraction that made us kiss in the damn bathroom as if we were two hormone-crazed schoolkids."

As he tucked a strand of hair behind her ear, she drank in the sight of him, the serious look always on his face, the slight scar that she found so sexy, his dark eyes filled with heat.

"You're very direct."

"Life's too short for me not to state what I want, and go after it." He gave her a pointed look. "Shall we eat out or order room service?"

She licked her mouth again. "Room service sounds terrific to me."

* * *

The meal had been delicious, but food wasn't on his mind. Gray set the tray in the hallway. When he returned inside, locking the door, Peyton stood near the bed in sleep shorts and a sleeveless flowered shirt. The bedcovers had been turned down and her eyes were bright with anticipation.

She snapped off all the lights but one, plunging the room into dimness. Hell yeah.

Gray went to her. He ran a thumb along her lower lip, making her tremble. Peyton leaned forward, kissed him gently. They kept kissing, as he deepened the kiss, his tongue moving between her lips. Peyton fumbled with his belt buckle, drawing it out of his jeans. Oh yeah, he didn't need a GPS to see where this was headed.

Too impatient, he stepped back and in his eagerness, almost popped buttons off his shirt, then tugged it off. Gray kicked off his shoes, removed socks and jeans, tossing them aside. She sat on the bed, her hungry gaze devouring him. In his black boxer briefs, he joined her, taking her into his arms and kissing her.

It felt so right, so good. Hell, he couldn't remember the last time he'd had a woman in his arms he cared about. Since Andrea's death, he'd shied away from relationships. Sex was only to ease his body's needs and the women he'd dated knew his terms up-front.

They usually vanished after a night or two, wanting the same thing he did.

Not with Peyton. He cared about her, maybe too much. Gray kissed her, his body ready and straining toward her. He rolled over to his side, cupping her breasts and gently kneading them to arouse her.

With an impatient sound, she sat up, and pulled off her sleep shirt. Her breasts were full, the nipples erect. Gray drew her into his arms, kissing her again, his blood racing. He caressed her body as he dropped tiny kisses along her neck and shoulder, then he climbed atop her, his hands on her wrists as he stared down at her. Ready for this.

But as he lowered his head to kiss his way down her perfect, soft body, her gaze went from glazed with passion to sparking with panic. Barely had he registered the change when she writhed beneath him.

"No, no, stop it! Get off me, get off!"

Damn! Immediately he slid off her perspiring body. He held up his hands, palms out. "Peyton. I'm not going to hurt you. I'm not touching you anymore. It's okay, sweetheart."

Gulping down breaths of air, she was too pale, too upset. What the hell happened? Insight struck him.

Gray slid to the bed's edge, careful not to touch her and send her into distress again. "Peyton, were you raped?"

Huge eyes met his. A head shake. Relief spiraled through him. Then he asked the second question he dreaded knowing.

"Did he threaten to rape you?"

This time, she nodded, tears streaming from her eyes. Gray released a volley of curses. He went and fetched his shirt, wrapping her in it, and made a snap decision.

"I'm taking you home. It's for the best. I didn't realize..."

The trauma she'd suffered had been buried deep. *I can't help her.* The realization hurt deep.

Peyton grabbed his arm. "No! Please. I know I should talk to someone about this, but I don't trust anyone yet. Except you. I can't go back yet. I feel like I'm starting to remember, and I've buried everything, but you're helping me remember. If I go home, I feel like I'll lose all the progress I've made so far with you at my side. I have to find my life again."

He hesitated. "Peyton, you're better off with family, and

a therapist who can cull the memories and help you heal. I can't do that."

She refused to let go, and implored him with a pleading look. "I don't need my family hovering over me or a stranger telling me how to heal. I need you. My GPS. Please, Gray. Don't send me away because of this. I'll be fine, I will."

"Sweetheart…"

"Promise!"

"Shh. I promise. I won't send you away."

She shivered. "I'm afraid to go to sleep now."

Gray thought a moment. "Try this. Empower yourself through active daydreaming. Imagine the person who hurt you, and then imagine you controlling the situation. You're attacking him and hurting him."

Her mouth wobbled. "I'll try. But I need you, Gray. Stay with me. I need you." She burst into tears, healing tears, not the inconsolable panic exhibited earlier.

He held her tight against his chest, letting her sob, letting her release all her anguish as he silently vowed to find her kidnapper and deal him a little justice of his own. Even though he already had a tarnished rep, it didn't matter.

We'll find him. I promise you, and when I do…

He's a dead man.

Chapter 17

The following morning, they were on the road again, but Gray made a short stop in Miami. He left his Mercedes at the Miami airport and then they took the rental car bus to a nearby rental car agency. Using one of his credit cards and identification cards under another name, Gray rented a sport utility vehicle. Ever cautious, he didn't want his own vehicle tracked.

Richardson was on the run from a loan shark. He did not wish to be found. Gray would find him.

Peyton had fallen asleep in his arms, her eyes swollen from crying, her lips puffy. He'd asked her if she'd wanted to talk about it, but she did not. So he let it go.

As they drove on the Overseas Highway, Peyton seemed more relaxed, looking at the water, the breeze from the open window billowing her long hair. Gray filled in the silence by talking about the beauty of the Florida Keys and the excellent fishing and diving.

He'd made a reservation at a hotel on the Atlantic with

a beach, a pool and lounge chairs set beneath an array of coconut palm trees. During his tours overseas as a navy SEAL, he'd learned patience and planning. Jace was tracking down Richardson's correct address, which would take a couple of days. In the meantime, he and Peyton would establish a presence as a married couple enchanted with the tropical allure of sunshine and water in the Keys.

They arrived at the hotel midafternoon and checked in at the tiny front office. Gray took the key and drove Peyton to their designated parking spot. She climbed out, stretched and gazed around.

Gray removed the two small suitcases from the vehicle and rolled them over, then inserted the key into the lock of the oceanfront suite. He cautioned her to remain outside. It didn't take him long to inspect the room. No hidden cameras, no microphones. Safe enough.

For now.

Peyton brightened as she went inside and he wheeled the two suitcases into the room. A small kitchenette was tucked into a corner, and a sofa sat beneath a bank of windows. The white paint, beach-theme bedspread and beach decor made the suite bright and airy. Then she saw the king-size bed and glanced at him.

Gray's heart raced at the tentative hope in her eyes. "There's a sofa. I'll take that."

For now, he silently vowed.

Peyton wheeled her suitcase to the sofa, and began unpacking. "How long are we staying here?"

"Three nights. Tomorrow we have a reservation for the turtle hospital. I thought you'd like it, and it might help to shake free more memories."

"Do I have time for a swim before dinner?" She shook free the bikini she'd purchased in Vero Beach. "Because that pool looks mighty tempting. Diving would be great because the Keys offer terrific dive spots, but I don't have my wetsuit or my tanks…"

Her voice trailed off. She rubbed her temple. "Diving. Did I like to dive?"

"Did you?" Gray unzipped his suitcase and pulled out some personal items, putting them on the white dresser.

"I must have, if I'm a sea turtle biologist." Peyton opened her suitcase and put her undergarments in the top drawer along with his.

He wondered if she realized how naturally she'd taken to doing this.

Gray pulled out a pair of navy swim trunks from his suitcase. "I think a swim sounds excellent. It will help you relax and maybe recall some additional memories."

She slammed the drawer shut. "I'm tired of trying to make my brain work on recalling memories. Can't I swim just to have a little fun? Pretend this is a vacation for a little while?"

The sudden outburst made him realize he had been pressuring her, perhaps too much. "Of course."

Swim trunks in hand, he vanished into the bathroom to change his clothing. When he emerged, Peyton stood there in her shorts and sleeveless tank top, staring at her swimsuit.

"Everything seems so contrived. Even my clothing doesn't seem familiar, all this new stuff. It's like I'm a stranger wearing someone else's life."

Her words stopped him in his tracks. Nothing in his plans had accounted for her feelings, the wild seesaw of emotions she must be experiencing after the trauma of escaping her captor.

If he could have her kidnapper at his hands, he'd break his neck. Gray squeezed her shoulders gently. The move seemed to soothe her in the past, but not today. Tension radiated from her in waves.

"I'm sorry it feels like I'm rushing you through the process. Let's swim. No pressure, no trying to remember anything. Just two people enjoying this perfect weather."

Big blue eyes met his. "Thanks."

She vanished into the bathroom with her bikini in hand.

I need to slow it down a little for her emotional wellbeing. She was almost raped by a man who wanted to kill her. Why would she want to recall that trauma? I'm asking her to recall the worst moments of her life.

Peyton emerged a few minutes later. The blue-and-white-striped bikini made him bite back a groan. Damn she was sexy. He hoped the pool was cold. He needed cold water. Hell, a bucket of ice water would be great at tamping down his sudden arousal.

"Gray, I never did thank you for all you're doing for me. Everything you've done is to help me, not hurt me. I'm sure it is coming at great personal cost to you. I mean, taking this time away from your work and loss of income. My family is supposed to be wealthy, so I'm sure they will compensate you."

Nothing like a woman indicating he was poor to dampen his ardor. He almost laughed. Peyton thought he was struggling for money.

Trying to keep a straight face, he shrugged. "Thanks. Appreciate it. But I'm good."

Her needs, not his, came first. Needed to make sure she was okay with their plans for the next few days.

"Peyton, there's still time for me to return you home if you're uncertain about being here alone with me."

Because that outburst in bed and her heartbreaking sobs still echoed in his mind. She'd been hurt enough. He wouldn't cause her any additional pain.

She picked up a striped pool towel, draped it over her arm. "I'm not. I'm fine as long as you're around. Let's go."

The pool water was warm from the constant sunshine. Gray treaded water as Peyton did laps. He surveyed the hotel. Small mom-and-pop place, but the suite was large and offered a splendid view of the ocean and a nearby pier and tiki hut. Only two other guests were there, the owner had informed him. It was midweek, and summer, off-season in the Keys. Lobster season wouldn't begin for another two months.

Satisfied they had privacy, he dived beneath the water, hovered for a few seconds and, as Peyton swam, kicked upward and grabbed her foot. Squealing, she kicked free as he playfully pulled her downward.

They splashed each other and then Gray grabbed her around the waist. "Gotcha."

Peyton didn't struggle. Instead she reached down and cupped his groin. Lightly squeezed. His eyes went wide and he went instantly hard. Holy crap. She caressed him again and his entire body went rigid with need.

She winked, then swam off as he groaned. Damn.

When they climbed out of the pool, she had a knowing look on her face. Struggling to find his wits and regain his composure, he climbed out as she sat on a lounge chair. Peyton gave him a serene smile.

"I told you I'll be fine as long as you're around."

The seductive promise in that smile made his groin ache further. Gray headed for the freshwater shower used to rinse off salt water. He ran it for a moment and then the water turned cooler. After standing beneath it for a moment, he could think.

Almost.

He joined her on another chaise lounge and they lazed

in the sun for a few moments. Then they headed inside. Gray dried off while Peyton showered.

After dressing in black board shorts and a blue polo shirt, he pulled free his laptop that Jace had tucked into the suitcase. He glanced at Peyton, sitting on the bed in white shorts and a turquoise shirt that echoed the blue in her eyes.

"I have a little work to do. The Wi-Fi signal's strong enough, so I'm going outside."

She glanced at the laptop as if it were a snake. "I thought we were going to pretend we're on vacation."

"I'm always working, even on vacation, sweetheart."

Two white rockers overlooked the Atlantic and the beach. Towering sea grape trees provided shade for a picnic table and lounge chairs. Gray accessed the Wi-Fi, then went on his VPN to ensure a secure channel. He looked at the world news, checked the portfolios his father wanted him to look over, considered the risks and made a few trades, then emailed his father.

His father emailed back immediately. Good to hear from you. All okay? Can you talk?

Peyton watched the placid pelicans sitting atop dock pilings. He emailed back.

No, but text or email me if something critical pops up. How's Mom?

Good, the reply came. She's worried about you.

His mother worried about him. She might fret publicly about getting her nails manicured for a social event or how her new shoes did not quite match the dress she'd bought for a black-tie dinner, but it was all superficial. Her true concern lay with her three children. His older brothers,

Jon and Gary, were investment analysts. Both married, with children. Gray was the youngest and the maverick.

The black ops sheep, Jon always joked. Jon, who worked for their family's business, was conservative and predictable. His wife and children were as stoic. They didn't quite know what to make of "quiet Uncle Gray, who makes bad guys go away."

Still, they loved him as fiercely as he loved them back. They were blood. Family.

Shutting down his laptop, he looked at Peyton, smiling as a pelican flew over the water. He understood her father's obsession to keep her safe and her family's worry.

I won't let anything happen to you.

The fierceness of that thought startled him. It was more than his failure when Andrea died. This felt richer, deeper and more emotional than dedication to an assignment. Contentment filled him. Maybe this was meant to be.

"Do you think moments like this, that seem perfect, are a gift to counter the bad times when they come? Lately I've been thinking that I got a second chance at life, and I don't want to waste a single minute, Gray. Because you never know how long you'll have." She hugged her knees as she rocked back and forth. "I may not remember much about what happened to me, but I could have died that day."

Damn. Contentment vanished as he set aside the laptop. "Every day above ground is a gift, Peyton. It's a tough lesson to learn."

Gray understood, because he'd learned it as well, but he'd experienced more of life's hard moments in his military career.

If you didn't get tough, you'd let your guard down and the enemy could wound you. Or kill you. Or when you returned from a tour of duty, the haunting memories could immobilize you. One of his friends never fully recovered after a mission. Gray tried to help him with words of advice and financial assistance, but only after agreeing to get extensive counseling, which Gray paid for, did his friend finally start to recover.

She was a rare creature herself, not caring that she had ruined a designer dress that night on the beach during the gala, and refusing to hide from the trauma of her kidnapping.

Wanting to coax her out of this mood, he considered their dining options. "How about the Lorelei for dinner tonight? They have excellent seafood and a terrific sunset."

Her smile lit up her entire face. "I love that place. I've always eaten there or had drinks when I visited the Keys. The mahi-mahi tacos are fantastic."

"Good. Shall we?"

As he took the laptop inside and grabbed the car keys, Gray wondered if she realized she'd started to recall more memories. Perhaps they wouldn't only find Richardson on this trip. Maybe Peyton would find herself again as well.

Dressed in black board shorts and a green-and-red tropical shirt with parrots, Gray looked like a tourist. Peyton had to laugh. The serious Gray had vanished, replaced with a man whose company she enjoyed more and more.

She twirled around, displaying her white sundress with pink flamingos as they headed for the vehicle. "I sense a theme here."

Gray smiled. "You look lovely."

As she basked in the compliment, he added, "Good choice. We look like a married couple on vacation."

Her enjoyment faded a little. Of course. Part of his job—looking the part. Suits when he was the shadow, and this to act the part of their disguise.

Peyton wondered who the real Gray was, alias or no alias.

At the restaurant, they seated themselves at one of the tables shaded with bright turquoise umbrellas. Sunset was not for an hour, so the outdoor restaurant wasn't crowded. Peyton scuffed the sand beneath her open-toed white sandals. A beach for a floor... Something else tugged at her memory.

Not the horrific memory of her abductor jeering at her as he pinned her down, feeling her with his hands, grinding himself against her...something else that happened prior to that horror. A phone call. She remembered now. He had to leave. He knocked her out and then he must have left.

That's when I escaped. The thought comforted her. She hadn't been a helpless victim.

They ordered tropical drinks, a mai tai for her and a rum punch for him, and they both agreed the mahi-mahi fish tacos sounded delicious. Gray leaned back in his chair, studying the water. Sailboats moored in the bay rocked peacefully with the tide, their masts soaring upward like exclamation points.

"I remember the first time I saw you in a sundress," he mused. "It was white with big orange sunflowers. You took my breath away."

Peyton's own breath hitched. "I did? Did you do the same to me?"

He gave a lopsided grin. "I don't think so. I was wearing a business suit with a red tie and you looked at me as if I were a process server."

She laughed. "I doubt it."

When the waiter served their drinks, she lifted hers.

"To us," she said.

Gray looked surprised, then smiled. "To us."

The balmy breeze and the turquoise water soothed her. Palm fronds rustled overhead as shorebirds combed the

Gulf waters. The cloudless blue sky and the warm sun made for a perfect day.

Gray pointed out a black cormorant fluffing his wings as he rested on a piling. He talked about the birds in a deep, soothing voice.

"Every time I go fishing, I try to clean up whatever plastic or trash I find on the water." He shook his head. "It's horrific how many water bottles you'll find in the ocean."

"Single-use plastics are deadly to sea turtles."

Gray fell silent, simply gazing at the water.

"I know this. I was dedicated to eradicating single-use plastics in my family…"

She rubbed her now-healed temple and frowned. "Baby sea turtles, hatchlings, can ingest tiny bits of plastic floating into brown seaweed… No, it's called sargassum. They stay there and eat what they can find and plastic gets caught in the sargassum. Trash is deadly to hatchlings. Even cigarette butts… Why can't people stop littering?"

He didn't ask if her memory was returning. Peyton found that more reassuring than the fact she recalled bits and pieces from the past.

On a nearby stage, musicians played Jimmy Buffett songs. It was almost a cliché, being in the Keys with tropical drinks, sand and Buffett songs. Peyton watched a boat drift past. A couple at the next table talked of their day on the water and the loggerhead sea turtle they saw while scuba diving. Wistfully she thought of what it would be like to experience seeing one of those magnificent creatures.

I wonder if it was Jolly, the turtle we released last year.

The thought startled her. It came out of the blue, a streak of recall fleeting, but there.

Peyton closed her eyes, trying to imagine what it would

be like to dive. Pressure, weights, buoyancy compensator, *mine was bright pink…*

She was swimming through the warm, shallow waters on a drift dive when she saw her. Jolly, the turtle released only hours before. It was like Jolly returned to say goodbye, her large head coming close, liquid gaze meeting Peyton's behind her mask.

Jolly bumping her before swimming off into the deeper waters of the Atlantic, pulled by thousands of years of instinct. But in those brief few moments, they had connected.

Peyton's eyes flew open. She drew in a breath.

"What's wrong?" he asked quietly.

She smiled. "Nothing. I had a memory of a sea turtle. I was here before, Gray. A group of us from the institute drove down to the turtle hospital last year to watch the release of a loggerhead. I'd discovered her in distress while diving in the Keys on vacation. They invited us to join the release. Martin, myself, Adam, Claudia and Riff, one of the interns. We released Jolly on the boat and then we dove and watched her take off into deeper water."

"It must have been a magnificent sight, watching a turtle swim freely, knowing she was rescued."

She watched him intently. "Like how you rescued me. Not to keep me a prisoner, but to set me on my own path."

The quick smile he offered assured her he'd done exactly that. Recalling memories tugged her closer to her old life. She looked at Gray, his piercing gaze and handsome face, his air of authority and quiet confidence, and Peyton wondered.

Was her old life worth returning to if he was not in it?

Gray had been a perfect gentleman, letting Peyton have the bed while he slept on the sofa. Much as he wanted to explore the attraction between them, she needed rest. After dinner she'd seemed distracted, as if the memories of the turtle release bothered her. She'd asked to find a drugstore and asked for privacy to look at "feminine items." Gray had left her alone while she made her purchases.

To further give the impression they were tourists on vacation, Gray took her on a long drive to explore the middle Keys the next day. Their reservation to tour the turtle hospital wasn't until a couple of hours after lunch.

"Can we stop? I want to sit by the water," Peyton said.

A few miles down the road, he spied a small oceanfront park and pulled into the sandy lot.

Peyton clambered out with the eagerness of a child at recess. Seeing her finally lose the tension gripping her in Clearwater and Vero Beach was like watching sunrise. It did something for his soul.

He joined her at the water as she sat at a picnic table, gazing at the turquoise water. The beach was little more than a narrow strip of sand, but other than a family of four picnicking at another table, they were alone.

Peyton jumped up from the table and went to the water's edge, squatting down and touching it. The family, finished with their picnic, began packing up. The man went to the water close to Peyton, and Gray's awareness pricked. Still, he didn't want to crowd her, act overzealous. If something happened, he'd be there in seconds. Or shout.

The father looked around covertly, then reached into his pocket. Gray watched as he pulled out a pack of cigarettes and lit one. He smoked without the leisurely attitude of one enjoying an after-meal cigarette. Peyton glanced at him, returned her attention to the water.

He wondered what she studied.

The woman called to the man to help her. Sighing, the father shook his head, pitched the still-lit cigarette into the water. The white cylinder floated, a stark exclamation point of trash.

Peyton jumped up. Scowled. Retrieved the now-extinguished butt. As the man started to walk off, she confronted him, shaking the stub at him like a teacher with a pointer.

"Hey. Do you know what you just did, litterbug? I don't care if you smoke, but do not throw your cigarette butts into the ocean! Thousands of pounds of trash go into the ocean."

The father shrugged. "So? It's just one cigarette."

Here we go. You're in for it now. Gray compressed his lips in a tight smile, wishing he had popcorn to enjoy the show.

Peyton's gaze rounded. "Just one cigarette? Do you know what this does in the ocean? It floats and gets caught in sargassum, brown seaweed, where baby sea turtles hide after they hatch. The seaweed protects them from predators and the babies eat the seaweed as part of their diet. Along with eating the sargassum, they ingest whatever else gets trapped in the grass. Get it? That includes plastic. Trash. Cigarette butts! A baby sea turtle is going to eat your trash! It's going to get caught in his stomach and he'll most likely die before he's had a chance to live."

By now the man's children came over to watch. Peyton continued her tirade, shaking the butt at the man and asking if he wanted his children to bathe in water surrounded by old, soggy cigarette butts.

"I don't wanna bathe with that," the girl cried out. "Daddy, why do we have to take a bath with that?"

"Daddy, why are you killing baby turtles?" the boy asked.

The man's mouth opened and closed. Gray joined Peyton, saying nothing. The father glanced at his children, then glared at Peyton.

"You're scaring my kids," he snapped.

"They should be scared. With your actions, you're polluting the world they will inherit one day."

The man's expression went from angry to embarrassed. Gray almost felt sorry for him. Almost.

As a final resort, the father looked at Gray with a pleading look, man-to-man. "Hey, buddy, can you get her off my case?"

Gray shook his head. The father's gaze narrowed. "Are you gonna jump all over me, too?"

Gray pointed to the sign that clearly stated No Littering. "Not necessary. I'd dispose of that butt properly if I were you. I can think of better ways to spend $500, maybe a nice dinner with your family instead of paying a fine."

Red-faced, the man grabbed the cigarette butt from Peyton and walked over to the receptacle set aside for such trash. He hustled his children to a car that had seen better days, as his wife began to scold him for smoking when he promised to quit.

As they drove off, Gray turned to Peyton. She was not smiling.

"I guess I was a little excessive."

He cupped her face with his hands. "You were magnificent. I daresay he'll think twice about littering again."

Her shoulders lifted. "Does it do any good? Does it really make a difference that I stopped one man from littering and perhaps killing one sea turtle hatchling?"

Gray thumbed her soft cheek. "It makes a difference to the one you probably saved."

The courage of her convictions showed her true personality. Peyton might have lost her memory and didn't remember who she was, but the heart of her remained. He kept touching her, enjoying the texture of her smooth skin beneath his fingertips. Such a marvel, this woman. She'd been through hell and despite the trauma she'd suffered, retained her passion for what mattered most to her.

Not her own needs, but the needs of animals and the world around them.

Frowning, she pulled away from his touch, rubbing her temple. Lately she'd been doing that more often. He suspected it happened when a memory was triggered.

"What's in the water that you were looking at?" he asked.

"Nothing. I don't know." Her frown deepened. "I was looking for signs of trash...seeing if people tossed plastic or soda cans in the water. I remember a study I'd read about hermit crabs being attracted to a chemical additive used in plastics because it's the same smell as their food... It really bothered me. I think...after that I helped organize a beach cleanup that my work sponsored. On the mainland, at a public beach not far from my home. It must have been in the past few years because I clearly remember that study being recent."

Encouraged, he asked her about the beach cleanup.

But she shook her head and the despondent expression returned. "It's too fuzzy."

The doctor said her memory would return as quickly as it vanished. Whoever wanted Peyton dead still searched for her and wouldn't rest until she was cold in her grave.

Too many things about this case seemed odd.

It was almost as if someone wanted her dead because she'd witnessed something. But what? The beach was her family's private land.

Unless...

Gray tucked that thought away to entertain later.

She couldn't believe how she'd lectured a stranger on littering. It made her feel good, though.

They got on the road again and had lunch at a seafood restaurant he'd dined at previously. After lunch they drove to the turtle hospital. Gray bluetoothed his cell phone to the vehicle for his Keys playlist. Soon the strains of Jamaican music blared over the speakers. She grinned at him.

"Your favorites?"

"I always play this when I head down here on weekends." He tapped his fingers on the steering wheel to accompany the reggae beat.

"You come to the Keys every weekend?"

"When I can get away."

"Where do you stay?"

He glanced at her. "Lower Keys. It's quiet, and the sunrises on the Atlantic are spectacular."

At the hospital, a staff member named T.J. herded the tour group into the administrative building for a presentation on sea turtles. T.J. was filling in for the educational administrator, who had the day off.

Gray scanned the room, expression blank, but she knew he summed up each of the thirty visitors for threats.

Being around him gave her a sense of peace.

T.J. discussed the variety of sea turtles found off the waters of the United States. She felt a little hopeful. Every day more of her memory returned.

Next, their group gathered outside a surgical suite where veterinarians performed surgery on sick turtles. Nothing clicked here, but glancing at a neatly organized stack of file folders by a sink, she felt a flare of excitement.

"I know this," she murmured. "IDDEX. Blood work analysis. Liver, kidney functions."

"Blood work on the turtles when they are rescued?" Gray asked.

"Triage. Assess the turtle's condition…" Her voice drifted off as the group moved outside.

Memories kept teasing her, gray areas that she felt desperate to recall, but faded the harder she tried.

"Why don't you relax and enjoy the tour," he suggested. "You're trying too hard. It's like forgetting a song title and once you start falling asleep at night, your mind not as focused on trying to recall it, it comes to you."

"It's right there, I can feel it. If I don't recall what happened to me, and who did it, he'll come after me again and this time, I'll die."

"I'm right here and you're safe," he assured her.

T.J. took them to large, circular tanks enclosed by fencing and shaded from the sun. Each tank held a recovering sea turtle.

Gray glanced at her. She shook her head. Nothing. She might as well be watching a National Geographic special.

"*Carretta caretta*," he told her.

"Loggerhead," she replied automatically.

His mouth curled in a satisfied smile. "You're getting there, Peyton. Don't get discouraged."

She beamed at him. "Maybe you're right."

"I'm always right." His mocking smile assured her of his teasing.

"Except when it comes to getting directions."

He gave her a mock scowl. "Do not question my judgment, oh user of phone apps. My navigational abilities are mystic and require no satellite transmissions."

"Except when you get lost trying to find a gas station."

He grinned. "That wasn't getting lost. It was taking the scenic route."

Their group moved to an enclosure filled with seawater and netting to house the turtles that could never return to the wild. Each guest was given pellets to feed the turtles. Peyton tossed hers in, smiling a little as April, a blind turtle, snapped up the treats. A loggerhead turtle with "bubble butt" stuck his head out of the water and breathed. Enchanted, she leaned over the railing.

"Hi, Jammer. How're those weights feeling?"

Peyton blinked. Jammer. She knew this turtle. Remembered him from three years ago… He'd been struck by a boat prop off Sombrero Beach. The injury was so deep the turtle couldn't be treated with conventional methods.

"They used maggots," she muttered, staring at the turtle. "Maggots to clean out the dead tissue and it worked."

A staff member joined T.J. and the guide excused herself. They walked off a little ways. The tour group, talking excitedly about the turtles, snapped photos and pointed to the animals.

Gray walked a short distance away, peering into the water.

Peyton looked up at the newcomer with T.J. just as a woman called out a name in sharp anger.

Her heart raced. Fear immobilized her. She could not breathe and the open-air enclosure seemed to close in around her. She had to get out of here, had to leave, now or he would get her.

Hurt her.

Kill her.

Peyton's mouth opened and closed.

In desperation, she looked for Gray, but another visitor was chatting with him, asking him something about seafood restaurants nearby. Gray glanced at his phone.

Please, please, help me.

She had to flee, run far, far away. Get away because no one and nothing could stop this person. Safety seemed miles away. Peyton backed up against the fence and released a small whimper.

Gray glanced at her, pushed aside his startled companion, then ran to her side immediately. His hands gripped her shoulders.

Her mouth opened and closed again. All she could do was utter a tiny whisper.

"Get me out of here."

Gray wasted no time in hustling her out of the turtle sanctuary. Only when they were on the road, the open windows blowing warm air on her icy cheeks, could she finally breathe normally, the tightness in her chest easing.

"What scared you?" he finally asked when they were a few miles down the road.

She couldn't answer, only hug herself tight.

"I'm taking you back to the room," he told her.

Peyton shook her head, her insides cramping as the fear finally morphed into nausea.

"Pull over. Please!"

He nudged the vehicle onto a sandy shoulder by the water. Not waiting for a complete stop, she opened the door and emptied her stomach of its contents. The excellent fish sandwich, she thought with dim amusement, tasted much better going down.

Gray was at her side, holding back her hair, murmuring to her. When she stopped, he handed her a paper towel and uncapped a bottle of water.

"Better now?" he asked softly.

Peyton nodded. After wiping her face, she sipped water and then took a deep breath, knowing he waited for answers she couldn't quite give him.

"I heard something back there and it triggered a memory. A bad one and I lost it. I'm sorry."

"No apologies necessary. I'm glad you're all right. What did you hear?"

Pain filled her head as she tried to recall. "A name. Martin… I think."

Gray's gaze narrowed. "Martin. When you're ready, let's go."

On the drive back to the hotel, as the icy air-conditioning cooled the sweat on her face, Gray called Jace and told him what happened. He listened, nodded and hung up.

"Jace has a bead on the house where Richardson is staying. He'll find him."

Peyton licked her lips and sipped more water. "How?"

Gray's fingers tightened on the steering wheel. "Using my connections in the Keys. I have a few. The Keys are a tight-knit community."

When they reached the room, he hustled her inside, insisted she lie down and rest. Peyton slid onto the bed. Gray jingled the keys in his hand, seeming to struggle with a decision.

"I need to go to the grocery store, but I hate leaving you alone."

"I'll be fine. A nap will do me some good." And maybe get rid of her headache. She closed her eyes, the pounding in her head easing a little.

"As long as you promise not to leave the room, and call me if anything, and I mean anything, troubles you. I'm right down the road."

She opened one eye. "On one condition. Buy me some cookies. And milk."

His mouth quirked upward. "What kind?"

"Oreos."

Gray sat on the bed, kissed her forehead. "You got it."

After he left, she fell into a light, troubled sleep. Memories of a man, his face blurry, bending over her, threatening her...

Peyton did as Gray suggested. She fantasized about scratching the man's face and kneeing him in the groin. In her mind her attacker screamed in pain.

She smiled.

Then her fantasies turned direction. Instead she imagined Gray, naked, sliding into bed with her, kissing her, arousing her, making her cry out in pleasure instead of pain...

Her smile widened. Still deep into her fantasy, she barely registered a key opening the door. Gray walked inside, carrying bags into the kitchenette. He dumped them on the dining table. Peyton yawned, stretched, eyed him with hunger no groceries could satisfy.

"What did you buy?"

"I thought we'd eat in tonight. I bought scallops at the market, and I make a mean mushroom risotto."

Her mouth watered. "I love risotto."

"A memory?"

"Fact." Peyton felt the day's tension slide off her as she bounded into the kitchen to inspect the groceries.

Pleased Gray had bought her cookies, she grabbed the packet of Oreos and opened them. Gray snatched them from her. "No snacks before dinner."

"I'm hungry now."

"It will be worth the wait." His dark gaze twinkled. "Trust me."

Intrigued, she sat at the dining table to watch him work. The kitchenette was small, but he made efficient use of the space, cleaning the sea scallops, then sautéing them in butter. As he made the risotto, her stomach growled. While Gray busied himself at the stove, she snuck two cookies and tiptoed over to the sofa to munch.

He popped his head out of the kitchenette, gave her a mock scowl. "Oreos don't pair well with a seafood dinner."

"Oreos pair well with everything." She finished licking the inside cream and then devoured the cookie.

"Heathen," he murmured. "Oreos need milk to complete

the epicurean experience and I have a fine vintage to pair with our meal. Not Chateau de dairy cow."

Peyton laughed and licked a few crumbs from her mouth. His gaze darkened as he watched her. Then he vanished into the kitchen again.

A short while later, he instructed her to go outside. On the front porch facing the Atlantic, a small table was set with a white linen cloth, two china plates, two wineglasses, the scallops and risotto and silverware. Gray joined her and pulled out a chair for her.

"This is lovely." She beamed at him. "Thank you. Much better than eating at a restaurant with strangers."

"My sentiments as well."

He served her a large portion. As she slid the fork into her mouth, flavor exploded on her tongue. Peyton moaned with pleasure. "This is delicious. I feel like my mouth has experienced a first-class orgasm."

Gray's mouth twitched as she felt herself turn bright red. "Sorry. That was crude."

"No, it was the finest compliment I've received on my performance in the kitchen." His piercing dark gaze met hers, heat flaring there as if he subtly indicated his performance in the bedroom was equally superb.

The chemistry between them flared like a sizzling electrical wire. Peyton felt as if she'd been granted a rare second chance in life. Gray rescued her and where others pondered what should be done, he hadn't hesitated in springing into action.

That leap forward had saved her life.

Sliding her hand across the table, she gripped his palm. He recoiled a minute, looking startled. "Thank you for saving me, Gray. I'm alive today because of what you did."

His hand was slightly calloused beneath her trembling fingers. Gray looked down, nodded and then removed his hand, but first gave her palm a small squeeze. As if the moment had become too intense for words.

She focused instead on the dinner, changing the subject to cooking and how he'd selected the scallops and prepared them. He poured wine from the bottle sitting on the table.

"Try the wine. Pinot Noir 2018. Usually I serve white with seafood, but since you already ate dessert for dinner, we shall be heathens."

Peyton examined the bottle. "This looks familiar. You sure you didn't purchase this at the grocery store?"

The wounded look on his face made her laugh. "I'm joking, Gray."

After Gray poured two glasses, he handed her one. "Wine this exquisite is meant to be savored, not gulped down like beer at a sports bar."

They sipped. Her palate tingled with the wonderful flavor.

"What a distinguished, flavorful wine." Another memory flickered—tasting wine at her family's annual summer July Fourth dinner when her father's best friend brought a few bottles from his cellar. "This tastes as if it's private stock."

"Mine." Gray sipped again. "I have a small but exclusive collection."

How could he afford it? "Have you collected for a long time?"

"A few years. I enjoy a fine wine and started acquiring bottles from various vineyards."

"On your salary?"

Peyton clapped a hand over her mouth and felt color flood her face. "Sorry. Usually I'm more tactful. At least I believe my parents raised me to be more polite. I think. This wine… It must run about one hundred dollars a bottle."

Gray's mouth twitched as if he found her amusing.

"Try three hundred dollars. And as an executive protection agent, I would find my budget severely strained by purchasing more than a few bottles. But soon as my assignment with you is over, Peyton, I'm leaving SOS."

"Why? Because of what happened to me?" She set down her glass, deeply troubled by the idea of Gray quitting. Troubled even more by the idea of never seeing him again.

"You're good at what you do, Gray. You found me, and without you, I might be…"

As her voice trailed off, something flickered in his dark gaze. "Don't go there, Peyton. I promised to be your shadow and I never back down from a promise. I knew I would find you. But thank you for your confidence in me."

He glanced at the dark red vintage as if hiding his emotions. "Few have it, due to my reputation. You're one and Jarrett Adler, the owner of SOS, is another."

Peyton sensed a deeper level to Gray. "Then why leave? Give it a chance."

"This assignment was a last favor to Jarrett. I knew him from my navy days, served with him during two tours."

"Where will you go and what will you do?"

The enigmatic look he gave her signified he was about to tell her something significant.

"Back home. My father is chief executive officer for a large hedge fund. I investigate various investment opportunities for the firm. You might say I'm his research assistant." Gray swirled the vintage, studying the deep red color. "My enjoyment lies in investing in wine ETFs."

Fascinated by the revelation, she shook her head. "Sorry. I don't know what that is."

His gaze flicked to her. "You did. You actually told me about them."

A flush heated her face. "I did? I told you…and that's your area of expertise. Goodness, was I a snob?"

He smiled. "Far from it. You had no idea of my private life. ETFs are exchange-traded funds. Almost like a mutual fund, but an ETF has lower expense ratios and contains a variety of investments. Even commodities not typically found in the market, such as wine."

"Like this vintage." She picked up her glass.

"I found this winery on a tour of Napa Valley after I left the navy." Gray sipped some more. "I added a few bottles to my cellar."

Peyton sniffed the wine, inhaling the fragrance of cherries, blackberries and other rich fruit. She swirled the liquid, then sipped.

"To truly appreciate the flavor, swish it in your mouth. As if you're gargling mouthwash."

Nearly spitting out the wine with her giggle, she swallowed. "It's wine!"

"Swishing it in your mouth opens the flavor, spreads the wine to all your taste buds so you can fully experience it." Gray demonstrated.

She felt awkward but took another, larger sip and tried. Her palate exploded with the rich flavor. Letting it linger on her tongue after a minute, she finally swallowed.

"You're right! It feels as if my entire mouth is filled with berries."

He gave his first real smile of the night. "It's the best way to savor the flavor. Some things in life are meant to be enjoyed…slowly."

Gray's hooded, seductive gaze met hers. Her body tingled, and she felt warm, relaxed and yet so aware of him.

They finished dinner and went to the porch railing to watch the water. Gray did not sit, but took her hand. Peyton gazed at him, and then he kissed her.

His kiss was tender, so gentle it felt like a velvet brush against her mouth.

But she wanted more. She needed to show him she wasn't afraid. Not of him, her shadow who did everything to make her feel safe.

"Let's go inside." His voice was hoarse, filled with the same raw need she felt.

Once inside, Peyton went for her purse. She pulled free the purchases made at the drugstore. They landed on the table. He picked up a foil pocket, a question in his dark gaze.

"I want you, Gray." She felt heat rise to her cheeks. "I wasn't sure of what size to get, so I got them all."

A light laugh as he selected one condom, mischief now dancing in his eyes.

"Don't hold back on me, Gray. I can take what you want to give."

The thud of shoes falling to the hard floor was followed by the rasp of his zipper sliding downward. He undressed in a hurry. Peyton tore off her own clothing as he slid the condom over his erection.

Naked, they rolled onto the bed together.

His hands stroked over her skin slowly, with tenderness and possession. Her heightened senses took in the warmth of his skin, the masculine scent of him, the salty taste of his skin beneath her tongue as she licked his collarbone. He took her mouth again, demanding, insistent. Savage possession was in each deliberate thrust of his tongue. Wet heat gathered between her thighs. She ached, her body hot and yearning.

Gray dropped kisses across her naked flesh, each kiss inflaming her and pushing her desire higher. Deep inside, a tiny fear still lingered. Yet she trusted him, trusted this.

He put his hand between her legs and stroked, so gentle and deliberate. His fingers slid between her soaked folds. Clutching his muscled shoulders as he touched her aching, shivering flesh, she arched her back, giving herself over

to pure sensation. Each caress erased past fears. He slid
a finger deep inside her, teased. Fire mounted inside her,
licking and then roaring into an inferno. Peyton arched and
cried out his name as she shattered. When her body finally
ceased shuddering her climax, she saw frank satisfaction
gleam in his eyes as he mounted her, his intent clear.

Gray quivered, as if desire to touch and claim her as
his own had overtaken all his control. As if he threatened
to spiral out of control. Panting, Peyton tried to wriggle
free of him. He stopped.

"It's okay, sweetheart. You're in control."

The deep timbre of his voice echoed in her ear. He slid
a hand down her thigh, then rolled off her, onto his back.

"Ride me, Peyton. You've got this," he said in his deep
voice.

Desire nudged her into mounting him. Her Gray, who
would never hurt her. Peyton slid down on his throbbing
erection. A low groan tore from his throat as she sheathed
him. Bracing her hands on his muscular chest, she began
to move. Slowly. Each exquisite motion wrung another
groan from him as he reached up and cupped her breasts,
softly kneading them.

She gave a small, sexy pout to mask the tiny anxiety.

Shuttering the thought, she concentrated on teasing.
Drawing pleasure from each slow rise and fall of her hips.
Gray wrapped his hands around her waist, pushing her up-
ward. He let her have control.

For a few minutes more.

Then in an apt move, he flipped her over, spread her
legs open wide. In answer, she kissed him. Then he began
to move, his sure, heavy thrusts creating a delicious fric-
tion. Each slap of his flesh against hers heightened the
pleasure. He trailed his mouth over her neck, lightly licked
her earlobe.

She moved against him, nipping him as she tasted his salty skin. He leaned over, nuzzling her neck, and bit her on the sensitive juncture of her neck. She threw back her head and whimpered with pleasure. Wrapping her legs around him, she met his heavy thrusts as they tangled together. Peyton screamed his name as she climaxed, followed by his hoarse shout.

When they collapsed back onto the bed, she felt sated and satisfied. And knew with growing dismay that this wasn't merely sex.

She had fallen in love with Gray, her protector.

Chapter 18

Though tired the next morning, she felt utterly well-loved and happy. Peyton felt ready to tackle the world and everything in it, including Fletcher Richardson.

Jace had called this morning with an address, after finally tracking down the elusive Richardson. Surely when she saw him, he'd recognize her and her memory would snap back. Little images of memory surged: The times they'd spent sitting on the beach at night, watching and waiting for nesting sea turtles. The stories he'd told about the leatherbacks lumbering onto the sand in Malaysia, like seeing a submarine surface.

However, none of those distant memories were as pleasurable as when Gray had made love to her, with fierce, dedicated devotion. All night long, as he'd promised. Awareness of him sparked like July Fourth fireworks. Oh, there'd been fireworks last night. Even now, she entertained naughty fantasies of climbing all over him and licking him from head to toe like her favorite ice cream flavor. Whatever that was. Blood raced through her body, making her nipples harden and her sex feel soft and ready once more.

As they drove south, Peyton held a small, secret smile. Gray glanced at her, his own smile equally telling. Then the serious Gray returned.

"You ready for this meeting with Richardson? I'm still not convinced I should have taken you along until I checked him out first," he said.

Peyton waved a dismissive hand. "More than ready. I need answers."

She thought a moment. "I want my life back, Gray. I want to make it all complete, and I can only do that by remembering everything that happened to me. Fletcher is key to recovering those memories."

"We made good memories last night," he murmured.

Flushing at the thought of what they'd done in bed, Peyton felt turned on all over again. Gray could talk about the weather in his deep voice and she'd fall into his arms, ready to get naked again. Rain, sun, snow or sleet.

"I want those memories to mingle with the old memories."

He slid her a knowing glance. "There will be more, sweetheart."

Then he went quiet, consulting the directions on his phone's GPS as they neared Richardson's house. He turned off the Overseas Highway down a residential road leading to homes nestled against a deepwater canal.

Even though Peyton couldn't remember much about the Keys, Gray told her he knew these were luxury homes a wandering soul like Richardson couldn't afford. The man was house-sitting for a friend for the summer.

"I can appreciate the lifestyle. I lived here in the Keys when I was trying to find myself again."

She wondered what happened to make him so lost.

"The memories I have, they're of Fletcher. We used to hang out on the beach, watching and waiting for turtles to nest. He's eccentric, but a fun guy."

The two-story concrete home was built on stilts, with parking under the house on the first floor, as many island houses offered. Painted tropical turquoise, it looked welcoming, with white shutters and a garden shaded by coconut palm trees. Gray parked in the brick driveway. A small fishing boat sat on a trailer off to the side, along with a battered sedan.

Gray started to get out of the car, opened the door. Then he hesitated, looking at the house. Not moving.

"What's wrong?"

"Nothing. Everything. I've got a feeling and it isn't good."

Gray pulled out his handgun. Peyton's breath hitched. Oh God, he sensed trouble and even she knew it was too quiet. Her memory pricked. No music blaring from speakers as Fletcher worked on his boat or one of his woodcarvings, singing off-key to some oldies tune from the '60s. No sounds of activity inside the house. Not even a cackle from a seagull swooping down to investigate the half-cleaned fish left on the dock. Her nose wrinkled at the smell. Days-old fish left in the hot sun?

Something was dreadfully wrong. Maybe Fletcher was sick.

"It's too goddamn quiet," he muttered. "Stay behind me."

They went around the back, skirting the pool, and climbed the stairs to the second floor. Heavy hurricane-resistant sliding glass doors showed a living room with a toffee-colored sofa, entertainment set and wide-screen television. The rug on the white tile floor had turquoise and tan accents.

"Don't touch anything." Using the edge of his shirt, Gray opened the slider. "Fletcher Richardson?"

No answer.

The fact the door wasn't locked didn't bother her. She sensed this neighborhood seldom locked doors when the occupants were home. But the stench was thicker now, making her gag. Gray left the door open. The living room was open, airy, with an adjacent, modern kitchen with granite counters and gleaming appliances, rattan chairs pulled up to a breakfast bar where one could dine while looking out at the canal. A pretty house.

But the smell…

Gray held his gun out, cupped in his hands. Peyton's throat tightened with the stench. Maybe Fletcher had left fish out to clean and forgot… He must have forgotten how fish stunk after a little while…

Pointing his gun, Gray rounded the corner, then ground to an abrupt halt. Lowering the gun, he cursed, turned, tried to shield her view.

Peyton pushed past him.

The gleaming white tile extended to the hallway and main bedroom. Heavy, masculine furniture filled the room, and the bed was covered with a duvet with a seashell pattern. It wasn't the bed or the furniture that she spied.

But the blood. Red, viscous, a river streaming from the body on the floor…a man clad in gray shorts, a wrinkled blue shirt with anchors that must have been white but were now painted crimson, and dirty white sneakers.

One lace trailed into the pool of blood. She kept staring at it, seeing the white against the crimson, the life fluid that had leaked out of Fletcher, who lay supine, staring at the ceiling.

Gorge rose up. Peyton clapped a hand over her mouth

and fought her nausea and shock. She ran out of the room, outside, coughing.

Gripping the metal railing, feeling the sun-warmed metal beneath her shaking hands, she tried to keep from retching. Gray hadn't followed her. Oh God, Gray was still inside?

She couldn't do it. Couldn't return, see Fletcher lying on the cold white floor, his body leaking crimson…

Peyton stumbled over to the rattan outdoor sofa and sat, rocking back and forth, holding her stomach. Finally Gray emerged from the house.

"We have to call the police," she said, her voice cracking. "Oh God, who could have done this?"

The handgun was back in its holster, tucked against his lean hip. He helped her stand. "Did you touch anything?"

The railing. She pointed to it and he tugged off his black T-shirt, and wiped the railing before putting it back on. "That'll erase your prints. Come on. Let's go."

Making sure she didn't touch the railing, Peyton headed down the stairs, but at his car, she hesitated. "We can't just leave him here. We have to call the cops."

"I've already been arrested once," he muttered. "Not going there again. You call the cops now, we'll be here for hours while they question us. Don't worry. I have a plan."

Much as he'd wanted to rush out of that house, Gray had remained behind, searching for clues, careful not to disturb the crime scene or leave any fingerprints. A bottle of half-drunk whiskey rested on the nightstand. He guessed that's how someone got the drop on Richardson. The man's body was soaked in blood. He'd been stabbed in several places. Stabbing was personal, indicated someone was mighty pissed off at Richardson.

His wallet had been on the dresser. Nothing much inside,

only a little cash. But after opening a nightstand drawer, he found a receipt for rope.

He photographed it with his phone, his suspicions rising because the hardware store was close to Peyton's home.

Why would the man buy rope last month from a hardware store near Peyton? Unless...

Richardson wasn't innocent. He had a hand in Peyton's kidnapping. He looked further and found a credit card in Richardson's wallet. Not his. Name on the card was one Martin Gauthier.

Martin, Peyton's boss.

Gray called Jarrett, studying the position of Fletcher's body, the lack of defensive wounds on his outstretched hands. Looked like blood on the back of his head. Someone had gotten the drop on Richardson, then stabbed him to death.

Peering under the bed, he found a cracked glass globe the size of a baseball. Blood and hair caked it. He recognized it as the artwork he'd seen on Martin's desk.

"I'm here at Richardson's house. Peyton's outside. Richardson is dead. Stabbed." Quickly he explained to Jarrett what he'd found.

Jarrett cursed. "I'll call the cops."

"No. Don't get involved. I'll call Detective Sims, tell him what I found. I'll have someone else call the local cops."

He hung up.

While driving back to the hotel, he called in a favor of a friend in the Keys. Jane was an old salt, a curmudgeon who disliked almost everyone but her four cats. He'd let her use his Keys home when hers had been destroyed during Irma, and helped her secure a loan to rebuild.

Jane was happy to hear from him, more than willing to call the police about screams she'd heard at the rental house where Fletcher's body lay, and extracted a promise from Gray to stop by for dinner next time he was in town.

"And not getting into trouble," she cackled, then hung up.

Soon as they returned to their room, they packed in a hurry, tossing everything into the suitcases. After checking out, Gray drove back to Miami. He called Detective Sims on the way back.

After returning the rental, they took an Uber to the airport parking lot where he'd left the Mercedes. When he told Peyton about Martin and what he'd found, she grew quiet.

He glanced over. "Do you remember anything about Martin?"

Frowning, she pressed a finger against her temple. "A little, maybe. He came to see me in the hospital. He seems so...ordinary. Businesslike, not like he actually harbored any great feelings for me. He was concerned, but more about if I could return to work eventually. His love really seems to be the institute. You think he kidnapped me and used Fletcher as well?"

"I don't know but it looks suspicious." He softened his voice as he passed a slow-moving recreational vehicle lumbering north. "I'm sorry, sweetheart. I know Fletcher was your friend but it looks like he had a hand in your abduction."

Her face fell. "I thought he was my friend. Is anyone in my corner anymore?"

Gray reached over, squeezed her hand. "I am."

Peyton called her parents, who were delighted to hear she was headed back.

"My parents want to put me on speakerphone so they can talk to you." Glancing at Gray, she did as they asked.

"How's Peyton, Gray? Did she get her memory back?" This from her mother.

Gray raised his brows. "Dr. Bradley, she can answer for herself."

"I didn't, Mom, but I'm remembering some things…"

"Peyton, honey, what's wrong? You sound shaken up," her father said.

She burst into tears. "It…it was horrible. He's dead, Dad. Fletcher's dead. We went to the house where he was staying to talk to him and…someone killed him. Oh God, there was so much blood on the floor…"

Silence for a moment. "You saw the body?" Her father's voice was low with fury.

Realizing her mistake, she backpedaled. "Only for a moment. It's okay. The police were called."

"Peyton, tell us where you are and we'll come pick you up. I know what's best for you and I don't want you with that man anymore," her father snapped.

"We're headed home. Gray's taking me home. I'll see you soon." She hung up.

Gray's jaw tightened.

Too pale and quiet after hanging up with them, Peyton kept twisting her hands. He got it. Her friend, hell the only friend who could tell her what happened and why she'd been mixed up in this mess, was gone. Her friend who hadn't been a real friend after all.

He glanced over and saw her quietly weeping. Fat tears rolled down her soft cheeks. He wanted to pull over, take her into his arms and tell her everything would be okay.

Even though it was not.

Grief was a funny thing. It seized you by the throat at first, and you pushed it aside to deal with stuff. Funerals, wills, arrangements, telling everyone. But it lingered deep down, like a shark lying in wait. The moment you stopped to think, it attacked.

The same way it attacked him when he'd walked into

his home and saw Andrea lying on the floor, beaten to a
bloody pulp, and he'd vowed to do the same to her killer.

He couldn't help Peyton anymore. She needed family
surrounding her.

All he could do was accelerate and speed her home.

Her worried parents met them outside soon as Gray
drove through the front gate. Seeing them, Peyton gripped
her hands tight. Everything had been a dream until this afternoon.

Until seeing the blood on the white tile floor, the body...

Shuddering, she hugged herself. "That could have been
me," she whispered.

"No." Gray parked a short distance from the house,
turned in the seat, his expression fierce. "I promised you,
Peyton. I wouldn't let anything happen to you."

"Can you be sure of that?"

His jaw tightened. "I would, if your father..."

No time to finish his sentence because her parents came
running toward the car. Peyton stepped out and they engulfed her in their arms, forming a tight circle. Basking
in their love and concern, she hugged them equally tight.

Gray wasn't part of the circle. After depositing her suitcase on the driveway and shutting the trunk, he hung back,
waiting. Watching.

Her father finally released Peyton. Splotches of color
darkened his tanned face. Fists bunched, he stalked forward. Gray tensed. Stopping a few feet away, her father
seemed to struggle with his emotions. Get his temper under
control. Finally he lowered his hands, but glared at Gray.

"You promised to protect my daughter and keep her
safe. You led her straight into danger instead. Into a murder scene!"

Peyton started to protest. Gray shot her a warning look,

then studied her father with his cool, dark gaze. "I did. I apologize, sir."

"And she still doesn't have her memory back!"

"Dad, leave him alone. He didn't kill Fletcher." She pushed a hand through her hair. Could her father ever see reason when it came to her welfare? Vaguely she remembered all the past times he insisted he knew what was best for her.

I've never been my own person.

"He shouldn't have taken you to the house. You'd have been better off staying with us, honey."

"Gray never let anything happen to me!"

"He could have!"

Her mother, in control and calm and reasonable, shook her head. "Honey, listen to your father. He only wants what is best for you. We found things out about Gray Wallace, I mean Grayson Mitchell."

It was as if Gray were invisible. Expressionless, he stood nearby in silence as her father berated him. Peyton turned her back on her parents and went to Gray.

"I don't want to lose you. The thought of losing you... I can't bear it." Peyton stared at him, her heart racing as she thought about how he'd stuck to her side all this time. "What do you want to do, Gray? Are you sticking by me? I need a new beginning and I hoped it would be with you. I don't know if I'll ever get my memory back. Or if I even want it back. All I know is that I want you, with me."

Are you going to stand behind your promise to be my shadow?

Gray touched her cheek, his piercing gaze filled with torment. "Peyton, I don't know if I'm the right man for you..."

Her father glowered at him. "Knew it. You made her fall for you, you bastard. You didn't take her on the road to regain her memory and find Richardson. You did it to ensnare her. Tell her, Gray Wallace or Grayson Mitchell, whoever the hell you really are. Tell her who you really are. Tell her about how you got arrested. My daughter deserves the truth."

Her mother shook her head. "Gray's a violent man, Peyton. He killed a man with his bare hands. I want you to stay away from him."

She searched his face, silently pleading for her parents to be wrong. "Gray?"

Gray faced her square-on. "They're right, Peyton. I did commit a violent crime. The truth is… I was arrested for killing my fiancée and her lover."

Her chest went tight. It had to be a mistake. "Gray… Did you kill them? Please, tell me the truth."

As he opened his mouth, her father stepped forward. "The facts are clear. The police found him standing over his fiancée's lover, beating him to death!"

His broad shoulders lifted in a slight shrug. "I did kill him."

Tears clogged her throat. "Gray, please, there has to be an explanation… You're a good man."

The cynical look returned to his gaze. "Am I? Maybe your parents are right. Dad knows best, right, Peyton?"

"That's not fair. You can't expect me to hear all this and not react or be upset."

He shoved a hand through his short black hair. "No, I can't. I should go."

"Yes. Give me a little while. I can meet you later."

"Go for good, Peyton."

Moisture blurred her eyes. "You're leaving me?"

"You deserve better," he said quietly. "I should never have taken you to Richardson's house. It only caused you more distress. You deserve someone without a tarnished reputation who won't cause whispers when you're with him out in public. Someone who will never let anything happen to you, not just to protect you physically, but from emotional damage as well. I can't do that anymore."

"Where are you going?"

"Back home, to New York." He went to the car and sat in the driver's seat, the motor running, his window rolled down.

Tears clogged her throat. She wanted to beg him not to leave her. He waited, as if expecting her reaction. Her parents stood nearby, looking worried. Torn in half, Peyton hesitated. "Gray…"

Expression tight, he glanced at her, rolled up the window, and his car roared off, out of the driveway.

Out of her life.

Chapter 19

He should leave town. Pack up and go. He'd already told Jarrett what happened and quit his job. No reason for him to hang around, unless he wanted to torture himself with thoughts of Peyton. It was over.

Life was empty. Numbness wasn't bad. Kept him from feeling anything, feeling the crush of hopelessness. For a while he thought he'd found his way again, a navigational beacon back to normal in the form of Peyton. Her laugh. Her smile and how bravely she forged ahead, trusting him, trusting herself.

But her family came first, and they ruled her life. Couldn't blame her. He understood about familial obligations. His past made people avoid him. Including Peyton and her family. No one cared to know the truth. The painful facts.

He'd return home to New York, take his place in his father's business. Keep advising from the sidelines. Quiet Gray in the shadows. Ah, the irony. As long as investors didn't deal with him personally, his father's multimillion-dollar hedge fund company would continue to thrive.

Maybe tomorrow he'd leave. Gray called Peyton to check on her. Her voice was dull and listless. "What do you want, Gray?"

"I need to know you're okay," he said softly.

"Yeah, well." She gave a bitter laugh. "Not that it matters to you. I have to go, Gray. I'm headed for the institute. I need my life back, even if I don't know what that life is."

She hung up on him.

For a moment he stared at his cell. Call ended. Relationship, budding as it was, ended as well.

Martin had been arrested and brought into the sheriff's office for questioning. Gray needed to hear what Gauthier had to say. He couldn't get over this niggling feeling Martin might not have abducted Peyton after all, despite the evidence. It was all circumstantial, but enough. Sims called. Two detectives from the Monroe County Sheriff's Department were present at the interrogation, since Richardson's homicide fell under their jurisdiction. Sims wanted him there as he grilled Martin.

Gray couldn't leave until he was assured Peyton would be safe. Never leave a man behind, they always said in the teams. Never leave a job half-finished, Jarrett always added to that.

Now, hovering against the wall as Sims sat at a metal table facing Martin, he watched Peyton's supervisor. Sweat beaded his face, dampened his polo shirt. Yeah, the man looked guilty. Yet Gray was good at reading people and sensed Martin wasn't nervous because he'd stalked and abducted Peyton and killed Fletcher.

He was too ambitious about his career at the institute, making his résumé shine. Martin wasn't a man of great passions obsessed with Peyton. Even the charges of sexual harassment against Martin at another job proved to be a dead end.

"Your institute credit card was found in Fletcher Richardson's wallet," Sims told Martin.

"My credit card was stolen a month ago!"

"You never reported it."

"I didn't want the board to know…" Martin looked away. "I was on track to becoming permanent director after they fired the last director. But I screwed up a few times. The board put me on probation. I was walking in a minefield. If I didn't get the institute back on track with funding, I'd be out. A stolen credit card would show I wasn't responsible."

"Or you gave it to Fletcher Richardson to purchase everything needed for Peyton's kidnapping, promised to pay him off and then killed him to keep him silent. We found a paperweight from your desk near Richardson's body. It was used to knock him unconscious." Sims glared at him.

"Anyone could have taken that. It wasn't me!" Sweat poured down Martin's pale face. "I only wanted to keep things together, try to keep up appearances. Dammit, the institute couldn't afford another scandal, not after the former director was accused of having an affair with an intern. I tried to keep it quiet about Adam and his gambling. He had such a crush on Peyton, I thought about firing him, but it looked like they were friends… She always treated him like a friend."

Gray's heart raced. He leaned on the table, brought his face close to Martin's. "Adam was in love with Peyton?"

"Tried to hide it. But it was pretty damn obvious to me the way he made sheep's eyes at her when he thought no one was looking. I thought he wanted her for the money. Her family is loaded and the guy owes probably six figures in gambling debts."

Martin gave a grudging laugh. "Peyton always treated him special. Let him access her family's private beach at any time, gave him a key so he could count sea turtle nests. I could get in there, but Peyton insisted I go with her. Only Adam could go alone and take an intern."

Everything clicked together like tumblers in a lock. Gray checked his handgun. "Keep him here," he told Sims. "I'm going to the institute to check on Peyton."

Without waiting for an answer, he raced to his car, hoping and praying he was wrong.

Because if he was right, Peyton Bradley was alone in the institute, with the man who wanted to kill her.

Chapter 20

Life had been restored to normal, except she still didn't remember. Maybe that was for the best. A new normal. Her parents told her Martin was arrested and charged with her kidnapping.

Remember how Martin had betrayed her, and her family? How he'd desired her and then wanted to kill her? Why would she want to remember that?

Nor did she want to remember the guarded look on Gray's face as he'd confessed what he'd done in the past. Her rescuer. The one man she'd trusted since this nightmare began. No one else trusted him. And then he walked away.

It hurt to think he'd kept the truth from her, hadn't trusted her the way she'd trusted him with her life, with everything.

She needed alone time with her work, with the creatures whose lives she tried to save. Sea turtles were uncompromisingly simple. They had no motives, other than what nature provided them.

It was past closing time, but she knew staff would be there until nightfall. As she drove to the institute, the setting sun turned the sky rose gold and violet. Streaks of clouds painted the western horizon, reminding her of the magnificent sunset she and Gray had witnessed. The thought depressed her. He was gone for good and she needed to forget him.

Even though she could not.

Peyton used her key to unlock the lobby door, careful to lock it again, and then used her keys to access the gated area guarding the tanks for recovering turtles. Molly was there, swimming in circles. Immediately her stress faded. This was what mattered. Not Martin's betrayal.

Or Gray's abandonment of the truth, and her.

Peyton leaned over the tank, smiling at Molly. "Don't worry, girl. You're getting better, day by day. And we'll get things right here again. Everything is going to be fine."

The overhead canopy providing welcome shade from the intense sunlight during the day also protected the tanks from rainfall and dew at night. Nighttime…beach…turtles…something in the water she knew was dangerous…

Peyton's memory flickered like a movie projector. She checked the tank and the water supply, and accessed the turtle's logs from her phone to see her progress.

Another memory surfaced as Molly dived under the water. Going to the ocean, watching the waves at moonlight, feeling annoyance as her bodyguard joined her on the beach. Not Gray. The other one, who enjoyed eating more than tagging along after her. But that night he'd stuck to her side…

Black blood in moonlight, sticky sand, horrified screams ripping from her mouth…

Peyton pressed two fingers to her temples as Rafe, one of the interns who greeted her at the entrance, called out.

"Hey, Adam! Can you give me a hand with locking up? I have a hot date."

"Give me a minute, dammit!"

Peyton froze. Adam...that voice. Deep voice threaded with impatience. *Give me a minute, dammit.* Give me a minute...as the gag slid over her mouth and she fell into unconsciousness, but not before hearing the sickening thud of bullets hitting Ed's body, seeing the moonlit black blood stain the gray sand...

The name she'd heard at the sea turtle hospital. Adam Martin, called by an impatient mother scolding her wayward son using his full name as some mothers did. It wasn't the name of Martin that sent her spiraling into panic.

But the name of Adam. Her friend, Adam Russell. Her stalker and would-be killer.

Must not let him know she remembered. Ignorance was a good defense. Peyton eased away from the tank as Adam sauntered over. A hank of blond hair flopped into his face and he pushed it away with an impatient hand.

"Hey, Peyton, you're back!"

Couldn't help stiffening as he hugged her. Adam stood back, holding her upper arms. Frowning. Oh God, did he know?

Everything rushed back like a cresting wave, breaking over her and threatening to topple her downward. Peyton forced a smile while inside she wanted to retch.

Rafe called out. "Okay, I'm done with everything. I'm headed out. Can you guys lock up and secure everything?"

Her mouth opened and closed. She wanted to scream out to Rafe to stay, oh God, please stay, don't leave me alone with him...

"Sure, have fun!" Adam called out.

They were alone.

Adam's smile dropped as he dropped his hands. He

backed away. "You got your memory back. I can see it on your face, Peyton. You remember. You know."

Anger nudged aside fear. "Adam, it was you... How could you? You're a biologist, you're dedicated to saving species like I am! And you sold out for money?"

Shame flickered across his expression. "I didn't want to, Peyton. I had no choice. It was Fletcher's fault. He got me into it. We were gambling on sea turtle nests. That's how it began. Friendly bets, me and Fletcher. A few dollars on if a turtle was going to nest that night. Then it got bigger. He took me to the track, and then... Fletcher knew these people who needed a favor and needed the beach."

Then his gaze hardened. "You have money. You'll never know what it's like to owe six figures to a guy who would break both your legs if you miss a payment. I can't let you go, Peyton."

He reached into the back of his shorts. Overhead lights gleamed on the metal barrel of the handgun he pointed at her.

Peyton backed up. She kept her eyes trained on the weapon, the same one he'd used to kill Ed. He killed Ed. Not the three drug runners he'd accompanied to the beach that night she sat on the sand, waiting for her beloved sea turtles to nest.

The drug runners who were there with packages of cocaine to bury in the sea turtle nests, knowing they'd be protected by the signs and tape Adam placed there...until the cocaine could be moved.

"Adam... Don't do this. Please. I thought you cared about me."

His gaze dropped. "I did, Peyton. But I care more about getting my life back. I'm not going to prison. You're the only one who knows."

Her only chance lay in diverting him. Peyton gasped

and pointed at Molly's tank. "Molly! She's climbing out of the tank!"

He turned for a minute, all she needed. Peyton ran, zigging and zagging as Adam turned, fired, bullets whizzing past her. One grazed her arm. Burning pain lanced her but she didn't dare scream.

She ran for the light switch, pressed it and the lights went out. Darkness was her friend. Peyton headed for the educational exhibits as she heard Adam behind her, cursing, as he struggled to reload.

The giant replica of a leatherback shell standing upright that children loved to duck behind provided cover. Peyton hid behind it, dialed 9-1-1.

"He's shooting at me. Marine Institute on Ocean Boulevard. Hurry," she whispered.

Peyton muted her phone, not daring to say anything more, knowing Adam would find her.

"Pey? Hey, Pey, come out. You can't hide forever."

Oh yes I can. She gauged the distance to the back entrance. Might be able to flee… But she heard him approach. Then splashing sounds.

Frantic, she looked around for any kind of weapon. Nearby was the sandbox where she'd stored trash found on the beach to show visitors the dangerous ocean debris that harmed sea turtles. Peyton grabbed the glass jar of cigarette butts.

"Pey, come out. I've got Molly and it doesn't look good for her."

Molly? Panic exploded in her. Holding the glass jar behind her, she came out from behind the leatherback shell.

Adam held Molly up. The juvenile turtle's flippers waved madly. Peyton inched closer to Adam. She had to get closer.

"You cared more about these damn turtles than me."

Adam dropped Molly on the hard concrete. The turtle lay there on her back, flippers pawing frantically at the air. He kicked it away.

"You bastard," she breathed.

Adam raised his gun. "Bye, Peyton. I loved you, you know."

Now! Peyton threw the glass jar filled with cigarette butts. It hit the gun, shattered, shards hitting him in the chest and face, making him stumble backward. Adam yelled. Peyton ran.

Gunfire exploded. Peyton froze. It didn't hurt. Nothing hurt, except the stinging pain on her arm.

She turned.

In the dim light, she saw him.

Gun cupped in his capable hands, Gray stared straight ahead at her. Cool. Resolved. Unflinching. Peyton's heart raced as she looked down at Adam writhing on the ground, clutching his leg.

"Peyton, get his gun, kick it out of the way," Gray ordered.

She did. Blood leaked from the bullet wound in Adam's leg. "You shot me, you bastard!" Adam screamed.

"You'll live," Gray said calmly.

Running over to the wall switch, she flipped on the lights.

Gray spied the blood on Peyton's arm and he cursed. "Peyton, you got hit."

"It's just a graze. I'm fine."

"He hurt you." His voice was low, ominous.

Gray's expression turned dangerous. Her breath hitched. *Please don't kill him. Don't be that man my father says you are.* Peyton backed away, clutching her arm. It was all up to Gray now.

He walked over to Adam, gun aimed at his head. "I could kill you for what you did to Peyton, how you terrorized her and almost took her life. You hurt her."

Gray glanced at her. "But I won't. This time, I'll let the law deliver justice instead of taking it on myself."

Something inside her eased.

"It hurts!" Moaning, Adam clutched his leg.

"Not as much as it will." Peyton kicked him in the wound, satisfied to hear Adam's moan turn into a scream.

"That's for terrorizing me, you son of a biscuit."

Gray's mouth twitched in amusement. "Good for you. And you got him with that jar filled with cigarette butts."

She grinned at him. "Like I always tell the kids, ocean debris is deadly."

As the police arrived, Gray felt a tremendous weight lifted from his shoulders. Yeah, the cops would say he should have waited. But if he had, Peyton would be dead. As it was now, she was injured. "Over here," he yelled.

"Molly!" Peyton rushed over to the tank where the Kemp's ridley juvenile wriggled on the ground. "Oh no… Gray, help me get her inside so I can examine her."

Gray slid his handgun into its holster and helped her gently carry the turtle into the building's surgical unit. They set Molly on an examining table as Peyton snapped on a light, turning the turtle over. Outside in the lobby, police and paramedics had arrived and were dealing with Adam.

"Let me see your wound, sweetheart." Worried at the blood dripping down her arm, Gray examined the bullet graze. He found gauze and wrapped her arm.

"We need to get you to a hospital."

"I'm fine. Never mind me. Hold her steady." Peyton washed her hands and snapped on latex gloves.

After examining the turtle and doing an X-ray, she was relieved to find the hairline crack on Molly's carapace was the only injury. No internal damage.

Peyton focused, studying the turtle with intensity. "Hand me the raw honey."

She applied a line of the sticky golden substance to the crack in the shell. "Raw honey has amazing healing powers. It actually fosters healthy tissue growth. We use it for cracked shells."

Together, they returned Molly to her tank. Peyton removed her gloves. The adrenaline rush had ceased, and she trembled. Her pupils dilated and her breathing hitched.

"You're coming down from an adrenaline high." He signaled to a police officer. "She's injured and needs medical attention."

As the officer went to find a paramedic, Peyton shook her head. "I don't need a hospital. I need you."

Opening his arms, he swallowed past the terror that had gripped him when he'd spied Adam pointing a gun straight at Peyton. Gray closed his eyes and engulfed her in a hug as she nestled against him as if he were a lifeline.

"I remembered everything soon as I heard Adam's voice. Everything. I've never been so scared in my life, even when he'd kidnapped me. Then I remembered all the things you taught me, and how to survive if I got attacked again. You did more than rescue me, Gray. You helped me rescue myself."

Marveling at her faith in him, he kept holding her tight. His greatest fear had been losing her to the mad man who stalked her, and letting his own personal rage consume him instead of keeping a level head.

He'd finally made peace with the past, and proved he could remain in control of his emotions, even when someone he loved was endangered. No longer would he react in fury. He could rein in his personal feelings as he'd done all those years with the teams.

For the first time in years, he felt free.

Chapter 21

Two weeks later, her arm healing nicely, Peyton took charge of her life again.

Adam had made a plea deal with the district attorney in return for his testimony. He gave information on the three drug runners who used the Bradleys' private beach to hide cocaine and they were arrested. The same drug runners had been the ones following Peyton after Adam placed a tracking chip in her clothing while she was showering at the institute. He'd planted the notes in hopes of scaring her into going to Nantucket for the summer and leaving the beach to him to keep running drugs.

Adam confessed to knowing the drug dealers had killed Fletcher when the man had contacted him, wanting to go to the authorities. They wanted to frame Martin for the murder, so Adam had stolen the glass globe from Martin's desk for them. Fletcher had never wanted Peyton harmed.

That news gave her a little solace.

She signed a lease for her own apartment and made

plans to move out of her parents' house. It felt good to know who she was, and embrace new goals. Much as she loved her family, she no longer felt tethered to them or their advice. She felt ready to forge ahead in new directions.

For now, college was on hold. The board of directors had offered her the position as director of the institute after Martin resigned. She accepted on a temporary basis until a new and competent administrator could be found. In the meantime, she hired a well-known public relations firm for damage control. Overcoming the institute's scandal with Adam became a priority, along with reassuring the public they were still dedicated to saving sea turtles. Her PhD could wait.

As she packed books in her room, her father poked his head in the door. "Honey, there's someone here to see you."

Peyton glanced up as Gray walked inside. A wide smile touched her mouth. Her father hovered in the room, looking at Gray. Damn, if he was going to say something against Gray again…

Surprised, she watched her father stick out a hand for Gray to shake. "Gray, I apologize for all the things I said about you. I misjudged you. You saved my daughter's life."

Gray glanced down at the outstretched palm. "I told you, sir, I wouldn't let anything happen to her."

Her proud father looked ashamed. "I know. Will you forgive me?"

After a few seconds, Gray slid his hand into her father's. "You were being a protective dad."

After a fierce handshake, her father withdrew his hand and sighed. "Overprotective. I have to let Peyton be her own person. It's the toughest part of being a parent, letting go."

With a nod, he retreated out of the room, closing the door behind him.

Gray walked over to the desk. He arched a dark

brow. "Should you be lifting anything heavy with your wounded arm?"

"I'm good. Doc says I can lift things as long as they aren't over twenty pounds. It's only books. The movers will take them to the van, and bring them into the new apartment."

She gave him a long look. "I'm moving out, Gray. I can't stay here anymore, taking their advice, letting them dictate my life. I love my parents, but it's time."

Still wearing his serious look, Gray nodded. "Good. I'm glad to hear it."

"It's time to trust myself as well and go after what I want in this world. Go out on my own, free of the expectations my parents—and others—place on me. I love them and always will, but they've hovered long enough. I never realized how much they shadowed my thinking about others…until I saw my dad's mistrust of you, my shadow."

Peyton tilted her head at him. "And you? Back to New York?"

She dared to hope he'd changed his mind.

"No. Jarrett offered me a full-time position, investigating cases for SOS Security. It means remaining in Florida." He picked up a textbook on marine biology, turned it over in his hands. "I'm not returning to New York, Peyton. I accepted his offer."

Her heart skipped a beat. "I thought you were going to work for your father's business."

"I can still make recommendations on ETFs and make trades remotely as a side business. But I believe in SOS and the work they do, not only to provide security, but help women and children find new lives, away from the trauma of their pasts."

It sounded too good to be true. She knew Gray was a noble man. But she had to know why he'd kept from trusting her.

"Gray, why didn't you ever level with me about what happened to your former fiancée and her lover? Why couldn't you trust me with the truth?"

He took a deep breath. "I spent years struggling with my temper, Peyton. I put up barriers to keep people, especially women, away from me so I wouldn't get involved again. You threatened to break those barriers down.

"And then I started falling in love with you and couldn't bear you judging me the same way your father did, thinking I was a violent man with an explosive temper. I'm not, Peyton."

"I know," she said softly. "Will you trust me now with the full story? I need to hear it."

"Yes. You need to know...though I haven't talked about this with anyone, except Jarrett and my family."

He beckoned to the bed. They sat on it and, knowing he needed support, she held his hand. Gray stared down at it.

"Andrea and I met at a party five years ago. I fell in love with her, and she fell in love with me as a navy SEAL. Or the idea of being a SEAL. We moved in together, and I asked her to marry me."

Gray made a dismissive gesture. "I tried to tell myself she loved me for who I was, not what I was. But I was blind to the truth. Then I kept leaving on missions. The letters and emails trickled to nothing, and I suspected she was having an affair. It didn't bother me because I realized it was over. Figured I would break up with her on my next leave. A good friend investigated for me and discovered she had a lover."

"Jarrett was that friend."

Gray nodded. "But Jarrett told me the guy was abusing her. Beating her up. She'd show up for work with bruises on her arms. I talked with Andrea, and she begged me for help. I promised to keep her safe, but I had to leave on a mission.

I sent her to Jarrett so she could leave the guy through the network he runs with Lacey, his wife, to assist women in domestic abuse situations.

"Before Jarrett could arrange for Andrea to escape, I came home on leave. She called me, begging me to help her. Her lover had broken into the house. I drove as fast as I could and ran into the house. She was dead on the floor, blood everywhere."

He simply looked at her. "The bastard beat her to death in a rage and then shot her. He was standing over her body, saw me and laughed. Then he pointed the gun at me and said he would get off and be free, and everyone would blame me. Murder-suicide."

Peyton inhaled. "Gray… You killed him instead."

"Yes." No shame in his matter-of-fact tone. "The whole time he was bragging, I jumped him. Broke his neck. And kept hitting him postmortem…and that's how the police found me. They arrested me. Eventually the truth came out and charges were dropped because it was self-defense. My father pulled strings, got my arrest record wiped clean, but there were rumors. So I changed my name to protect what was left of my reputation and didn't re-up. I began working for my father. But it was just a job, not what I really wanted."

"You're a very good bodyguard. I mean, executive protection agent."

He gave a wry smile, then grew serious again. "It's why I want to work for SOS. You have caring parents, Peyton, and resources when you faced danger. There's a world of women with children running from abusive spouses who don't have anyone to help them. I need to help save them, if I can."

She felt a surge of pride in him, knowing he finally found his calling, just as she'd found hers. Gray would put the same dedication and zeal into helping others as he'd helped her.

Gray cupped her shoulders so she faced him. His serious face, the firm chin, the small scar on his cheek, the intensity in his dark gaze. Her shadow. Her Gray.

"I'd like to remain in your life, Peyton. It took almost losing you to realize I'd fallen in love with you. You were no longer an assignment."

"You're the reason I'm alive today, but that's not why I love you, Gray." Peyton wrapped her hands around his wrists. "Your honor and loyalty and dedication made me realize what a good man you are, a rare soul in this world."

A twinkle lit his dark eyes. "So it wasn't only my devastating charm and good looks?"

She considered. "No. But you do have a very nice butt."

Gray kissed her. It was a long, drugging kiss, a promise of pleasures to come. When he pulled back, she gave a breathless laugh.

"I suppose a real date would be a good start. I'm free for dinner." She made a face. "Anything but seafood. I get tired of seafood after working with turtles all day."

He smiled. "A quiet steak house sounds good."

"I like beef. I had forgotten how much I did until I regained my memory. I'm grateful for that."

Gray ran a thumb over her lower lip. "So many reasons to be grateful."

"Yes. You're the best one of all. I found myself again," Peyton murmured. "Thanks to you."

He drew back, framed her face with his hands. "I found myself again as well, sweetheart. Thanks to you."

* * * * *

#2255 CSI COLTON AND THE WITNESS
The Coltons of New York • by Linda O. Johnston

When Patrick Colton's fellow CSI investigator Kyra Patel sees a murderer fleeing a scene, he vows to keep the expectant single mom out of the line of fire. But will the culprit be captured before their growing unprofessional feelings tempt them both?

#2256 OPERATION TAKEDOWN
Cutter's Code • by Justine Davis

As a former soldier, Jordan Crockett knows the truth about his best friend's military death. But convincing Emily Bishop, his deceased buddy's sister, exposes them both to a dangerous web of family secrets...and those determined to keep Jordan silenced.

#2257 HOTSHOT HERO FOR THE HOLIDAYS
Hotshot Heroes • by Lisa Childs

Firefighter Trent Miles *stops* fires—not starts them. But when his house burns down and a body is found inside, he becomes Detective Heather Bolton's number one murder suspect. Their undercover dating ruse to flush out the killer may save Trent from jail, but will Heather's heart be collateral damage?

#2258 OLLERO CREEK CONSPIRACY
Fuego, New Mexico • by Amber Leigh Williams

Luella Decker wants to leave her heartbreaking past behind her. Including her secret romance with rancher Ellis Eaton. But when the animals at her home are targeted and a long-buried family cover-up comes to light, Ellis may be the only one she can trust to keep her alive.

Get 3 FREE REWARDS!

We'll send you 2 FREE Books plus a FREE Mystery Gift.

FREE
Value Over
$20

Both the **Harlequin Intrigue®** and **Harlequin® Romantic Suspense** series feature compelling novels filled with heart-racing action-packed romance that will keep you on the edge of your seat.

HARLEQUIN
PLUS

Try the best multimedia subscription service for romance readers like you!

Read, Watch and Play.

Experience the easiest way to get the romance content you crave.

Start your **FREE TRIAL** at
www.harlequinplus.com/freetrial.